One look at that blanched face was all Beck needed to confirm the urgency of the message

The State Department being what it was, the note was cryptic—HP/NSB B-1; RSVP—but the Israeli hand holding it out to him was as white as the paper.

The prefix HP was familiar, even routine: Home Plate—Washington; following it, instead of an operation's cryptonym, was the acronym for Nuclear Surface Blast; after that came the standard letter-number intelligence appraisal, B-1, which told Beck that the information was from a usually reliable source and confirmed by other sources; the RSVP appended was somebody's cynical joke.

He would never remember the cars he ran off the road into the soft sand, and later into one another; he only remembered the sky, which he watched through his double-gradient aviator's glasses for some sign of thermal shock wave, a flash of light, a mushroom cloud; a doomsday darkening in the northeast over Iran—and the radio, which was stubbornly refusing to confirm or deny what the little piece of State Department letterhead in his pocket said.

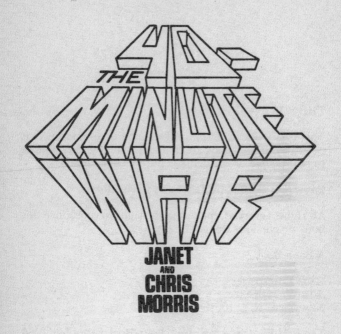

THE 40 MINUTE WAR

JANET AND CHRIS MORRIS

BAEN
SCIENCE FICTION
BOOKS

THE FORTY-MINUTE WAR

Copyright © 1984 by Janet and Chris Morris

A Baen Book

Baen Enterprises
8-10 W. 36th Street
New York, N.Y. 10018

The first hardcover printing, Baen Books, October 1984

First paperback printing, October 1985

ISBN: 0-671-55986-9

Cover art by David Mattingly

Printed in the United States of America

Distributed by
SIMON & SCHUSTER
MASS MERCHANDISE SALES COMPANY
1230 Avenue of the Americas
New York, N.Y. 10020

ACKNOWLEDGEMENTS

We would like to thank Jim Baen, who read the manuscript in progress and made astute suggestions; David Drake, whose DU rounds came in handy; and Dean Ing, whose up-to-the-minute expertise in the area of nuclear conflict and kind assistance were invaluable.

PROLOGUE

It was cherry blossom time in Washington and from the air the clever planning of the city's French architect was clearly visible: no horse army would have an easy time storming revetments well placed along those concentric circles. Capitol Hill and its buildings, as the young nation's fathers had intended, would be prohibitively expensive to take and the last to fall to an enemy infantry slogging up the slope.

But this was of little concern to the airborne warriors of the Islamic Jihad in their commandeered Royal Saudi airliner. There were only six martyrs aboard—three Iranians, two Libyans, and a Palestinian woman who, despite her sex, was their commanding officer.

Numbers were an extraneous consideration in their battle; so was survival of the warriors. This was as it had always been and it bothered none of the suicide commandos in the big Boeing's cockpit: they had been chosen by their mullah for just this reason—with, of course, the additional proviso that they be technically capable of performing their mission.

Each one of them was a certified pilot capable of flying the jumbo jet to its rendezvous with history if only one was left alive; all were fluent enough in the dialects and customs of the despicable Saudi moderates and the American Satans to pass for a commercial jet's crew; each had been drilled and redrilled in the arming and detonation of the tactical nuke they had on board until any one of them could have delivered it to its target from the depths of sleep or death's door.

It was a simple matter, really, as it had been to commandeer the jetliner without one of its two hundred and fifty-seven passengers suspecting anything: every move they made had been thought out by other, wiser heads far in advance.

The jet wasn't altered; it bore no rocket launchers under its wings; it needed no complicated targeting electronics or heads-up displays. The martyrs weren't up to that and their dispatchers knew it—hence the complex and painstaking ruse that assured the complete normalcy, to all appearances, of the final approach of Flight 319 from Riyadh.

What the commandos *were* capable of doing was vectoring from their approach to Washington International Airport and crashing their jumbo jet into the very lair of the greatest Satan of all: the White House, home of the President of the United States.

The entire operation, from the moment the jet veered from its flight path to the moment it crashed into the White House among a tardy hail of antiaircraft fire from stunned soldiers in nearby emplacements, took fourteen point nine seconds—just long enough for the woman who led the martyrs to let the world know who should get the credit for eradicating its greatest evil in the cleansing fire which the American Satans had so long used to hold the Islamic peoples hostage to its will.

"Allaho Akbar," the woman whispered—"God is Great"—just before she armed the suitcase bomb they had with them on the flight deck.

She died smiling, which was more than could be said for the jet's pilot who, despite his revolutionary fervor, voided in his pants just before he was incinerated as the bomb went off milliseconds before impact.

Her smile was the last smiled around Washington that day in April or for many days afterward, for the terrorist bombing of the White House by the Islamic Jihad had certain unforeseen consequences:

The electromagnetic pulse from the blast knocked out communications in the immediate area and wiped data from a number of computers, including those used by the flight controllers at Washington International, all of whom were killed by debris riding the shock wave radiating from Ground Zero, with the result that the Jihad's message was never delivered to higher American authorities or anyone else: the Libyans, whose bomb it was, had been a little too zealous, the bomb a trifle overpowered for its purpose.

The President of the United States, who was— fortuitously or not—in Air Force One on his way to deliver a speech to dairy farmers in Wisconsin, received the news that his wife and two young children had been annihilated with something less than aplomb: he got up from his orthopedic leather recliner, bumping a brilliantined head against the luggage compartment, and stormed over to the shocked Air Force officer who had the ill-fortune to be the man carrying the Football—the briefcase containing the codes and electronics to arm and fire America's nuclear arsenal—that day and snapped, white-faced, "Open it."

The Air Force officer had no choice but to obey his Commander in Chief.

The other five passengers aboard sat stunned and silent. No one argued that it wasn't the Russians, that it might be better to wait—the US and the Soviets had long ago given up the option of waiting: the two superpowers maintained a state of readiness called Launch on Warning.

If a nuclear attack on the White House—the President blinked away visions of his wife's face transported in ecstasy the night before in Lincoln's bed—wasn't sufficient warning and clear provocation, the President didn't know what was.

He bent over the Football, open on the Air Force major's lap, and did what he'd prayed fervently to God he'd never have to do. President Alexander Claymore was a devout man, a good man—as good as any who runs for so high an office could be; unfortunately for the civilized world, he was also a family man and an ex-military man with a peculiarly military outlook on life, the world in general, and the Soviet Union in particular.

As a family man, he was devastated by his loss. As a military man, he knew that any war was lost as soon as it must be fought—a nuclear war wasn't that different in theory, just in consequences. As a Soviophobe, he'd always known, in his heart of hearts, that it would come to this.

And he'd promised himself and his wife—might she rest in peace—that if it ever came to this he'd put bullets through both their heads. He squeezed his eyes shut as he straightened up from the instrument of Armageddon called the Football and, through his shirt, the soft inside flesh of his arm brushed the little PPK he always carried in a shoulder holster.

The Air Force major stared at him wanly; when the square-jawed, crew-cut youngster opened his mouth to speak, strings of mucus stretched across his lips: "We've still got seven minutes, Sir . . . to verify . . . to abort."

That was true, technically. But Claymore was thinking about the bathroom, the clean finality of a nine-millimeter slug crashing into his brain: he was Commander in Chief, and he'd lost his war. Honor demanded a quick exit. And his wife, sweet Linnie, was waiting. So was little Jenny, and Bobby, his son.

"Verify *what*, soldier?" Claymore slugged the major with his stare. "It ain't easy to learn Russian, boy. You think maybe it's a mistake? That Ivan'll say he's sorry?"

"No Sir, I didn't—"

"—didn't *think*. Check."

Claymore looked around. All of his people were staring at him: the Undersecretary for Agriculture, a pure hayseed with a stain on his chinos he was too terrified to hide; his Press Secretary, a walking mouth without a brain in his head but possessed of an autonomic gift for gab that had been crucial during the campaign; a woman speechwriter who sat quietly, chin up, with tears running down her rouged cheeks like gray worms; a Special Assistant who wasn't particularly special and now had his knuckles jammed in his mouth; and two Secret Service men who watched everyone else with bleak eyes, ready for any sort of trouble.

But there would be no mutiny aboard Air Force One that spring day and the trouble their President was in wasn't the sort that a pair of loyal, athletic men with sunglasses and wires in their ears could hope to fix.

If there had been one intelligence specialist, somebody from Defense or State, along to remind Claymore that the Iranian crazies had threatened to "roast the greatest Satan in his lair," maybe Claymore wouldn't have gone into the bathroom and blown his brains out.

But no such person was on board that day to avert World War Three by aborting the launch-and-arm sequence within the seven minutes required.

When the shot rang through Air Force One, however, the entire situation changed: the Vice President was informed and a cooler hand took the helm.

Unfortunately, even that wasn't enough to avert all the consequences of what would be called, forever after, the Forty-Minute War.

Book One:
FOREIGN PORTS

Chapter 1

The question people asked one another after that day in April was no longer, "Where were you when Kennedy was shot?"

But like that earlier and, by comparison, milder tragedy, everyone remembered exactly where they were when they got the word that the Forty-Minute War had begun—and ended.

To most Foreign Service officers, even in the Mediterranean, word came earlier than it did to Marc Beck, who was babysitting a convention of genetic engineers with astronomical security clearances being held at a private estate on the Red Sea when an aide slipped him a note.

The State Department being what it was, the note was cryptic—HP/NSB B-1; RSVP—but the Israeli hand holding it out to him was as white as the paper and shaking like a leaf: the aide, loaned to him from Israeli Military Intelligence, was seconded from a Saiyeret crack commando unit and one look at that blanched face was all Beck needed to confirm the urgency of the coded message.

The prefix HP was familiar, even routine: Home Plate—Washington; following it, instead of an operation's cryptonym, was the acronym for Nuclear Surface Blast; after that came the standard letter-number intelligence appraisal, B-1, which told Beck that the information was from a usually reliable source and confirmed by other sources; the RSVP appended was somebody's cynical joke.

Given the above, he left the genetic engineers to their Israeli hosts and RSVP'd toward Jerusalem at a hundred eighty klicks per hour, eschewing a driver and pushing his Corps Diplomatique Plymouth well beyond the laws of man and physics in exactly the way every new diplomat was warned against when first posted overseas.

He would never remember the cars he ran off the road into the soft sand, and later into one another; he only remembered the sky, which he watched through his double-gradient aviator's glasses for some sign of thermal shock wave, a flash of light, a mushroom cloud, a doomsday darkening in the northeast over Iran—and the radio, which was stubbornly refusing to confirm or deny what the little piece of State Department letterhead in his pocket said.

Beck wasn't naive but he couldn't believe that the bombing of his nation's capital wasn't newsworthy. Damn it to hell, Ashmead's report had been right on the money: the Islamic Jihad had actually done it! Nobody believed they could—or would . . . nobody but a handful of Ashmead's field-weary counterterrorists who couldn't write a grammatical report.

Beck, in fifteen years of overseas postings, had never been party to an error of this magnitude. He'd signed off on a negative analysis of Ashmead's intelligence, along with everyone else whose opinion he respected, right up to CIA's Regional Commander for the Middle East and his own Bureau Chief, Dickson. It wasn't going to look nearly as bad in his superiors' files as it was in his. He was praying that Muffy and the kids were safe in East Hampton as he wheeled the competent Plymouth past an Israeli convoy on the move, their desert camouflage reminding him, if he needed the reminder, that he was posted in a war zone.

The worst that could happen, he decided, was that he'd be sent Stateside—headquarters wouldn't sack the lot of them, even if old Claymore was a puff of radioactive dust wafting over the Mall by now.

And that wouldn't be all bad, as far as Beck was concerned—he was ready for a rest. The only cure for the craziness that seeped into your bones when you lived in a terrorist environment was to leave that environment. He'd been here seventeen months as State's liaison without portfolio, trying to reduce friction among the various intelligence services crawling over Israel like ants on a picnic table.

And he'd been doing pretty well—Ashmead had trusted Beck, and Ashmead, the Agency's Area Covert Action Chief, didn't trust anybody; Mossad and Shin Bet honchos invited Beck to weapons tests and gave him Saiyeret commandos, no questions asked, when he needed security boys, as he had

for the genetic engineering conference—pretty
well, until today.

He focused through the Plymouth's tinted glass
on the sun-baked road ahead, blinked, then cranked
the steering wheel around and the Plymouth went
up on two wheels to avoid a woman and a donkey
crossing the road directly in his path. Beyond them,
eucalyptus whispered, their leaves shimmying in a
white-hot breeze.

Pretty well, Beck knew, wasn't good enough when
you were in the field. Beck's official post was that
of Special Assistant to the Ambassador and he did
perform some nebulous duties in that capacity; his
real status was that of Assistant to the Chief for
Operations of State's Bureau of Intelligence and
Research, Middle East. The Bureau, called INR by
those who worked for it, was going to take a lot of
flak over this botch: by fragging CIA's high-priority-
flagged warning of an imminent terrorist attack
on Home Plate, they had end-run themselves.

He hoped to hell they hadn't end-run the whole
intelligence community—or the whole blessed US
of A: a "Nuclear Incident" like this could start a
damned war.

The thought made him nervous and he began
punching buttons on the Plymouth's multiband.
When the radio chattered on blithely in Hebrew,
Arabic and English of quotidian affairs between
musical interludes, he could only assume that stringent Israeli security measures were in effect.

And that made good sense: only the parental
and unceasing care of the US kept Israel from
destruction by her enemies. But then again, it was
ridiculous to assume that even the Israelis would
censor news of that magnitude. So it had to be

something more: sensitive negotiations must be in progress.

And this, finally, cracked Beck's calm: in the air-conditioned sedan, he began to sweat. There was something really wrong and Beck, a high-powered polymath with an MIT education who just happened to be a Senior Arab Specialist because languages and history to him were recreational drugs, was beginning to realize what it might be.

By the time he careened into East Jerusalem, he was getting visual confirmation: too many of the wrong kind of official vehicles on streets not as busy as they should have been; too few of others.

Driving up to the new temporary American Consulate—the last one had been car-bombed three weeks before with no casualties, thanks to another of Ashmead's terse and profane warnings—he was praying in nonsectarian fashion for the English-language radio commentator to drop even a hint of the nuking of Home Plate.

But it wasn't forthcoming. He told himself that there was no way it could be as bad as he was assuming it was—at home, once Defcon Three was reached, the whole country would have known about it. A state of actual war ought to leak, even in Israel.

RSVP. Right. Check.

A pair of stone-faced Marines stopped him at the compound gates, their M16s on full auto. It was the weapons which told him for sure, before one Marine said, "I guess you know we'd really appreciate a confirm or deny on this, Sir, if and when you can—some sort of damage estimate . . . we've all got family—"

"As soon as I know, Sergeant. What are all those people doing in there?" Beyond the guardpost, a queue of civilians had formed. Beck could imagine what the Americans in their rumpled polyesters wanted; he was just trying to cover his own confusion.

A glance in the rearview mirror showed him too many cars with rental plates parked on the street outside the compound; as he watched, a taxi pulled up and a woman with a boyish haircut and the custom-tailored bush jacket of a press type got out, a carryall in hand. She was crying.

"Just citizens, Sir—you know you can't keep something like this ... rumors, that is ... quiet long," said the Marine sergeant thickly.

When Beck looked up at the guard, he saw that the man's chin had doubled and his lips were white. "Hey there," Beck caught the Marine's anguished but disciplined gaze and held it, "when the going gets tough ... Right?"

The Marine squared his shoulders: "That's right, sir," he replied, and Beck wished that individual courage such as the guard's could make any difference in something like this.

As if reading his mind, the Marine offered, "As long as we've got a government ... well, you know—it's got us."

Haven't lost your touch, anyway, Beck told himself, feeling something akin to love for the Marine in that instant.

Then the woman with the carryall hiked up the drive, hallooing, then breaking into a trot. She had on sensible tennis shoes and the bag was now over her shoulder but tears still ran down her face and it was too swollen to tell if it might have been pretty.

Beck was about to put the Plymouth in gear when she put a hand on its fender, then on the half-open glass of his window: "American?" Her voice was husky, but it might have been from emotion. She ducked her head to peer into his car and he decided she was probably very pretty—she knuckled her eyes and said, "Thank God . . . I saw the CD on your car . . . look, let me go in with you. I can't stand in that line. Please?"

The Marine was telling her with firm politeness not to bother Beck and the way was clear before him, the Plymouth idling. All he had to do was drive on.

But there was something so urgent and so helpless about her, like a lost kitten, that he motioned to the passenger side even though, by then, he'd noticed the press credentials clipped to her breast pocket.

So had the Marine—he didn't delay them.

The woman got in, slammed the door and slouched against the seat, her head back, pulse pounding in her throat, fingers splayed in her short chestnut hair: "Christ," she said. "Christ. I still don't believe it." Then she turned her head and stared at him fiercely: "Do you, Mister—?"

"Beck. And you probably know more than I do, unless *The New York Times* isn't what it used to be, Ms. Patrick." He'd read it on her press pass, automatically checking the photo—of a pretty girl trying not to be—against the face above: Christine Patrick of *The New York Times*—the enemy.

One of the first things State taught its people was how to give a nonbriefing. He wouldn't have

to worry about that this time; but another was
how to extract information from the unwary without giving any signs that an interrogation was
under way.

He was gearing up to do just that as he wheeled
the car slowly toward the staff parking lot past the
queue of anxious faces when she volunteered,
"We're at war with the Soviets—nuclear war. That's
all I know, except I'm wondering why I'm not
dead." She sniffled and wiped her face with a
crooked arm in an angry gesture. "I guess we'll be
the ones who die slowly. . . ." She turned in her seat
to look at him. "Beck, you said, right? Do you have
a gun, Beck?"

"Me?" he said innocently. "Why, whatever for,
Ms. Patrick?"

"Shit, the world is ending and you're Ms.-ing
me? To blow my head off, that's what for, like . . ."
Her lower lip quivered and she stopped, then be-
gan again, eyes flashing: "And people call me
Chris—or, anyway, they did. And I'm—I was—a
Miss, not a Ms., whatever that is."

"Chris," he amended, grinning in spite of himself as he pulled into his slot before a sign that
said "Reserved"—they didn't advertise reserved
for whom, not in Jerusalem.

"So?"

"So what, Chris?" He turned off the ignition and
removed his key.

"So, do you have one or not? Can I borrow it?"

"Aren't you being a little premature, Chris?" He
was used to dealing with other people's problems;
her manic distress had a calming effect on him,
despite what she'd said. The press was paranoid;
all she had were assumptions and a grandstander's

instinct he couldn't help liking: she was providing him with some comic relief.

She grimaced and the grimace turned into a canny pout: "I don't know, that's what I'm saying—you tell me, Mr. Beck. Beck . . . that's German, isn't it? Isn't that kind of—inappropriate, here? Can't we get on a first-name basis? Life is looking kind of short. . . ." A gamin smile came and went on her sun-freckled face. "Let's make a deal—you tell me everything you know and I promise I won't report it until . . . until—" Her throat closed up and she shook her head miserably as she fought to clear it. "—until there's somebody to report it to . . ."

"Whoa, slow down." One leg out of the car, Beck wondered why he was wasting his time—RSVP—but said kindly, rolling back his mental tape of her remarks with professional ease, "Call me Marc, if you want, but everybody calls me Beck. It's no problem and it's not German. As for a deal—I really don't know as much as you do, yet. You must have a local chief to report to—if there's been any megatonnage released, the EMP will have put satellite links and all sorts of other semiconductor-driven com channels down . . . temporarily. Don't assume so much, okay?" He reached out and squeezed her arm.

"EMP?" She made no attempt to open her door, just sat in her seat, watching him.

"Electromagnetic pulse. Are you coming? You said you wanted to get past the civilians on line and I said I'd take you in—but once you're in, you'll have to wait for me . . ." He didn't know why he was doing this, except that he didn't want to leave her in his car and she had a nice uptilt to the breast under her plastic press pass, ". . . if you want more than the official story, that is."

"Great! Thanks!" She flashed him a look the kitten might have if he'd taken it home to a saucer of milk, then opened her door; as she got out and he power-locked the Plymouth, he couldn't help noticing that she had a fine ass, muscular thighs under her desert cloth pants, and that because she'd taken his mind off . . . things, he'd probably promised more than he could deliver: the crisis committee meeting he was walking into would probably last well into the night.

He hoped not. Beck wasn't above the occasional indiscretion and he realized what he wanted most in the world right now was to think it would matter if he got his ashes hauled by a newsie: he wanted things to be normal once again.

By the time they reached the ad hoc consulate's front steps, that hope was nearly eradicated: the people on line were hysterical, each in his or her fashion, and hysteria communicates itself like nothing else.

He'd wandered through Sabra and Shatilla with some very unhappy Israelis one morning and seen much worse among the living as they counted the dead—but those weren't Americans. Until that moment, he hadn't realized how privileged he'd always felt, how much of his professional calm was based in the assumption that *his* country was safe from the horrors he drifted among, always half a world away.

His stomach began to churn and he felt his solar plexus shooting adrenalin into him as, hand on Chris Patrick's trembling arm, beneath which an unladylike stain of perspiration was beginning to spread, he shepherded her through the crowd, ignoring everyone who reached out to him or called to him because he looked as if he were in control, as if he knew what he was doing, as if, in his accustomed economical way, he could make everything all right.

But this wasn't a matter of a lost passport or stolen luggage—this was lost faith and stolen dreams. Damn the Islamic Jihad! Damn Dickson! Damn himself, too—and Ashmead, for not going to the wall when his net's report wasn't believed.

Still, as he guided the reporter he'd befriended through the outer anteroom, he hadn't come to grips with the situation—not because he was emotionally incapable, but because he reflexively refused to consider situations about which he had no information.

And it was this internal discipline, this forcing of his perceptions outward, where information could be gathered, that made him realize what no one—not the civilians waiting in the anteroom or the three harried clerks trying to keep order there—had realized: that there was trouble of a more immediate sort beyond the sharp turn in the corridor directly ahead.

He couldn't explain to Chris Patrick, whom he should have left behind in the anteroom, what alerted him—he didn't want to make a sound.

He touched a finger to her lips while taking hold of her chin and turning her face toward him: *Quiet*, he pantomimed. *Stay here*.

Quizzically, she flicked a glance ahead, then nodded that she understood and would comply. As he moved silently past her, she was clutching her carryall in both hands.

Then he forgot about her: the sounds of scuffle he'd heard were gone now and he was about to walk blindly into he-didn't-know-what.

In Jerusalem, he never carried a side arm; it was a perk he maintained he didn't need, a regulation he disagreed was necessary, even if he was dealing all too often with people who understood little else: he was from State, not CIA, and he liked to keep the definition clear, wanted no guilt by association.

But he was armed, after a fashion. As he slid down the corridor, he unbuckled his belt and slipped the buckle-knife from its integral sheath of crocodile leather, grasping the wicked three-inch blade by its handle as he sidled around the corner.

Before him was a scene from a very standard nightmare: a crazed, burly civilian in a Hawaiian shirt and shorts was holding a balding man in a custom-tailored suit in front of him; beyond the big tourist who was holding Dickson in a hammer-lock stood four very unhappy-looking consulate staffers—two of them plainclothed security people with their issue S&Ws at their feet and their fingers entwined on top of their heads.

One of the security men was blond and Beck worked out with him on occasion; his expression of relief was so palpable that Beck thought the big civilian would surely notice and that would be the end of Dickson—and probably Beck.

The overweight six-footer in the howlie shirt was sobbing truculently, "—get me on some frigging plane with this asshole, now, do you hear me! I've got to get home! I've got a wife and kids, a business to run! Now kick those damn heaters over here or I'm going to crack this s.o.b.'s neck like so much . . ." in a Brooklyn accent.

Beck was moving with as much stealth as he could muster toward the sopping Hawaiian shirt stuck to the huge back that, as he closed, Beck realized was trembling.

He felt a moment of pity for the panicked man from Brooklyn as he closed the final distance and grabbed a handful of the hostage-taker's graying hair with his left hand while shoving the little buckle-knife to the right of the base of the man's skull.

"Freeze, old man," Beck said evenly, letting the point pierce whitening skin.

"Fuck!" said the man from Brooklyn. "I'm frozen, I'm frozen." He began to sob in earnest now and pushed Beck's chief away from him with enough force to send Dickson sprawling on the floor, saying, "I just want to go home, that's all. See what's left. Find my family. Nobody will *tell* me anything! The phones aren't working! I've got to call my wife—*Do* something. . . . Go *home*, I just want to go home— find out if—if everything's all right." As if he'd forgotten that he was held at knife-point, centimeters away from certain death, the big man from Brooklyn buried his face in hamlike hands.

"That's what we all want, old man, believe me," Beck said gently, though his grip on the hostage-taker's hair was still painfully tight. "And that's what we're trying to do here—find out what's what, make sure everybody gets home, if . . . *when*," he amended savagely, "it's possible—safe and possible. Now you be a good old guy and let us help you."

Meanwhile, the security men were retrieving their guns and the staffers their chief.

Beck was aware that the man he was holding wanted to slump to the floor; the Brooklyn voice was whining now, calling the names of his family each in turn, and bewailing the state of the world in New York Yiddish.

Beck removed the point of the knife from the thick bull neck and, with a glance to make sure the security men were ready to take over, released his grip on the old fellow's hair.

The man slumped and everyone started talking at once.

Dickson was on his feet, brushing furiously at the arms of his silk suit, a look of sick fury in his eyes: "Beck," he said tartly, "we've been waiting for you. In my office."

No "thank you," no "glad you happened along," just business, as if it were an everyday occurrence for Beck to interdict a hostage-taker single-handedly.

It wasn't: his fingers were shaking and swollen and he had trouble slipping the buckle-knife back in its housing, especially while trying to convince the security men that, under the circumstances, they ought to content themselves with escorting the bereaved man to the front gates.

The staffers were scurrying back to their desks and to a luckless civilian seated at one of them whom Beck hadn't noticed in the heat of the moment, when he heard a pair of hands clapping directly behind him.

He wheeled around and confronted Chris Patrick, leaning against the wall, clapping her hands in a slow and measured fashion with a wide but sardonic grin on her face: "I thought I told you to stay where you were, Patrick. What do you think this is, a youth hostel? A refugee camp?" Since the consulate was about to become a little of each, Beck brought himself up short and apologized sheepishly: "I'm sorry. But remember our deal—you've come about as far as you can right now."

She ignored everything he'd said: "You were *fantastic*. And my mother always said I couldn't pick'em."

Beck, in his turn, ignored that: "Pickwick, see what you can do for this lady. All the courtesies and whatever you can manage above and beyond, on my say-so, all right? She's going to wait here for me. . . ."

Pickwick, the senior staffer present, was straightening his desk's paperwork fastidiously. "If you insist, Mr. Beck, though I've fifty people out in the outer office with prior—"

Beck was already heading toward the door through which Dickson had disappeared.

Inside it, seated on a makeshift, make-do collection of bad furniture borrowed from half the missions in town, was the consulate's senior staff, sharing a certain pallor not in the least lessened by the pile of gas masks, counter-biochemical warfare suits, radiation counters and plastic film-sensitive badges on the table before them.

"Jesus," Beck said, fingering the compendium of last-ditch nightmare preparations. "That bad, is it?" Looking around, he realized that he was the only man in the room who didn't have a small red radiation-sensitive badge pinned to his lapel: he took one from the box and put it on, took three more and slipped them in his pocket, feeling as if he was in the middle of a bad dream just waiting to wake up.

The Second Secretary, who had been polishing his gold-rimmed glasses, stared up at Beck with an expression of glum horror that made his sharp, beady eyes seem like an imbecile's.

"Beck." Dickson was rod-straight, standing at the head of the table: "Why the fuck won't you carry your damned gun like you've been told to? Your degrees aren't bulletproof, and it's going to be open season on Americans as soon as the rest of the world realizes how thoroughly we've pissed in everybody's drinking water."

The four other senior staffers were like limp rag dolls. Beck had the impulse to find some cold water to throw on them.

"Answer one question for me, Dickson, and I promise I'll strap on my government-issue iron—*if* I like the answer."

"Go ahead, smart-ass." Dickson's reaction to personal danger was always fury after the crisis had passed. During one, he was anybody's best man.

"The question is, do we still *have* a government?"

The First Secretary, a black man with distinguished graying temples, turned his face to the window and began quietly to weep.

"Of course we've got a government—we've got a roaring mad ex-Vice President who's taking the Oath of Office—" Dickson glanced at his watch "—even as we speak, safe as he can be underground at . . . you know where."

Beck didn't: the new President could be at the Aerospace Defense Command Center, Norad, or any of a half dozen other sanctuaries. "Beggs, you mean?" Beck said distastefully: Claymore had been a hothead, but comprehensible; Beggs was a politician through and through, a viper.

"Beggs. Claymore put a bullet in his mouth after he pushed the button. The war lasted," Dickson sat on the table, running his fingers absently through the gear meant to protect them from chemical warfare, and began Beck's briefing with acid precision, his previous emotion gone now as he began doing what he knew he did very well, "exactly forty minutes—one salvo each, unrecallable, of course, mostly submarine-launched, we think: our Deltas, their SS-NX-20s and SS-N-18s."

Beck digested that, trying not to let his emotions show: any missiles launched from submarines had a CEP—circular error probability—of as much as a mile, and these were MIRVed missiles: the SS-NX-20s carried twelve MIRVs with a five thousand mile range; the SS-N-18s, three MIRVs with a maximum range of four thousand miles. The strikes would hardly have been surgical. His mind threw up images of fireballs rising forty thousand feet in the air whose "Rem"—Roentgen-Equivalent-in-Man—was as high as four thousand. Seven hours later, one tenth of that radiation would be present, and every seven hours thereafter it would decrease until it reached a low level of three or four Rems per hour, where it would stay for three or four months. Absorb four hundred Rems in a day or a week, and your chances of survival were fifty per cent or less; absorb less than a hundred, and you might pull through with modest care and live another thirty or forty years, though your odds of getting cancer within fifteen or twenty years increased drastically. All he could think of was his family—Muffy, the kids.

But Dickson was still talking: "Beggs and his opposite number—I'm not quite sure who that is just yet—in the Kremlin, did their best to minimize the damage. We can't get a damage assessment of any consequence, won't have one for a while: the electromagnetic pulse and some of the Soviets' first impulses—killer satellites and the like—knocked out almost everything . . . all communications, anyway. We do have some satellites which were transiting the southern hemisphere, but . . . well," and suddenly Dickson slumped and his compact, upper-class little body seemed almost to melt, "we'll just have to play it by ear."

"By ear," Beck repeated numbly as what he was hearing sank in. "You wouldn't happen to know exactly how many nukes hit us, would you? Where the red zones are?"

"Not yet, I told you. We think there were a lot of misfires, as many as one out of three—old weapons will malfunction—but I'm not suggesting you fly home tonight to take your wife for a carriage ride in Central Park . . . or that you'll be able to do so any time soon."

"Not in this lifetime," the First Secretary muttered.

"We can do without any defeatist talk, Sammy. Beck's missed all the fun. We were just about to start collating what reports we've got—" Dickson's hand waved aimlessly and Beck realized that Dickson wasn't taking this as well as he was pretending.

And neither was he: there was a lump in his throat and he kept seeing TV fireballs rising up to heaven. He thought, in a moment of private despair, that if he were lucky, his wife and kids would

already be dead. Then he thought about the catas-
trophe-theory model that purported to prove that
any nuclear detonation of consequence would
plunge the entire world into an endless night of
icy death.

Then he said, "Do we have to put this stuff on?"
and poked at the protective masks and suits.

"It's up to you. It's kind of hard to work in it.
We'll have enough warning, the Israelis say, of any
serious radiation hazard blowing this way." Dickson
blinked like a rabbit in Beck's headlights. "There's
still—something, you know ... there's the Red
Cross, and there's a UN, sort of, though God knows
we can't raise the building it used to be housed in.
That's what we're doing, trying to find out what
we can do to help. . . ."

Abruptly, Beck sat down. "Right. Well, let's see
what we've got for assets." And the words reminded
him: "You realize that this whole thing, unless
I've got my signals crossed, happened because none
of us had the guts to put our careers on the line
and back up Ashmead's people?"

Nobody said anything for a long time. Beck
wanted to get it over with, though: "So it's our
fault, gentlemen. In pursuit of a Palestinian solution,
and with a careful eye to the feelings of our oil-
producing friends, we may have destroyed the civilized world."

It wasn't until much later that Beck remembered Christine Patrick or his convention of genetic engineers.

The first was understandable—she'd just appeared in his life and didn't bear on the problem

at hand; the second was inexcusable—the brain-power sequestered by day on the Dead Sea but allowed the freedom of Jerusalem at night might be the extent of America's remaining brain trust.

Chapter 2

Five hours later, Chris Patrick was having dinner on Beck's balcony and watching him stare defiantly out over the American Quarter into a blazing Israeli sunset that made you understand why three of the world's great religions claimed this spot as their spiritual home, listening while Beck explained why the lights were on in Jerusalem, and in general fed her the official line.

"... so you see, Chris, wherever old tube transformers are in use or where defensive hardening of long lines has been undertaken or those lines are fiber-optic or underground or shielded by certain types of porous rock or by the earth's curvature from the force of the blast, communications and power stations are pretty much intact."

"Pretty much," she echoed, and Beck looked away from the darkening horizon of purple and gold to assess her face—that was what Beck did; he didn't look at her, he evaluated her and then took the appropriate measures.

She knew he was using her as an *ad hoc* stringer— a conduit for information the US government wanted to float, but she couldn't imagine who it was he wanted her to tell. The world was ending and this very bright, disconcertingly attractive man of the inaccessible type that used to give her a terse "no comment" on the way to a waiting limousine from a meeting in the Tank or the White House didn't seem to realize it.

Now he said, his even-featured, supremely American face composed and his eyes delving into hers so that she sat back in her chair with crossed arms: "It could be worse, you know. Cheer up."

"How? How could it be worse?" He flustered her: she was sure he could see right into her soul, knew that, in the midst of Armageddon, all she wanted was to go to bed with him; that, as life as she'd known it was ending, all she could think of was getting laid by some career diplomat who undoubtedly had a wife who routinely spent fifty thousand a year on clothes but never looked dressed up, and who paid for it all with stock dividends from the portfolio she'd brought to their marriage.

"Somebody could have won," he replied, saw the shock on her face and reached out to enfold her hand, squeeze it quickly, then break contact: all very professional and earnest. "Does that sound subversive? It's not. It's practical: both sides realized the unworkability of continuing hostilities, admitted their mistake—there'll be no retributive strikes, no incursions of ground—"

"Practical?" Chris couldn't believe her ears. "Mistake? Continuing hostilities? What's to continue?" She fingered the little red-film badge he'd given her; not to worry, he'd said, until and if it clouds up: in her purse she had a pocket-sized Geiger counter—just a precaution this early, he'd told her; the local jet stream would carry the radiation downstream at a speed of one hundred miles per hour at forty thousand feet initially, but ground-level winds carried fallout at normal windspeed and that was an average of fifteen miles per hour— they had days to prepare, he'd smiled.

Beck sat back and loosened his rep tie. He had made the dinner while she watched—Salade Nicoise—telling her cheerily that she'd better eat all the greens she could before they became suspect; his manner now was similar and he seemed genuinely hurt that she was questioning his unassailable truths.

"Chris." He sat forward and there was something of the priest in him now, the zealot of unshakable faith. "You've got to stop feeling sorry for yourself if you want to survive."

She imagined saying, *I don't—just fuck me and I'll die happy*, but she wasn't that brave. In the five hours Chris Patrick had sat waiting for Beck in the inner offices of the consulate, she'd learned a lot: she was, after all, a trained observer. She'd learned that the consular staff had all been issued protective clothing and breathing apparatus, as well as Geiger counters and badges, but that they'd decided that wearing them would terrify a populace who must do without, so they were waiting for some sort of last-minute alert; she'd learned that their best advice to American citizens was to depart for southern hemisphere destinations if possible; if not, to collect as much food and drinking water as they could and plan to stay indoors for at least a month, wear protective clothing (hoods, hats, raincoats, high boots), carry paper masks when they went out, and seal their windows with duct tape.

"I told you," she said, hoping checked hysteria would pass for an imitation of his unflappable calm, "the nicest thing you can do for me—besides this wonderful dinner, of course—is lend me your gun."

Now Beck's eyes narrowed with an almost paternal outrage; black pupils seemed to swallow the smoky irises around them: "You're fixated. What makes you think I have a gun?"

"Well, you're a spook, aren't you?" she said defensively.

"Try sleeping pills, if you must—it's cleaner." He put down his fork and it clattered against the faience plate. "But if you're that intent on throwing your life away and you're not afraid of dying, I can offer you an alternative."

He was like a snake, striking; then he sat back and waited for her to respond.

"What do you mean? What kind of alternative— something for God and Country, I bet." She'd kept her temper in check through all his obscene references to second strike capability and subsequent incursions; she hadn't said a word, though she'd turned over the cassette in her little recorder on the table between them when the tape ran out. Now her horror got the best of her: "Do you think it matters that there won't be Soviet shock troops in Langley by morning? Do you think it helps that only the northeast seaboard, Silicon Valley and the northwest as far as Utah have been confirmed as your stinking . . . your fucking filthy radioactive red zones? It's over, can't you see that? God knows you *seem* intelligent—can't you get it through that handsome head of yours that this is the—"

"I told you to stop feeling sorry for yourself," he said quietly, and yet it was as if he'd slapped her across the face.

He stood up and went to the balcony's edge; the high-rise compound might have been in any of a number of cities she'd visited but somehow, she knew, Marc Beck would only have been here. He leaned with both hands on the hip-high concrete wall, then faced her again, his back to it: "Answer me," he said like an army officer to a soldier facing court-martial, and she realized he had her little tape recorder in one hand, the cassette in the other, and was methodically pulling the tape from its spindles.

"I don't understand the question—Christ, I don't even *remember* the question."

She stood up uncertainly and her napkin fell from her lap. He was angry and she didn't want him to be angry with her; the terror of his displeasure was more immediate than the terror of lingering death by radiation poisoning, and not only because she remembered what he had done to the panicked tourist in the consulate.

"Come here, Chris."

She did and he was holding yards of unwound recording tape over the balcony's edge, where it fluttered like ticker tape. Her neck was hot and she was so close to him she could have reached out and grabbed the loose tape as he dropped it and it wafted downward. She didn't and it disappeared into the dusk.

He probed her with his stare: "I could use you.

If you're angry enough, when you understand enough, if you're willing to die *for* something rather than as a victim *of* something."

She'd thought this before, now she said it: "You want me to be your stringer. You *are* a spook."

He shrugged: he didn't like her choice of words but that was a minor irritation and he was willing to bear with her—she was ignorant; he was patient.

He didn't say anything, so she went on: "But why? What's the use? No, I'm sorry; I do remember: don't feel sorry for myself. But my bureau's in a mess; there's no use in propagandizing, whether it's gray, black, or even white propaganda you've got in mind—"

"There's still an international edition of your paper; I've checked it out," he interrupted. "We want to set the record straight, for starters. We want to protect our people overseas in more substantial ways than having the Israeli government declare American money to be as good as shekels and make it a crime not to take our paper or our plastic." He faced her now, something like fervor glittering in his eyes so that he seemed like a priest again: "I keep telling you this isn't the end of the world and you keep refusing to register the input."

"You got that right, buddy," she muttered. And that stopped him, so she said, "Again, my apologies for not acting like a trooper. Please go on. You know all us girl reporters fantasize regularly about working for the CIA—"

"State."

"State. Tell me about the 'giving my life for something meaningful' part." She purposely misquoted him. Levity seemed the only safe refuge but, God, he was getting to her and she didn't even understand how or why. He'd thrown her interview tape away and at any other time, with anyone else, she'd have scratched his eyes out, or at least hollered that her First Amendment rights were being infringed upon. Where was all the hardboiled investigative cool she'd cultivated so long? Blown up, that was where, along with Boston and Washington and whatever else in between—Cuba, he'd said with a cynical smile, had taken a hit meant for Kennedy Space Center; both Kennedy and Vandenberg would be operational, he'd said, in seventy-two hours, as soon as new electronics could be flown up from Houston.

Flown? she'd asked on the tape that now blew through a Jerusalem street.

Flown, he'd replied with satisfaction, as if MIT had just beaten Harvard in the season's big football game. *We've had plenty of time to devise hardened shelters for our surveillance and other ... critical aircraft. We'll even have new weather and photoreconnaissance satellites up and running within a couple of months.*

Suddenly, these and other things that he'd said began to sink in: Mark Beck, whose information was much better than hers could hope to be, was certain that the world would go on; more, that the US would continue to exist as an entity despite the, *oh*—she remembered him estimating the numbers, the way his eyes crinkled at the corners—*eight or nine million initial and fifteen to thirty million subsequent related casualties.*

"I can talk to you only in general terms until we reach an understanding, Chris." This was his professional voice and he spoke to her with all the care he would have used with an enraged foreign potentate or an angry superior. "We need to send an on-site inspection team back home—some of our people to accompany UN representatives, the International Red Cross, various do-gooders and gloaters. We want a reporter on that team, someone we can trust, someone who's going to have the right instincts and take the right direction."

"Holy fuck," she breathed, forgetting her manners. "Do we get Geiger counters, neat little radiation suits like you've got in the consulate? Security clearances?"

He grinned obliquely. "All of that and more—except for the security clearances: most of the others won't have them; they won't need them. You will. So we've got a lot of talking to do and the inevitable forms to fill out ... if you've got the requisite amount of sand in your craw."

"Will *you* be going?" she asked suspiciously, though she wanted to ask how long she'd live, afterward, if she agreed.

"You bet," he said and for the first time put a hand on her waist in other than a professional manner.

"There's more to this than what you've told me, of course."

"Of course, but you'll know everything you need to know when—"

"—I need to know it," she finished for him, giggling. Then she leaned against him and rested her head against his shoulder: "Once we get there, how long have we got—will the radiation kill us, or what? I'll need some pretty special communications gear. . . ."

"Getting in and out are going to be the hard

parts—there are lots of hysterical people over there right now. It won't be the radiation that kills us; we can protect ourselves against that, and if everybody follows their instructions no one will get sick; it's physical violence and the possibility of mechanical failure or human error we've got to worry about, just like on any other . . ."

She wondered what he had been going to say: mission, operation?

But then his hand, which had been demurely on her waist, slipped upwards and his face turned into her hair and he said, "And ourselves, of course."

Before she could ask what he meant, Beck kissed her, tentatively at first and thereafter with all of the fervor that hid behind his eyes.

When her tongue was free for speech, she was breathing heavily: "God, I thought we'd never get to the good part. It's okay if you sleep with one of your agents, then; this is by the book? Good spook procedure?"

"Hell, no," he said. "Sleep with a newsie? I'm about to commit treason. Come on, Mata Hari; it's time you saw the site of my fall from grace."

His bedroom faced west, toward Tel Aviv and the sea; he opened the glass sliding doors and thin curtains blew in the wind, showing her a starry night so beautiful her eyes filled with tears and she hugged herself.

He noticed and said, "Just for tonight—tomorrow I'll have the windows taped, even sealed with lead foil, if it'll make you feel better." Now it seemed that when he looked at her there was nothing else but her body on his mind.

Under that kind of scrutiny, as he unbuckled his crocodile belt and she remembered that it housed a deadly weapon, she felt naked in soiled work clothes. She hadn't thought, until then, about how she must look—dirty and sweaty and wrinkled.

Pulling off his desert boots, he peered up at her: "Change your mind?" His tie was gone, shirt unbuttoned and hanging loose over a short-sleeved T-shirt.

He'd caught her off-guard. What was it with him? She was as accomplished a sport-fucker as the next. Resolutely she pulled her shirt overhead to prove it: she had no bra on beneath and her nipples rose sharply in the cool air. It was the end of the world, and she was wondering if he liked her breasts.

She liked his buns, his muscular thighs and the shimmer of muscle under his belly hair as he bent to pick up his clothes and hang them neatly on the back of his chair.

"A shekel for your thoughts?"

She'd been thinking that it had been a long time since she'd made it with someone who wore white jockey shorts and a matching undershirt: she was wondering if he got high, or did this often, or ever let the lady be on top. She couldn't say that and she didn't want to watch him appraising her body, so she said, trying to be graceful as she pulled off her sneakers without untying them, belly held in, "Are you married, Beck—Marc?"

"Either am or used to be, hard to tell. Is that a problem? If you're having second thoughts . . ."

He came over to her and she thought that if he told her to forget it, she would, and run out of here, clothes in hand if she had to; she wasn't used to feeling vulnerable, or clumsy, or shy, and the way he watched her made her feel all three.

And then he slid his hands around her waist and up her spine, saying, ". . . it's a little late. I'm not letting you out of here until we both feel a whole lot better about life in general and one another in particular."

He was just under six feet and his erection pressed hard against her crotch as he held her, keeping her mouth too busy for questions, letting his hands ask her body what he wanted to know.

Her one extravagance was outrageous silk bikinis; when he'd peeled her down to them he got on his knees for a closer look and at some point judiciously declared that he was sorry, but they weren't going to make it through the night.

By then, in a stranger's hands on the last night of the world as she'd known it, she was weeping freely, staring out beyond him at the universe which had witnessed mankind's birth and now, probably, its death.

Standing, he saw her tears, tsk'd softly, picked her up in his arms and carried her to the bed she'd been studiously avoiding.

Like Beck, his bed looked appropriate, serviceable, but nowhere near as accommodating, as strong and supple and welcoming as it was.

The sheets were white but they were linen; the springs didn't make a sound as he lay her down. On the night table beside it she saw a copy of *Orbis*, open face down, the only sign here of what he did or what he was.

Then he switched off the reading lamp and sat quietly beside her, in the breeze that might be killing them as he stroked her and she found herself rising to meet his hand, her tears drying, and her hunger for him erasing all her fears.

As he bent down to her, lowering himself carefully but in such a way that his knee was between
her thighs, he told her, "Now you're going to forget about all this bullshit, all your troubles and
my troubles and the world's troubles. You're going
to relax and let me prove to you that there're still
some things worth living for," and guided her hand
onto him.

"Christ," she muttered, clasping him.

His knee tight against her crotch, he said, "Now,
rookie agent, if you'll just turn over and let me
drive, you're going to find out there's not a damn
thing to be afraid of when you're with me."

He was very good at it, so good she forgot to
pump him about his real reasons for inviting her
on his suicide mission, and everything else except
the feel of his strong hands on her buttocks and the
life he was pouring into her.

Chapter 3

The following day, Beck earned his keep: he called in every marker he had out among the Israeli intellectual community and convened a classified meeting of expert climatologists, physicians, geneticists, plasma physicists, mathematicians specializing in catastrophe effects, and military scientists who couldn't have talked to anyone but him and his under the kind of security he could promise.

He handed out masks and badges and everyone put them on, so that they looked like a bunch of medical students, until a climatologist remarked that he didn't really feel the masks were necessary because the jet stream was blocked—the plumes of short half-life radiation were locked into a pattern over the strike zones and the poles. There was an audible sigh of relief and the meeting began in earnest not, as Beck had expected, with his pathetic precautions-at-hand lecture, but with the climatologist's cheerful assessment that thermals had caused the jet stream to block and, if the jet stream stayed blocked for a week or two, Israelis would be exposed to no more than three or four Rems per hour and no less than one and one half Rems, for the three or four months it would take for the count to drop to point four Rem—a survivable level, certainly, if people minimized exposure of skin and lungs to unfiltered air.

Then a genetic engineer named Morse, whose specialty was cancer research, picked up the ball, and the meeting was alive and rolling.

At the end of that session, the joint report wasn't published; it was delivered by Beck and his opposite number from the Israeli government to Dickson verbally and concisely: "We think the jet stream will block—we think it *has* blocked," said Beck to Dickson, who didn't know what the hell he was talking about but had learned that, with Beck, if you kept your mouth shut long enough, you found out. "So the salvage operation is feasible, with enough Israeli support," and Beck's glance flicked to the Slavic-looking Israeli beside him.

"And that support we are willing to give," the broad-faced Israeli said grimly. "This blocking of the jet stream, everyone agrees, will mean that the worst radiation effects will be locked into an area relatively small for you, though gigantic by our standards."

"That's right," Beck said with equanimity. "When the initial blast occurred, the thermal effects— superheated columns and so forth—caused the jet stream to freeze in place. Now the weather conditions everyone was bitching about ... fierce cold up north, from Washington State to Moscow ...

are doing us a favor. If the jet stays blocked, the updrafts severe, then the worst of the radiation hazard will be limited to the American and Soviet north, where the plumes blowing downstream are dirtiest because the missiles were going after hardened sites."

The Israeli pulled a map out of his pocket and, saying, "With your permission, Mister Secretary?" spread it on Dickson's desk.

On the map were wide yellow lines like a stylized snake in mid-slither which covered the upper northern hemisphere in such a way that certain areas were free of what Dickson rightly assumed to be the radiation hazard: the yellow line dipped down across Alaska, covered Utah and Kansas, snaked on to loop around Cuba and Washington and up toward Greenland; then it swooped down again over the Urals and undulated toward the Sea of Japan before rearing its head again toward Alaska. The Middle East, South Asia, the southern hemisphere, and NATO's southern components would be spared the worst of it, if the projections were accurate.

"And if you're wrong?" Dickson said, his voice sick and brittle to his own ears, his eyes darting from his sealed windows, the filtration unit Security had installed to purify his air, to his little film badge, then to the Israeli.

"Then we shall all glow in the dark," said the Israeli with an air of fatalism. "Radiation goes where God sends it; after seven hours, it is one-tenth as severe; after seven times seven hours, a tenth of a tenth; after three days, the hazard decreases somewhat more; after fifteen days, it is down by a factor of ten. God is good; soon we will know for sure . . ." His eyes were welcoming Dickson like a new brother to the family of the holocaust, fond and understanding.

Beck said, "Look, Dickson, we're not pretending that this is the best news you've ever had. We're talking about initial, low-half-life radiation. When the polar caps melt—which they'll surely do at a higher rate than normal this year—everybody's going to give up fish and there'll be a run on Halazone tablets and whatever other precautions people think will help. The cancer rate's going to be astronomical. But that doesn't mean we shouldn't do whatever we can."

"And since we Israelis understand your loss as no other people, and have our own interests in seeing America through this most trying of times, all the resources of the State of Israel are at your disposal," said the Israeli Dickson knew as Netanayhu, who wore khakis as if he'd been born in them and probably grew up on some kibbutz playing cowboys and Indians with real guns and Palestinian kids as the Indians.

"That's very white of you, Mister Netanayhu," said Dickson, "especially since Lockheed and the rest of our military-defense establishment built, serviced, and just about *gave* you people everything you've got." Dickson hated Jews when they got superior, and that was all too often. To Dickson's way of thinking, Beck and his crew were just marking time until their hair started falling out.

"Not *all* of it, Chief Dickson," Beck said with an insubordinate edge to his tone, but didn't elaborate. When Beck "chiefed" Dickson, it was a warning that the ice was getting thin. "The colonel," Beck flicked his unholy stare at Netanayhu and then back to Dickson, "and I are going to go ahead with this, unless you've got a countermanding order. . . ."

"No, suit yourselves. It's your funerals, gentlemen. Just don't tax our meager resources. And . . ." The heavy-set Israeli colonel was rolling up his map; if he was smirking, Dickson couldn't see it. ". . . Colonel Netanayhu, on behalf of the United States, I guess I have to thank you—"

"Thanks are not necessary, Mister Secretary," said the Israeli, stuffing the map in his rumpled khakis; "not necessary at all. Did you thank us when we went into Beirut after the Palestinian murderers? Did you thank us in '73? Then don't thank us now. Even, if you want, be surly. We understand. We have been there. We may be there again," said the Israeli without a hint of condescension, centuries of warriors looking out through his eyes, "if your country does not recover. So, as it turns out, what we have is yours—even our sympathy."

Beck got the Israeli colonel out of Dickson's office before Dickson, white with fury, could think of something sufficiently scathing to say; then, making excuses to Netanayhu that the colonel assured him were unnecessary, Beck helped Netanayhu into his bulletproof and now spray-sealed raincoat and walked his Israeli ally to a waiting limo before going back into Dickson's office, forebearing to knock and slamming the door behind him.

"What the fuck did you think you were accomplishing, Dickson?" Beck, who almost never used foul language to a superior, strode across the Indo-Tabriz carpet and glowered down at Dickson, who had evidently put on his breathing mask as soon as Beck left and hurriedly ripped it off now, his eyes defiant and his thin hair askew as he slouched at his desk, snapping the mask's elastic.

"Accomplishing? Nothing at all, Beck. Which shows that I'm saner than you are. What's the use of this? Any of it?" *Snap*! went the elastic. *Snap*!

"If you keep this up—Sir—I'm going to have to suggest that you take a leave of absence until you're thinking more clearly."

And Beck could do it—had his own channels to those still putatively in control. But he didn't want to do it; he wanted to put his Bureau Chief back on track, shake him out of his funk.

"I . . . I can't stand it when those greasy little bastards start treating me like an idiot son."

"Then don't act like one. Look, I know how you feel—things are tough." Beck wished he didn't know how Dickson felt; there were lots of anti-Semites in the diplomatic corps, but having one at the helm in Jerusalem now, when America desperately needed Israeli help and protection for its citizens from angry Arab mobs in the Middle East, might turn out to have the opposite of the balancing effect intended by State when they'd sent Dickson here. However, Beck didn't have time to do much more than say, "No American likes it when he's face to face with somebody who thinks we're about to become a nation of refugees. The Israelis are probably the staunchest allies we've got right now. Try to remember that."

"Oh, mother of God, why me," Dickson whispered, not an answer Beck considered to be confidence-building.

"Because," Beck said, "I need you." It was a standard ploy, but Dickson raised his bleary, sick eyes. "I want to explain to you what you've got to do in—" Beck consulted his black chrome watch "—fifteen minutes, and I want you to do it as perfectly as you've ever done anything in your life. A lot of other lives depend on it."

Dickson was nodding slowly, like one of those glass birds that dip into a water glass for hours once you get them started. "Righty-O, son." He straightened up. "And thanks for . . . covering my lapse. It won't happen again. Let's hear what you've got."

"I've got a genetic engineer coming over here, a man named Morse, one of ours, who was at the conference. His clearance is Top Top and he's got an anti-cancer drug: it's a sort of vaccination . . . unproven, of—"

"He's got a *what*?" Dickson's face was lit from within as if someone had just rolled back the clock seventy-two hours.

"Recombinant DNA—you've heard of it, surely?" Beck said wearily. He'd been running on nerves for the last eighteen hours and he needed fuel—food, coffee, an enemy he could fight, something else besides Dickson's slow vapidity. He conjured Chris Patrick's ass and the vision buoyed him. "My conference, remember? On the Dead Sea? This morning I had breakfast with Morse and briefed him on the situation at home—the news will be out momentarily in any case."

Beck waited for a roar of outrage from Dickson at this flagrant violation of security, but none was forthcoming.

Instead, Dickson murmured, "A cure for cancer, well, I'll be damned."

"An experimental drug which the Israelis have agreed to help us produce in sufficient quantity to do a test—on Americans. It won't help those already dying, but it will prevent fragmentation of DNA, inversions, inhibit free radicals from—"

"Speak to me in English, Beck," Dickson said with disgust. "If this . . . Morse has got something, and the Israelis will loan us facilities, what's the problem?"

"Problems. A half dozen of them. First, security clearance—Morse can't give the formula to the Israelis without permission until you tell him he can. Second, waivers of some sort: Morse still thinks there's an FDA; he figures about twenty years of testing are in order before trying this stuff on humans. He wants it in writing that the Food and Drug Administration won't pull his license. Third, he's got family back there and he wants them out, if they're alive. Fourth, he wants to go along to make sure we get to his family, give them preferential injections, and bring them out. Fifth and sixth, he wants a lot of money and a position at one of the universities here under our auspices—" Beck raised his hands—this sort of morass was Dickson's territory, not his own—and looked at his chief, hoping for some sign in that flaccid face of Dickson's former sharpness, an indication that what he was saying was getting through to Dickson.

"I can't guarantee this Morse a visiting professorship at an Israeli university," Dickson mused, head down, tapping his Cross pen on his terrifyingly clean desk—Dickson's desktop was always invisible. Then he looked up and Beck knew that everything was going to be all right, or as all right as the two of them could make it in a world determined to destroy itself even though it might just have a second chance.

Dickson's small-featured face was a convolution of wrinkles that extended well up into his balding pate: "You'll have to romance the Israelis, after what I said to Netanayhu." Dickson got a notepad and started jotting. "As for the rest of it—screw the FDA, if we've still got one."

Excitedly, Dickson got up from his desk and Beck, relief like a dose of fatigue wastes flooding his system, sat heavily upon one corner of it.

"You'll see Morse, then? Convince him? Give him carte blanche? It's just for two weeks or so while the Israelis produce the material and I find the other people I need. . . ."

"Other people?" Dickson said warily.

"I told you I'll want the reporter, Chris Patrick; the paperwork's being done for her."

"I remember," Dickson snapped, his old self. "I'm not addled or senile."

Beck didn't comment on Dickson's state of mind: what he had to say next wasn't going to go down well. "I'll need some support types—people who can handle the logistics, security, and anything that might come up in the field. If this leaks, we'll never get out of Israel with that serum, let alone as far as the US: the Russians don't want us any better off than they are; everybody in the world is living in his own I'm-going-to-die-of-cancer nightmare. Morse, his project, and that crate of serum are going to be the hottest intelligence targets since the paperwork from the Manhattan project."

"How about your Israeli friends?" Dickson asked hopefully.

"No dice. They're doing enough and we're not telling them exactly what we're doing—we're faking it, saying the serum arrests the progress of radiation sickness."

"Mother of God," Dickson moaned. "You're using them for this and you don't trust them?"

Beck bared his teeth: "I don't trust anybody—not on this. I'm not sure I trust you. I'll bet your first thought was how soon you could get your shot."

"You mean . . . I'm *not* going to get one? Beck, we've got to take care of our own people first. Those we *know* will survive—it's triage. . . ."

Beck put up a hand. "You'll get it, don't worry. But how did you feel when you thought you might not? There's no way in hell we can produce enough for every man, woman and child on what's left of the earth in time. . . . So we've got to be particular. And we've got to be very careful about security."

Dickson rubbed his eyebrows: "I agree." Relief was still evident in his voice. "When's this genius Morse coming? Fifteen minutes, you said? I can probably put together a citation for valorous service; he'd like that. . . ."

"Five minutes from now. Never mind the citation, Dickson. I want an operational budget, no receipts required. And I want a free hand: if this blows and President Beggs never gets his shot, you don't want it to be your head that rolls. Okay?"

"Certainly. And about your security people? Do you know whom you want?"

This was it. Beck slid off the desk and faced Dickson squarely: "Sure do. I want Ashmead and whoever he wants."

Dickson turnd ashen. "Ashmead. *Ashmead*? What are you expecting, to be interdicted by an entire Soviet division? Absolutely not. Find someone else."

"There's no one else I'd trust," Beck said flatly.

"But he's CIA! He's a murderous, insubordinate cowboy! He's ... he's barely human; he's got no feelings, no—"

"He'll do the job with me and he won't ask me to give him his shot first. And, CIA or not, he and I get along."

"Well, it's impossible. You can't let the Agency in on this: their shop's so full of holes you might as well send a telegram to—"

"Don't give me that interagency rivalry crap. Not now. It's Ashmead or I'll just sit here and blow this thing off so completely that, even given what you know, you'll never be able to put it back together—not with Morse, or the Israelis. And don't think I won't do it."

"Look," Dickson, his mind on his own inoculation, approached Beck with something akin to desperation. "It's not that I don't think Ashmead's a good choice ... or even that the two of you couldn't keep a lid on things. But I had occasion to talk to the Tel Aviv station chief, and Ashmead—*and* his nasty little operations team—have disappeared. It seems they've taken out after the Islamic Jihad on their own, figuring that it's every man for himself and, for their parts, they want to take as many of the Jihad with them to Paradise as they can manage."

"That's Ashmead, all right," Beck said drily to cover his shock. "Well, then, I guess I'll have to go find him. Hold the fort, Dickson, and be nice to my biogenetic engineer."

Beck made for the door as Dickson, still wheedling, demanded to know how Beck thought he was going to find a CIA agent when the CIA couldn't, how long he'd be gone, and where he could be reached.

"Don't know, Sir," said Beck to all of those as he left Dickson's office at the very moment Morse arrived.

Chapter 4

The dusky air blowing south off the Persian Gulf into Abu Dhabi had death in it—Ashmead could smell it and it raised the tempo of his pulse while all around him the capital city of the United Arab Emirates prepared for another languid Arabian night.

He and his team were professionally unremarkable in the narrow shadowed street of coffee bars and market stalls; the street itself, restless in twilight, churning in slow motion as it made the transition from day to night, was another of his agents, part of the team, accommodatingly providing them perfect cover in an imperfect world.

Down the street, drinking sweet coffee and waiting unknowingly for the death Ashmead's team brought like a tin of sweetmeats wrapped in newspaper, was the quarry, one of the Islamic Jihad's revolutionary heroes. He was their mullah's son, a sullen-faced boy with lamb's eyes who had studied nuclear physics at Caltech and done his graduate work in Libya, who dressed Western in blue jeans and gold to flaunt his intellectual's status but didn't have enough common sense to go into hiding or even wear a kefiya to ward off the radioactive dust he'd helped blow into everybody's sky. He sipped and sat in blissful ignorance while around him Ashmead's *reshet*—network—tightened like a noose.

If ignorance were truly bliss, the world would be at peace.

Ashmead felt an almost sexual attraction to the bomb-maker he was going to kill: the death on the breeze from the Gulf tonight was Ashmead's to give and the Iranian's to receive—if there was another, subtler taint to the sea wind, the counterterrorist refused to think about it: his team and he had decided there wasn't a damned thing you could do to better your odds; they weren't going around in paper masks or worrying about hours of exposure or holing up in basements; they were getting in their last licks.

Now he was browsing among the stalls, buying vegetables, looking for a yam. He'd rather have had a nice, firm Idaho potato but his specialty was weapons at hand, and he didn't have his carry-gun, with its threaded muzzle, on him: he was going to kill the kid they'd nicknamed Schvantz, in case any of their low-tech communications were intercepted, with a throw-away scratch-gun he'd bought on the gray market and the old 9mm Tokagypt 58 was going to need some kind of silencer—this wasn't a suicide mission.

Lazily he fondled fruit and produce, buying pomegranates and other exotic delicacies he didn't need along with the yams, desultorily haggling with the vendor, in desert headgear he hoped would protect him from this newest American threat to the very air, who wanted to finish with Ashmead and two other late customers behind him and go home.

Ashmead's Arabic matched the black-and-white kefiya on his head: Palestinian in accent, like the aghal binding it to his head and the desert fatigues he wore tucked into combat boots. He wanted the street peddler to remember him, to give a Palestinian's description, and so he would: *Yes, yes*, the peddler would say to the police, and then to the secret police, and then to the national guard—a *Palestinian; no, I don't remember the face, it was late, his kefiya cast shadows ... who can tell one Palestinian from another?* And then, when pictures of uniforms and men were shown to him: *But perhaps ... yes, I am sure now that he was bearded, that he wore his kefiya in the manner of Habash's PFLP fighters.*

And that description, plus the fact that the gun was not a Beretta 92, Fatah's issue weapon, would place the blame for Schvantz's assassination squarely where Ashmead wanted it: on the doorstep of Habash's faction, the very same Palestinians who had helped the Islamic Jihad blow the fucking lid off Home Plate.

It was a matter of honor to Ashmead's team; they'd been pulled back by their own superiors in Tel Aviv and Langley when they could have intervened.

Ashmead had been sitting with his thumb up his ass on Cyprus, drinking Turkish sludge in Nicosia and watching the beginning of the end of every damn thing he cared about, when one of his team, a kid they called Slick, had slipped into the wrought-iron chair beside him and, fingering brown olives to find the firmest in the bowl on the checkered table, had said, "Bugger all, Rafic. Let's get the lot of 'em—the mullah and all his chickens. We've talked it over, and we figure that in fourteen hours there's not going to be any Agency, at least not enough of one for us to be sweating any disciplinary action. We estimate we owe it to those holy warriors to give 'em a head start to Paradise. . . ." Slick's sight-picture eyes had been shining like a laser. "We're not pushing you, Sir, you understand—this isn't a fucking mutiny. We just thought you ought to know how we feel—that we're game to play until we drop from . . . well, you know. And we'd really appreciate it if you'd run us this one more time. We'd sure like to die happy—fulfilled like. Let's grease as many of those cocksuckers as we can in the time we've got left. Why not?"

Why not, indeed. Looking at Slick, like a hunting dog straining at the leash, knowing the grouse were out there, Ashmead couldn't think of a single reason why not. His covert action team was the best America had; maybe there was one Saiyeret team as good in the Middle East. They knew what was going to happen; he'd known they'd been talking things over. When Slick came to him, he'd half expected it to be with a fond farewell and an apology because they wanted to go home, spend the last of it with their families.

That had been what he was about to tell them to do; he didn't want to sit in Haifa watching them drop, one by one, mooning around until they did, pretending it mattered if they ran through the killing house one more time, or spent as much time as they could in the basement, or scrubbed down when they came in from outside, or sprayed their flash hoods and double-thick uniforms to minimize porosity, or kept their gear in shape, or wrote readable after-action reports.

So they'd kicked butt out of Cyprus before the shit hit the fan, straight as the turbojet flies, and begun operating.

Schvantz was number three of seven, and the seventh was the impossible dream—the head motherfucker in Libya, the crazy who could only be gotten by someone willing to die in the attempt: part seven was the suicide mission. Schvantz was just a warm-up: Ashmead's. They'd decided on one apiece before Libya, and Schvantz was Ashmead's personal pick.

With his yams in his bag, Ashmead wandered a crooked path toward Schvantz's table near the curb, stopping again to buy some lamb grill (from an open stall—no one on the streets in Abu Dhabi seemed to understand that exposed food could kill you; the old ways would die with them) and thus having a reason to get out his knife and squat down, his bag beside him.

Slick, on a BMW motorcycle, puttered up the street and stopped opposite him, helmet on his head, booted foot on the kickstand, while Ashmead used his knife and a previously prepared paper circle the diameter of the Tokagypt's muzzle to dig an appropriate hole in the yam and channel a slot for the front sight to hold it in place.

Yael, her butt swinging provocatively under a mass of honey-colored hair that ensured no Arab on the street would be looking at anything else, got up from Shvantz's coffee bar and straddled the bike behind Slick. With a macho revving of the BMW's engine, the pair of lovers roared away, altogether too fast for the confines of the twisting, littered street and the Arabs on it, who jumped out of the way, cursing and gesturing obscenely.

Meanwhile, Ashmead eased across the street, lamb in the dirt behind him, yam and Tokagypt mated in the bag he held in one hand, the other gloved hand inside, on the gun, easing off the safety as he got a shooting grip on its plastic handgrips.

Schvantz was gazing after the pair on the BMW, indolent and stupid: this was the third day in a row he'd come here, waiting for a contact he didn't know to be dead. Routine kills people in the Great Game. His Libyan trainers had neglected to impress this lesson upon Schvantz strongly enough, or Schvantz assumed that his privileged status among Allah's chosen youth would protect him.

It wouldn't; not from Ashmead. Between the coffee stall and the bolt-cloth vendor to its right was an alleyway; right now the BMW was stopping at its far end, Yael hopping off and disappearing into a cheap hotel where she had a rented room in which to change her clothes and hair color while Slick waited, playing with his throttle, not for her but for Ashmed to come running down the alley and climb aboard. Three streets away, a nondescript Mercedes idled, ready to take them to the Hilton, its windows smoked so that Ashmead could change clothes in the car.

Two more of his team were riding shotgun in case something went wrong: one at one end of the street in a Ford with reinforced bumpers and bul-

letproof glass; the other, a sharpshooter named
Jesse, on foot a hundred yards behind Ashmead, a
machine pistol under his djellaba.

Schvantz was looking at his huge gold wrist-
watch; his second coffee came. This close, Ashmead
could see the acne scars on his face, the thick
lashes around almond eyes. Another few steps and
he could pull the Tokagypt casually up with the
bag as he sidled past Schvantz's table toward the
alley, shoot the kid in the brainpan, and be on his
way.

"Rafic! Hey, Rafic!"

The sound of an American voice calling his
workname—his god-fucked workname!—was like
coitus interruptus; unexpected, unwelcome, and
maddening.

Worse, he turned his head to look back—to see
who the hell was bawling his name.

Worst, Schvantz, in a clatter of crockery, cutlery,
and furniture, was bolting as if he were late for
prayer: the target, almond eyes wide in recognition and terror, stumbling over outstretched legs
of fellow customers as he went, was already in the
street, running and looking back over his shoulder
and howling to Allah to protect him.

There was a long moment in which Ashmead
considered taking down the kid despite the fact
that his name would be forever linked with the
killing. During this interval, he ignored the American hand outstretched to him in greeting. His eyes
were locked with those of the backup in the hooded
djellaba: Jesse wanted to know if he should swing
up his machine pistol and riddle Schvantz, who
was running toward him at breakneck speed.

Ashmead watched and considered, the Tokagypt

loose in the string bag now, his shooting hand on his hip. Then he gave the abort signal—he wanted Schvantz to be DX'd by a Palestinian, that was the damn point—and turned his attention to the American who had blown four days of intensive preparations by six devoted professionals.

Before him stood the State Department's boy wonder, Beck, wearing sunglasses, a radiation badge, and a baseball cap, his Ivy League grin and his innocence intact, gloved hand out to greet him: "Rafic, let's get out of the open, have a talk somewhere clean. I've been looking for you for a week. You sure can be hard to find when you want to be."

"Not hard enough. What the fuck are you doing here, Beck? Somebody forgot to lock you in your crib last night?" He was seriously considering shooting Beck, and his voice reflected his mood.

Beck withdrew his hand; he wiped it on his brand-new Levi's; his smile faded, to be replaced by tardy comprehension: "I've interrupted something? I'm terribly sorry . . . but this is urgent."

"It fucking well better be, Beck. You've ruined my whole day. And a lot of other people's." He looked Beck over more critically: the buckle-knife Ashmead had given him fastened Beck's belt; the belt was a one-and-one-half-incher and it had the telltale sag to its right side that meant Beck was carrying, probably behind the hip with his weapon's holster tucked into his hip pocket; otherwise, there'd be no need for the windbreaker tonight.

His net bag in hand and Beck beside him, Ashmead sauntered down the alley without more than one backward and openly quizzical look at the Iranian who was now careening around the corner while Jesse slouched against the wall in disgust. *Plan B, folks,* Ashmead thought, and shrugged his disappointment away.

He had other things to worry about. Beck, in particular.

The INR man was pacing him obediently; Ashmead had handled Beck's "orientation"—meaning he'd tried to instill enough tradecraft in somebody who'd always been able to get by on his brains to ensure that Beck would survive his tour. Tradecraft, in this venue, meant defensive driving, weaponry drills, and a quick course in kitchen ballistics that none of the gentlemen who'd prepared this walking computer beside him for the field had thought he'd need.

And Beck had been a good student: he was nothing if not precise. The kid—Beck was only five years younger than Ashmead, but elapsed time had nothing to do with manhood, in Ashmead's scheme of things—was coordinated and as sharp as the knife in his belt. He'd studied diligently and practiced until he was black and blue in the appropriate places. The only thing Ashmead hadn't been able to teach Beck was that Ashmead was never wrong. Beck had given a negative assessment of Ashmead's last intelligence report on the Islamic Jihad, or Ashmead wouldn't have been pulled off the scent—the kid carried a lot of weight with the suits back home.

"I hope nobody knows you're here. I sure as fuck know nobody at the Agency could have helped you find me."

It wasn't a question, but Beck felt compelled to answer: "No, Sir. I was very careful. I assume you know about Home Plate—that you were right?"

Ashmead gave a disgusted snort; he was looking into a gloom for some sign of Slick. As they passed the midpoint of the alley, a cat jumped out of a garbage pail with a yowl and Ashmead's gun came up, yam and all.

"What the hell—?" said Beck, squinting at the odd shape in Ashmead's hand. "What's that?"

Without a word, Ashmead handed it to him: it would explain a lot of things.

"Oh, Rafic, I'm sorry," Beck said, as if he'd just run over Ashmead's best dog.

"It's not your fault, it's Jesse's." But that wasn't true—Jesse had never met Beck, couldn't have guessed, and had been implicitly instructed against interdicting anyone who might come up that street unless he felt it necessary to warn Ashmead of local law approaching.

"Jesus . . ." Beck's 50 Meg mind was beginning to work on the bits of data he'd accumulated: "The Arab kid—the one who left so fast when he heard your name—a target? Islamic Jihad? A controller?"

"We've been calling him Schvantz," Ashmead said glumly.

Beck, a linguist, chuckled, then said carefully, "Ashmead, I'm not here to apologize, though I take full responsibility for the way we mucked things up—I've got a go on the drawing board that won't fly unless you're part of it." Before Ashmead could explain to Beck that he wasn't interested, Beck rushed on: "And it beats the hell out of seeing how many terrorists you can put in your shopping cart before the clock runs out."

Then Ashmead, full of adrenalin from his aborted operation, snatched the Tokagypt back, shook the yam from its barrel, thumbed the pistol on safe and threw it into his net bag: "Why, whatever do you mean, Mister INR honcho?" he said with exaggerated innocence. "My boys and girls are just taking a little well-deserved R&R with their dear old surrogate-poppa. I promised them they could spend their vacation any way they wanted, and this is their idea of a good time. They've earned it, and I'm seeing to it that they get it—uninterrupted."

Ahead, a headlight flared: Slick's signal.

"Come on, Ashmead, you know I wouldn't bother you if it wasn't—"

"Kid, I don't know anything of the sort. Like you said, you interrupted me. I'm busy. Find somebody else for your cockamamie mission. Want me to recommend somebody—?"

"Rafic, please just hear me out!"

"Look, Beck, there's no room for you on that bike up there and there's no room for you on my team. So go away. Compute casualty figures or something. Fucking bastard." Ashmead, still moving, edged away from Beck before his temper got the better of him: "You could have rammed that report of mine up Langley's back channel and saved us all a long, slow death. Why didn't you?"

Beck's head lowered in the gloom. His shoulders slumped. He said, with the most emotion Ashmead had ever heard from him: "*I* made a mistake." The admission had an edge of incredulity to it.

"You're a master of understatement, Beck, you know that? You fucked up like only somebody as smart as you are could. Now say that."

"I fucked up," Beck whispered.

"Good boy," Ashmead grinned. "Lesson number two: when you fuck up, you don't come running to me to help you ease your conscience. You bit this one off by yourself, and you're going to have to swallow it by yourself. Now say bye-bye. Me and mine have got lots of rag-heads to grease while we still can."

Beck reached out to touch Ashmead, who was close enough now to Slick's bike that the driver's helmeted head was turned their way and Slick's hand was resting inside his leather jacket, just in case Beck turned out to be a problem Ashmead couldn't handle.

Ashmead dodged the touch: "Beck, you want me to kill you, just ask, don't make me guess. I'll be glad to oblige you."

"Jesus, Rafic, why won't you listen to me? I've got something on that could save untold American lives—maybe make up for some of the harm I . . . we . . ." Beck broke off.

"Do I look to you like some pussy from the International Red Cross, Beck? Covert action, remember? We don't save lives, we take them."

Beck said only, *"Please*, Ashmead?"

And there was something in his tone that prompted Ashmead to give him the name of the hotel where he'd be having dinner: "You bring anybody with you, Beck, you're history. Comprende? Even if it's people you don't know, somebody following you. We're not going to care; we're not going to ask any questions. We're going to get you very dead, very quick."

"Right. Nineteen hundred hours. I'll be there."

Ashmead, as he slipped onto the bike behind Slick and the BMW roared away, could have sworn that Beck was smiling.

*   *   *

The dining room of the Abu Dhabi Hilton faces the Persian Gulf; Ashmead's party had a table in the corner where they would probably survive if the glass window-walls imploded and from which Ashmead could see both the customer entry and the door to the kitchen.

His team kept glancing at the sky; he couldn't blame them. These were the best operatives he'd ever had, perhaps the best anybody'd ever had in Covert Action; they were young and smart and healthy and they had everything to live for.

Unlike the networks they'd set up for him, the terrorists they'd infiltrated and on occasion assassinated for him, or the agents they'd run for him, all five team members were stone professionasls: Jesse, at the far end of the table, who had been born in the Galilee and spoke more Semitic and Indo-European dialects than even Ashmead, was their paramilitary expert—the consummate adviser to anybody's insurgency, a hardware connoisseur. Yael, next to him, a Bennington-educated Sabra, was a specialist in explosive ordnance as well as their queen of black and gray propaganda—when Covert Action wanted to set up a newspaper or a radio broadcast or place an editorial, it was Yael with her clear blue eyes and Aryan beauty who got the job done through persuasion, seduction, or loyal intermediaries; solid, stolid Zaki, next to her, was their chief interrogator and a field collector as good with Arabs as Dulles had been with Germans—Zaki had a string of informants among every Marxist-Leninist group involved with terrorism, a face nobody would look at twice in the Mediterranean or South Asia, and a way with electronics which had earned him the nickname Elint, for

Electronic Intelligence; on Zaki's left, with a
Lockheed Hercules baseball cap backwards on his
scruffy head, sat Thoreau, their Signals and Communications man and transport/logistics maven—
Thoreau had been seconded to Ashmead five years
ago from the SEALS for a mission that needed a
very special pilot and Ashmead had point-blank
refused to return him; opposite Ashmead was Slick,
Ashmead's deputy, who could overthrow a dicta-
torship and replace it with a friendly government
single-handed—Slick had it all.

The team had a wolfishness in common, always,
but tonight there was a dullness to their edge that
bothered Ashmead, a frustration that had more to
do with the fact that the sun hadn't broken through
the Gulf haze for three days than that they'd lost
Schvantz: it saddened Ashmead inexpressibly to
see his covert actors up against a wall they couldn't
blow up, tunnel under, fly over, or maneuver their
way around—the Forty-Minute War wasn't their
fault.

If it was the fault of anybody at that table, it
was his own—he could have ignored the pull-back
and turned his wolves loose in time. They weren't
blaming him—discipline was their religion; you
followed orders, you played your part, you sub-
sumed your personal feelings for the good of the
team and the operation: it was the only way.

Right down to the end they'd been telling each
other that Langley knew what it was doing, that
somebody else was on the case, that some other
operations team was going to get the glory. They'd
been telling each other that until Zaki called in
from the Riyadh airport to say that the Jihad's
suicide commandos had their bomb and their tick-

ets and Ashmead had had to tell Zaki to come in, to scrub the interdiction.

Even when their Agency turbojet was screaming out of Cypriot airspace toward the Gulf, Slick was saying, booted feet up on the seat across from him as he looked out the window so Ashmead couldn't see his face, "Maybe they'll blow those terrs out of the sky—yeah, a nice mid-oceanic jetliner crash. That's what they'll do. Who'd ever know? The right parallel, and nobody'll ever find that jetliner's black box . . . clean as a whistle, not even a diplomatic incident."

But Langley had done zilch, and here they were, in an almost-empty hotel dining room in Abu Dhabi that ought to have been full of fat and happy oil types dealing from a position of superior strength with Western businessmen in impeccably tropical worsteds—six foreigners at a table for seven getting burning looks from the hotel staff, who didn't quite dare refuse to serve them but wished they could.

Yael Saadia was picking at a hangnail as she said offhandedly: "I wouldn't put it past them to poison us; anybody in Occidental clothing is responsible for what's happened, as far as they're concerned." They were all dressed like tourists, to make a clean break with their earlier, operational identities, and Yael, a Western-looking woman, had been bearing the brunt of Arab frustration on the streets: the damage reports and warnings in the news were terrifying enough to make Arabs feel about Americans as they had long felt about Jews. "So I'll taste everything first, and we'll wait awhile to see what happens."

Thoreau raised his head and turned his baseball

cap around, a sure sign that what he was going to say was the pilot's final word: "My ass you will, Saadia." Thoreau and Yael Saadia were clandestine lovers; when he called her by her last name, she cupped her chin in her hand and looked away out the window without saying anything more.

"Speaking of waiting," Slick said, "who are we waiting for, Rafic?" He sighted-in on the empty chair. "Who was that guy with you in the alley today?"

"That *guy*," Jesse said with soft murder in his voice, "blew the scratch for us—he's the one that yelled Rafic's name." Jesse's lips pulled tight, remembering.

Ashmead's entire operations team eyed him steadily now, waiting to be briefed.

"Casper the friendly spook," he told him. "INR," he told them. "He says he's got something that might interest us more than what we're doing. We'll listen, we'll be polite, and we'll get back to him if we like what he's got to say."

"Unless he wants to reactivate the time-travel project," Slick cracked, "he ain't gonna say nothin' I wanna hear."

The team laughed at that—CIA had spent an unholy amount of money trying to determine whether it was operationally feasible to send an agent into the past: it hadn't been—people and other material things didn't travel well through spacetime; rumor had it that it had cost lives to find that out.

Zaki, their electronics expert and a physics buff, teased Slick: "What use, to reactivate such a project as Task Force 159?" Every interested party in the Agency had known the name of the supposedly secret time-travel project, a glum commentary on the state of Langley's internal security measures. "You would then volunteer, perhaps? And we would be rid of you. Ah, my friend, it is a temptation—even though 159 could not send so much as a bullet back through time formerly, perhaps in your case, with God's help, they will make an exception to the laws of physics. You are, after all, neither so quick as a bullet nor so necessary."

Again there were chuckles, and a chorus of "Ayes," as if a vote could propel Slick into the past, and even Ashmead's deputy joined in good-naturedly, saying that anywhere Zaki went, Slick would gladly follow. For they wanted to laugh, needed to regain their sardonic insouciance, to feel that, even if they'd lost their quarry today, there'd be other days and other targets.

That was all Ashmead wanted from Beck: Beck was going to make up for the boner he'd pulled by showing Ashmead's team that they were still in demand, that a government of some sort still existed, that somebody, somewhere, thought the sinking ship of state was salvageable. Then Beck could go fuck himself while Ashmead's Assassins, as his critics had tagged the team, got on with the business of countering terrorists.

Just then Beck came in, tall and charismatic next to the hook-nosed Ethiopian maitre d', waved and made his way toward them between empty tables.

The operations team twisted in their seats, following Ashmead's gaze and answering wave.

For a moment there was total silence; no one breathed. Then, like one man, five fists were raised and five thumbs turned down sharply.

As Beck came around to take the empty seat beside Ashmead, Zaki hissed softly; Jesse joined in; Thoreau pulled his cap's bill down over his eyes and tipped his chair onto its back legs; Yael said in a cutting, drawn-out *sotto voce:* "Booooo."

Only Slick applauded, five African-style claps of his hands that sounded like pop-gun reports a hundred yards away.

To give Beck credit, his welcoming grin stayed firmly in place as he shook hands with Ashmead and slipped into his seat: "I see my reputation has preceded me," he said generally and without a hint of defensiveness; pinned to his jacket collar was a radiation-sensitive film badge. "Good to see you again, Rafic. Sorry I'm late. If you've already ordered, that's fine. I'm here to talk, not eat. Gentlemen and lady, I'm Mark Beck, State's Intelligence liaison—"

"We know who you *are*, Casper; what we want to know is why you should continue to exist," Slick said pleasantly.

Ashmead sprayed his people with a glare to shape them up and everybody sat up straight. "Beck, this is Slick, my deputy; Yael Saadia, my chief of station; Zaki, case officer and ELINT; Jesse, counterinsurgency; Thoreau, COMINT, SIGINT and chauffeur."

"My pleasure, Slick, everyone," said Beck, sizing it up as it lay.

"Wish we could say the same. I've bled out people for less than you did today. Look, Mister State Department, say your piece and split before we lose our appetites, okay?" For Slick, that was polite: Ashmead had half expected him to say, *while you still can.*

Ashmead could have intervened, controlled Slick,

but he didn't bother: he was doing this for his people, not Beck. He sat back in his chair and toyed with his fork so that Beck would know he was on his own.

"Right," Beck said with a sigh, still managing to appear friendly and calm: "Let's define the objective, then—"

"Let's," Slick agreed drily.

"After past wars, the United States rebuilt Germany, even Japan; now we're going to do it for ourselves."

Snickers sounded; Ashmead's deputy lifted his hand from the tablecloth—just a few inches, but the team quieted immediately. "That's the objective; what's the operation—a temporal insertion?" Slick asked Beck. "You going to draft us into Task Force 159? It was your baby, we heard. 'Cause nothing short of that's going to make a flying fuck's worth of difference."

Beck bared his teeth in a facsimile of a patient smile. "159? I don't know what you're talking about. The operation I have in mind is both structured and unstructured. In its simplest form, it involves getting a scientist named Morse and a quantity of drugs to President Beggs and his staff—in the US." Beck paused for any ensuing hisses, boos, or mutters of incredulity, but none were forthcoming. He continued: "This we want to accomplish under the cover of a fact-finding tour composed of members of the International Monetary Fund, which is meeting now in Singapore—" From behind his hip, where Ashmead had assumed a firearm was secreted, Beck took a pouch and laid it on the table in front of Ashmead. "Open that up, will you, Rafic?"

As Ashmead reached for it, Yael shrank back

infinitesimally and he took time to glower at her
as he took the pouch, much heavier than it looked,
and emptied out its contents for all to see: six rolls
of coins marked *Krugeraands*—probably the entire
hard currency supply from Beck's consulate, unless the INR man was using his personal trust
fund for this, because American money and American plastic were no good in the Gulf, probably not
anywhere except Israel, where Americans could
call in markers due.

"There's your operational fund, folks—we're on
the gold standard, by order of the IMF, in order to
prevent a collapse of the entire world banking
system," Beck explained.

Nobody reached out to verify the contents of the
red paper rolls or even estimate their value:
Ashmead had brought the entire coin petty cash
fund with him when he'd left Tel Aviv, but everybody had too much valueless paper money on them
not to be impressed.

"Besides the IMF reps," Beck continued, as if he
were briefing an embassy staff on banquet preparations, "we'll have UN dignitaries, as soon as
they finish fighting over who's who in the new UN
in Sydney, as well as causists from the World
Health Organization, NATO envoys who must be
convinced that reciprocal courtesies to those we
showed them after the Second World War are in
order, two honorable sirs from the Japanese Ministry of Trade—"

"We *get* the idea, Beck. You want us to wet-
nurse a bunch of dips and leftists who're going to
stand around in their shiny contamination suits
and gloat. No dice."

At Slick's flat refusal, Beck, for the first time,

turned to Ashmead for aid, his Ivy League feathers beginning to ruffle, perspiration beginning to bead on his forehead: "Rafic, is that your answer, or just his?"

"I don't know yet, Beck. Keep talking."

"Check. Slick . . . all of you: I really need you. There are several reasons why your operations team is my optimum choice, but you're not my only choice, so if I can't convince you, I'll be on my way, no hard feelings, no attempts to pressure you through channels. This isn't a CIA operation and neither the Agency nor INR is in any shape to be heavy-handed. I'm asking you, agents of the American government, to do something more important for your country than forcibly retire a bunch of—"

"Rag-heads," Thoreau said with bared teeth. "We're all friends here, you don't have to be button-down polite with us." Tipping up his cap's bill with a knuckle, Thoreau leaned forward: "If I'm copying you right, you're talking about flying a mission over the Big Water and across what must be at least five hundred miles of red zones, just for starters. You've got a plane in mind that can do that?"

"All I can tell you—until we've agreed on specifics and you've signed on to the mission—is that I've got everything I need but you people. And I'll go to any lengths within my power to convince you to help. Specialists in paramilitary, propaganda, counterterrorism, and security are going to be crucial to this mission's success."

Jesse drew a bead on Beck's face: "No way," he said judiciously, "are you going to get that many dips in and out of any kind of dangerous terrain without losing a few of 'em; they don't know how to take direction."

"That's secondary. I'll be happy with a seventy-five per cent survival rate—"

"If you have to, you'll make do with a ten per cent survival rate," Slick cut in authoritatively. "You can't negotiate real life."

"Whatever." Beck, Ashmead saw, knew he was winning; he was imperturbable: "The actual mission is the delivery of the material—a serum of sorts—to the Administration."

"What is this serum?" Zaki asked. "Water from the fountain of youth? An anti-radiation drug, perhaps? Is that why you speak so calmly of such absurdities?"

"Zaki, you're absolutely right. But I didn't tell you and you don't know what it is, because if word leaks, we're never going to get out of Israel with it, let alone all the way to the Houston White House."

"So . . . do we get shots? If we're going to take it that far, we'll need all the edge we can get." Slick was looking out for his people as best he could.

"Absolutely. From the first batch, well before takeoff—as soon as I get mine." Beck, his trump played, sat back and watched the operations team think about what he'd said.

For the first time, Ashmead took a hand: "You're going along, Beck?"

"Would I ask you to go, if I wouldn't?"

"But are you? Not would you."

Beck met Ashmead's gaze and it was as if electricity jumped between them: "Rafic, I wouldn't miss it for the world."

Ashmead nodded absently, putting deeper meanings together in his mind, already launched upon a catalogue of what they would need for weapons, com gear, protective clothing, and fallbacks.

Then Slick said, "Well, Casper, maybe we'll bite." He reached out and hefted one of the rolls of Krugeraands. "But tell me something . . . are you one of these guys who doesn't have enough sense to be afraid to die, or the type who fancies a heroic death in battle while he's sitting behind his desk? Because there's no way we'll come through this in tip-top operational shape."

"I know that. But you were all going to blow yourselves to bits in Libya, weren't you?"

"Maybe we were, maybe we weren't. Answer my question." Slick was beginning to realize that Beck was smarter than your average dip, but he'd never accept that Beck was smarter than he was.

"Fair enough," Beck's chin tucked in as he answered Slick; "since you asked—I'm terrified of dying, emotionally. But intellectually I understand that the universe is like a novel one might read, if you'll accept the analogy, in which each second of elapsed time represents one page of the story: you read from beginning to end and yet, if you go back to any particular page, the time and events on it are always happening in the present sense; so, to continue the analogy, everything that ever was, is, or will be, is always 'now,' somewhere in spacetime's novel—we'll always be sitting here, having this discussion, in a universe which allows manifold novels . . . eternities, if you like. Consequently, intellectually I know that everything I do will live forever and I try to do my damned best to make sure I'm proud of it."

"Shit," Slick shook his head. The rest of his team looked askance at one another.

All but Zaki, who sat forward: "So you understand Einstein, even maybe quantum mechanics. Are you, by any chance, a Jew?"

Caught off guard, Ashmead nearly exploded in laughter: Beck had them, even if he didn't realize it yet—Zaki, not Slick, would have been the only dissenting voice that could have queered the deal.

It was going to be, Ashmead thought, one fuck of an interesting way to spend his last days on earth.

Chapter 5

By the time Beck got back to Jerusalem he felt like a shuttle diplomat in the middle of some Gulf spasm war: his little four-passenger prop developed engine trouble over Qatar and when he checked in with Dickson on the Qatar section's secure phone, Dickson told him to report to Tel Aviv immediately: "A week out of contact, at a time like this? All that money? A contingency fund is one thing; every piece of hard currency we've got is quite another. I couldn't cover for you when it turned up missing and the loss was reported to Tel Aviv. I didn't know where you were I told them; everything I had on you was F-6, I swore up and down. Remember our arrangement, Beck."

And then he'd been listening to the seashore-whisper of a dead secure line. "F-6" was information about which the truth could not be judged, from a source whose reliability could not be judged:

Dickson was telling him that Beck was free to cover his ass any way he might when he was called on the carpet, but that Dickson expected Beck to leave his chief's name out of it: as per their understanding, if heads were to roll, Dickson's was not to be one of them.

Tel Aviv station told him to go to the Circle and wait to be met on the west side of the glass fountain, and by this he assumed that he was in only minor trouble: he hadn't been summoned to the Ambassador's residence; it was an intelligence snit, not a diplomatic one. So he waited there, in the shadow of the ugly modern hotels which occluded the beach, watching masked people in silver space-blanket suits scuttle indoors from their cars, for someone to take him to the little house on the northern end of Hayarkon, near the defunct old port, where tea houses and bars were open till the wee hours and agents in the de rigueur swaddling clothes of the paranoid could come and go without attracting attention.

Always when he was in Tel Aviv, Beck craved the real Israel, the gold stones of Jerusalem, the polished Roman paving stones of the north—anything but this facile, miniature cosmopolis scarred first by the Mandate, then by industrious Jews homesick for Miami or New York.

This time he was more than usually restless: he could feel the clock ticking away inside him; he had too much to do to waste time in a bureaucratic wrangle. So far as he knew, the jet stream was still blocked, but the spring sky was full of storming clouds and at the Tel Aviv airport he'd seen what looked like a riot in progress, then used his black diplomatic passport to avoid finding out if he was right.

On Kikar Dizengoff, Tel Aviv's Times Square, he'd smelled vomit and seen too many hollow eyes: people were making themselves sick or convincing themselves they were sick, because it was just too damn soon for any serious symptoms. To make sure, Beck checked his Geiger counter, which read a measly one and one half Rem, and began to get angry. Hysteria would kill more people in Tel Aviv than radiation; in Qatar it had been the same.

He kept conjuring Chris Patrick: she was his plus in a world of minuses—his agent; he wanted to get home and debrief her.

Instead, he was scooped up by two blank-faced men with civilians' paper masks and wires in their ears who said only, "Beck? Let's go," and hustled him into a waiting Dodge Aries with American military plates and a powerful air-purification system, who drove like deaf and dumb maniacs through a cloudburst, half the time in four-wheel drift, slowing only at the gates of an old villa Beck had never seen, and then only long enough to wave familiarly to the checkpoint guards and accelerate again.

In the villa's forecourt, while rain bounced a foot high off ancient stones and, on the roof, soaked soldiers in full anti-radiation kit and holding M16s looked on attentively, he was hustled inside, through cypress-paneled halls lined with relics, into a vacant room the size of a tennis court where he was told to wait.

Alone in that room with the whirring of the air purifiers in each caulked window, empty but for an ash partners' desk with a reading lamp on a Pakistani rug, three gilt Louis Quinze chairs and matching settee, and a battery of olive filing cabinets, he had plenty of time to wonder who had interpreted his behavior as subversive—whether the missing gold was just an excuse, whether Dickson was involved, and whether he had legal recourse—before the Ambassador himself, flanked by a Marine colonel with a camouflage film badge nestled among too many grimy ribbons and a pair of well-groomed civilians in Brooks Brothers suits joined him.

He stood up and they didn't tell him to sit.

"Beck, Beck," the Ambassador said with a shake of his leonine head and a pat to the silver mane that was his trademark: "What are we going to do with you?"

"Mister Ambassador?" he replied, while the Marine took the chair beside the desk, the Ambassador the one behind it, and the two civilians whispered to themselves over the low rumble a filing cabinet made as they opened it. "Can you tell me what's going on here?"

His attempt at innocent outrage didn't impress anyone: the Ambassador gave him a neutral cocktail-party smile; the Marine yawned and watched him the way combat commanders will, his gaze fixed on a spot on the wall some distance behind Beck's head; the two civilians continued thumbing through the files and chatting to one another.

"We'd like to know where you've been, Marc," the Ambassador said as if to a troublesome nephew who had finally created an incident that couldn't be ignored; "we'd like to know with whom, and why, and what, exactly, you did with the Jerusalem Consulate's contingency fund—assuming, that is, you don't have it?" Bleary-eyed, the Ambassador leaned forward.

Beck said: "Why? Do you think I hopped up to Monoco or Liechtenstein, started a numbered account? No offense intended, Mister Ambassador, but you're not cleared to be asking me these questions." Like Ashmead's protégé, Slick, the night before, Beck dodged and feinted; he wasn't going to cave. He knew what they wanted now—Ashmead. For openers. Maybe Beck's game plan, too, if Dickson or somebody else had leaked it.

Before the Ambassador could respond with more than a reproving blink, the Marine said: "He will be once we bust you to civilian, mister. Don't give me this INR—"

The two civilians, each with his load of manila red-bordered folders, intervened: "We told you this wasn't necessary, sirs," the first said.

"That's right," the second agreed smoothly, "we think you ought to let us keep this in the family. There's no need to be hostile. Marc was just doing his job, the best way he knew how."

The first continued when the second left off in a way that let Beck know this was an orchestrated team play: "Everyone's judgment is a little skewed right now. If Marc, here," he touched Beck's elbow familiarly, squeezed briefly, took his hand away— "had a judgment call to make and he made it, it's up to us, not the diplomatic corps or the military, to determine its validity."

The Marine snapped to, clicked his heels together, and with an outstanding show of umbrage, growled: "When you speak to me, spook, an occasional 'sir' is appropriate. And when you're done coddling your traitor," the fingers of his right hand went to his hip and tapped there, "I'll expect to see the entire verbatim transcript. We're under martial law—not just at home, but all Americans, everywhere. And no matter which way your Mister Beck has flip-flopped, he's still under my jurisdiction." Turning smartly on his heel, the Marine stamped out.

As the door slammed, the Ambassador winced and rubbed his face with both hands; when they came away, he was the picture of sympathy: "He's right, you know, Marc. You've had such an outstanding record until now ... I hardly know what to say. Consorting with the Israelis whom you must know are calling up their reserves and getting ready to kick a little Arab butt while the kicking's good, handing out national secrets like the recipe for Coca-Cola, sneaking off with embezzled funds to Mister Ashmead, whom you must have known is no longer—"

"What? You've got to be joking. I haven't—" Beck broke off, embarrassed at how easily he'd risen to the bait.

"Mister Ambassador," said the slightly more forward of Beck's protectors, who was graying at his well-groomed temples, "Marc will tell us everything we want to know once we've convinced him that it's safe to do so—appropriate to do so, in private. Now, if you'll be so kind as to leave us alone for a while ... ?"

Protector Number Two, the stockier and younger, said, "Maybe Marc's hungry. Thirsty. Tired. Want some coffee, Marc? I know I do. Sandwiches?" These were requests aimed at the Ambassador, who rose as if the world rested on his shoulders and came slowly toward Beck, affecting a limp it was well-known he'd gotten in Korea.

In front of Beck, he paused: "I hope they're right, Marc. I hope this is a simple overreaction, a misjudgment—on all our parts. You're just the sort of person we desperately need right now. We can't spare you, Marc. So we're willing to be generous. Give us a half-decent explanation and you'll be back in Jerusalem before you know it, full privileges restored. Otherwise . . ." The Ambassador squeezed his eyes shut as if the alternative were too distasteful to contemplate. Then, with a fatherly pat on Beck's shoulder, he left them alone, promising brunch in "two shakes of a lamb's tail."

"Phew," said Protector Number One: "Glad that's over with. Okay, gentlemen, let's get to it." File folders in hand, he took the chair behind the desk and opened them, pulled tortoiseshell glasses from his pocket, scanned the files quickly, and then peered up over the rims at Beck, "You went to ground for a week?" he said incredulously. "In a crisis like this? With all that money and after consorting openly with Israeli Intelligence? No wonder they're nervous."

Protector Two ambled over to the chair by the desk, a folder open in his hand, and put it down where his superior could see it, finger running along a relevant passage, before he sat beside the desk: "Nervous? They're scared to death. Why in damnation did you bring a colonel of Israeli Intelligence in on something you didn't share with your own Bureau Chief?"

Beck said numbly, "Mind if I sit down now?"

"Sure thing. We're trying to help you. We're—"

"On my side, I know. Look, do you really think

this is going to work with me, fellows? We went to the same damn schools. I know this drill as well as you do.''

The one with the graying temples leaned forward: "Good enough. We're here to play golf, not fuck around. Run it down to us from the top and save everybody a lot of grief.''

He sat back and both agents looked at Beck expectantly.

Beck said: "Mind if I see your credentials first?'' Even those could be faked but Beck had to put them on the defensive if he could; like Slick, Ashmead's prima donna agent, he wanted to get information, not give it: how much they knew, how much they only suspected, how much they wanted to know. Telling too much was always the danger; usually, interrogators knew next to nothing when they started; sometimes, they knew everything. He didn't dare lie but he wasn't going to give them any more than he had to. Most crucially—damn Dickson for not finding some way to prepare him for this—he needed to find out if they knew about the serum: if they did, he might have a bargaining chip; if they didn't, he'd be a fool to play it.

"If it makes you feel better,'' said Protector Number One, fishing out a plastic badge which he tossed across the desk.

Beck took it and sat in the chair before the desk: on one side of the ID was a number printed on paper patterned with the profiled eagle's head and shield of Central Intelligence; on the other side was a picture of the man he was looking at and the advisory that the person pictured above was an employee of the Central Intelligence Agency, but no name.

Protector Number Two's badge was more forthcoming: it announced that the person pictured on the obverse was a senior analyst named Watkins.

Beck fingered the badges with evident disgust: "How am I supposed to talk to you two guys? Couldn't they come up with someone from my own department—or don't my own people know I'm here?"

"We're the best they could scrape up," said the one who wasn't Watkins, the one from the CIA's black-sheep Covert Action Staff whose badge said no such thing because you don't advertise your grade when it's an operational one. "On such short notice. Here and now. We'll have to do and you'll have to cooperate, sooner or later. Do us all a favor and make it sooner."

Watkins, the good cop in this little charade, might actually have been a senior analyst: he had the spare tire around his middle and was now displaying an analyst's sensibilities: "Ease up, Dow. Look here, Marc, I can guess what you've been up to; none of us wants to be here any longer than necessary. Just lay it out for us in your own words and, believe it or not, you're free to go—to continue what you've started, if you like."

"You guess, then, and I'll nod if you guess right."

The last place he wanted to be was in the middle of a private CIA squabble. Perversely, his mind kept throwing up grisly pictures of Muffy and the kids in various stages of living decomposition, so he tried to envision Chris Patrick's ass; this time, when he imagined her, she was hugging herself in his apartment while the wind blew in off the sea.

"You know that's not the way it's done, Marc," said Dow. "And you think that, being an intelligence liaison and all, you can outfox us—that it's just a matter of time until your people take a hand and you're out of here." Dow pursed his lips as if what he was about to say wasn't pleasant: "Now, I'll level with you, to set the tone. Watkins, here, really is an anaylst and he likes to do things the civilized way. But you know what I am, and they've never been able to convince us that interrogations work best when no physical means are employed. So, if you're thinking about heroics, forget it. Watkins may have to leave the room while I teach you some things they never did at State, but I'll get what I want from you."

Watkins took a handkerchief from his pocket and dabbed at his forehead: "I wish the food would come, don't you?"

"I told you," Dow said patiently, "he can't have anything to eat or drink until I've determined whether or not I'm going to use drugs."

"Will you two cut out this fucking psychwar and tell me what it is you want to know?"

Dow scratched one graying temple, took off his glasses and meticulously returned them to his breast pocket. "Normally, I wouldn't. But since you're a . . . distant relative, let's say . . . I'll give you an easy out: tell me where Ashmead is and what you've got on with him, as well as what you and Netanayhu are collaborating on, and we'll shelve the rest of it."

"Ashmead? I haven't seen him since my orienta—"

Dow's flat hand hit the desk with a resounding thump. "We know you went toodling off to the Persian Gulf, Beck. We know he's out there, too.

What were you doing, visiting your maiden aunt for a week?"

"If you know so much, you tell me."

"Beck, I'm going to leave this surveillance file open on the desk, here, and walk out of the room with Watkins. When I get back, you and I are going to talk about Ashmead—either the easy way, or the hard way. It's up to you."

"Do you think that's wise, Dow?" said Watkins as he followed Dow to the door.

The surveillance file detailed a number of Beck's movements, but not all, during the time he'd been looking for Ashmead. In Bahrain, the bird dogs had lost his scent, then picked it up again when he reclaimed his plane. If this was truly all they had, they couldn't prove he'd met with Ashmead; they were grasping at straws, backtracking from the aborted hit on an Abu Dhabi street, fitting his face to an unidentified figure that had intervened, just guessing because they'd been caught with their pants down, because they needed Ashmead for something and couldn't find him, and because Beck had left himself wide open.

Armed with that information, he prepared to defend himself.

When they came back, bearing a tray of sandwiches and coffee, he ate heartily, casually, daring them to risk killing him by giving him pentathol on a full stomach.

They seemed relaxed; even Dow had lost his glower, and they talked of the general world situation ruefully, like the professionals they were, until they'd done eating.

And then, when the questioning began again, it

wasn't about Ashmead at all, but about Chris Patrick and Morse and Netanayhu.

And maybe there was something in the coffee, after all, for when they let him go in the early hours of the morning, everyone was very friendly: Dow clapped him on the shoulders and told him if he needed any help, just holler; Watkins was telling him it was really wise of him to level with them and helping him straighten his tie, and Beck didn't remember telling them any damn thing at all.

To his knowledge, he'd held his own, given nothing, and found out that all they had were typical bits of discrete intelligence, like a handful of jigsaw-puzzle pieces from different areas of the board, no two of which would interlock, let alone add up into any coherent picture.

And because they were at pains to part on good terms with him, to convince him there were no hard feelings, that everyone had just been doing their jobs, and that—if he kept his mouth shut—there would be no further repercussions, not even a notation in his file or an official query as to the disposition of the funds he'd appropriated, Beck couldn't figure out the truth of it: either they'd gotten what they wanted or were pretending they had, preparing to face their own superiors; either he'd outsmarted them, or they him.

"We'll be seeing you," Dow said as they walked him to a waiting car.

"You can depend on it," Watkins added with tired bonhomie; "it's a small country."

And that was that: he'd been let off at the glass fountain, told that his plane wasn't airworthy yet, and, as far as he could tell, followed no more than

thirty kilometers on his drive southwest to Jerusalem in his rental car.

He'd never been happier to see the Walled City,
though the rain was fierce and the roads slick and
he was feeling like he'd been handed one too many
nightmares. In the midst of all this chaos and
horror, it seemed to him ridiculous that he'd become the center of some interagency flap: but then,
his superiors were only human; in the vacuum of
solutions to problems not of their making, men
cleaved to their routines, did their jobs, made up
jobs to do which involved soluble problems and in
which they could feel effective, though in the larger
scheme of things, all action was probably impo-
tent—even Beck's.

He could have reported the entire incident, continued the game, caused some trouble for Dow,
Watkins, even the Ambassador.

But by the time he'd reached the American
Quarter, he'd decided he wouldn't bother: he needed
some sleep and then he needed to get to work.

The rain stopped as he pulled up at the compound's gate and when he parked in his slot, the
sky was clearing, hellclouds blowing away on a
wind that didn't know it was probably full of death,
which promised spring and rebirth and smelled of
cedar, eucalyptus, and a desert grateful to be wet.

Getting out of the rental car, he shrugged into
the heavy, bullet-and-radiation-proof poncho Netanayhu had given him, pulled up the hood and put
on his issue rubber mask, telling himself he needed
the practice. All this would have to become automatic now.

Overhead, a jet screamed and he looked up in
time to see a pair of contrails: he'd missed the

overflights; it was good to know that they were flying again. The EMP effect, in Israel, had been minimal compared to the damage it had done closer to the strike zones, but microcircuitry was delicate; for those titanium jets to be wheeling in formation above him, much of their relevant electronics would have had to be checked out, if not replaced.

They dove and he saw that they were desert-patterned Israeli jets. He gave them a thumbs up and went inside, somehow cheered by this evidence of resurgent technology so that the questions at the back of his mind stopped nagging him quite so fiercely.

Maybe he'd done all right in Tel Aviv. Maybe he'd won point, set and match. Neither of his interrogators had mentioned personal inoculations, so maybe Beck's recollection of that long, hazy night was accurate. Maybe they hadn't drugged him, just exhausted him.

He fumbled his key into his lock and fell asleep without taking off his much-worn Levi's, wondering if the jet stream was still mercifully blocked and how Morse and the Israeli biochemists were doing.

It wasn't until he'd showered and breakfasted ten hours later that he realized someone had been in his apartment while he'd been gone: his air conditioners had been retrofitted into purifiers, turned backwards in windows securely sealed with silver tape; on his bedside table, where he customarily kept no more than one current and nonclassified report or magazine for late-night reading, were several Agency pamphlets on secondary radiation effects and a Special Forces field manual on survival in Red Zones I, II and III; Zone III being a circular area (less Zones I and II) figured by using

minimum safe distance III as the radius and designated Ground Zero as the center, in which all
personnel require minimum protection—all skin
covered by protection equal to that of a two-layer
uniform.

Since the super swore that nobody had come
asking to be admitted to Beck's apartment on
grounds of a security emergency or for any other
reason, and none of his doors or windows showed
any signs of forcible entry, Beck had to assume
that the health precautions and reading material
were Ashmead's way of saying he'd reported for
duty.

Three days later, Beck still had not seen hide
nor hair of his Bureau Chief, Dickson (who'd been
out sick since Beck called in from Qatar, so Pickwick said) or of Ashmead or his team, but their
spoor was evident, if you knew what to look for,
and Beck did.

Chris Patrick called his office and asked if the
long-haired girl who had come to her apartment
to "fix" her air conditioner and "weather-strip"
her doors and windows was really a friend of his;
Morse wanted to know why his phones had echoes
on them.

And Netanayhu came to Beck's office in a fury
just before noon of the third day, saying: "Inexcusable. Following me. Your people have too much
chutzpah, you know, Beck? No attempt even to be
coy. If again I see these cars straddling me, everywhere I go, I will have their tires shot out."

Beck couldn't keep a straight face but he couldn't
say anything aloud or lie to Netanayhu: he wrote
"Ashmead," on a piece of paper, handed it to
Netanayhu, and said: "It's nobody from State; must

be your own people, looking out for you, some old Haganah friends who think the Arabs might take it in their heads to come after you—why not?"

Netanayhu chuckled as he tore the note into tiny pieces, then sobered: "Not funny, my friend. While you were gone, the terrorists stepped up their murdering: now it is our fault that your President pushed his button, yes. We are the lackeys of American Imperialism, and we are the enemy. So—" Netanayhu's huge, sloping shoulders wriggled philosophically "—they are onto us again, like the jackals the bull in the field. And we, of course, have to retaliate; we have martial law and full alert and again we will soon be very busy protecting our borders from our Arab neighbors: this is no time for making jokes."

"So I've heard—just a 'little' war, I hope—we're in no position to pull you out if you get in too deep or one enemy comes at you from behind while you're engaging another." Since Netanayhu showed no disposition to argue Beck's assessment of Israel's war-fighting capability and no signs of leaving, Beck decided that being bird-dogged by Ashmead's team wasn't really the reason for the Israeli colonel's visit: "Lunch time, isn't it?"

"I thought," said the colonel, "you'd never ask."

At lunch upstairs in a private house which was Netanayhu's counterintelligence section headquarters and thus had a busy ground floor full of chattering telexes and typewriters—his computers weren't operational, he said sadly, shaking his huge head—Morse appeared from somewhere, looking put upon and harried, one of the ubiquitous paper masks down around his throat like an ascot.

"Beck! What's the meaning of this! I've never

been so insulted in all my life." The short, plump, mole-faced genetic engineer blinked through trifocals so thick his eyes were distorted behind them.

Netanayhu, like a kid who'd gotten his hand out of the cookie jar just in time, had a self-satisfied, naughty look on his face.

"This . . ." Morse waddled over to Netanayhu, his finger shaking with rage as he pointed it at the Israeli, "this . . . *bully*, this officious Jewish mother, pulled me right out of my laboratory—or his henchmen did—and spirited me here without a word. Not an apology, not an 'if you please.' And those Hebrew scholars you've found me can't possibly do without my—"

"Sit down, Doctor Morse. If the colonel wanted you here, it was for a good reason. Now, Dov, what's the reason?"

"Security," Netanayhu said as if it was perfectly obvious. "We've had a bomb threat—"

"A *bomb* threat," Morse repeated, becoming livid. "Oh, that's just wonderful! What about my coworkers? I've taught them everything I know. They're irreplaceable. I swear I'll never understand you Israelis, with your cavalier attitude toward human life, after all you've been—"

"I thought you just said they couldn't wipe their behinds without you overseeing them?" said Netanayhu, who might take this kind of talk from Dickson, but never from a man like Morse. "Now, which is it—either they're bumbling Hebrew scholars, or they're irreplaceable co-workers—certainly not both?"

Even Morse knew that he'd screwed up. He appealed to Beck: "If the lab is blown up, we're back to square one. What about your timetable?"

"Timetables, in Israel," Beck said with more chill than he'd intended, "are subject to interruptions of this sort more frequently than any of us would wish." Then he turned to Netanayhu: "What about it, Dov? Did you leave the rest of those scientists to sweat it out?"

"We evacuated everyone, how could we not? But this fat little goy of yours was judged to be top priority. And, as it happened, there was no bomb, none that we could find—or it was a dud."

Again with that philosophical air which meant he was setting Beck up for something, Netanayhu reached out for a slice of pumpernickel and said, "But security is always a concern. Tell Doctor Morse this. He does not seem to understand that we are protecting his welfare. He is disobedient, he makes phone calls, he tried to use leverage to get information on his wife and children, he is acting not at all like a good team player. There is no possibility of protecting this operation if he insists on talking to all his colleagues as if he were still a civilian."

"That true, Morse? Have you been socializing with your confreres? Making a nuisance of yourself at the legation? Using the goddamned phone?"

"Secretary Beck," Morse miscalled him, puffed up like a cockerel, "I've never been treated like this. I didn't expect to spend my time here in total isolation, be followed everywhere, have people in my apartment, in my car, looking over my shoulder at all times. I can't work this way. It's impossible."

"Dov, got a notepad?" Beck's spine was crawling; he remembered his blurred night of interrogation and when he tossed the notepad Netanayhu fished from his khaki pocket across the table to Morse, he could barely control the impulse to throw it in Morse's face.

"Sit down in that chair, Doctor Morse. Good." Beck flicked a glance at Netanayhu: "Dov, I'm truly sorry about this and I thank you for everything you've done." Then he bore down on Morse: "Morse, you take that pad and this pen," Beck took one from his suit's inside pocket, "and you write down the names of everyone you've spoken to since I last saw you—on the street, in a public john, at the lab, the conference, the consulate, on the phone. I want to know what you said to whom, when and where, to the minute. Is that clear? Because you're not leaving here until the colonel and I are satisfied that you haven't jeopardized this entire mission beyond hope of salvage. Do you get my drift? If you can't make that list, or if it doesn't satisfy us, there's no plane ride, no expedition to find your wife and kids, no money, no perks—nothing. You can fend for yourself from now on, just like a tailor from White Plains or a mechanic from Kansas City. Now, start writing."

"In the other room, if you please," Netanayhu said, the only sign that he'd felt Beck's vehemence to be excessive or out of character.

Morse, as he got up, pen in shaking hand, gave it one last try: "You weren't around, Beck, when I had to negotiate this with your nasty chief, that Dickson person. There's no money—at least not the sort I'd hoped. And the other—"

"I don't *care*, Morse," said Beck with real surprise. "You're in too deep and you're a security risk. Now go dig yourself out of the hole you've dug, or I'll personally see to it that you're buried in it."

As the little scientist stomped huffily away, Beck

put his face in his hands and realized that his fingertips were so cold that they were numb. "God help us," he told his palms, and he didn't take them away until Netanayhu's hand touched his.

"Beck," said the colonel avuncularly, "do you want to tell me about your trip?"

"I can't— Yeah, I'd like that. I'd like to tell somebody."

And when he'd finished telling Netanayhu about his forced debriefing in Tel Aviv, Netanayhu was scowling as if Beck were his son and had been dishonorably discharged from the army for reasons not his fault.

"So what shall we do, Beck? How to protect you from your own—this is not an easy question. They obviously were not buying the cover story of the fact-finding trip, were not buying it in any way whatsoever."

"Obviously. Maybe Morse is the leak. Maybe it's Dickson—he's been out sick since I got back. Maybe . . ." Beck spread his hands, saw that they still trembled, and put them in his lap.

"You were right to recruit Ashmead," Netanayhu said firmly. "All of this only proves how right. Don't worry about the bomb threat; it's not unusual; just Palestinians, who hate technology and now have good reason beyond their previous reasons. Eat. Such food should not be wasted. And I think better on a full stomach." He patted his.

So Beck ate, knowing that with Netanayhu briefed, to the extent that Beck could brief him, and Ashmead and his team out there somewhere doing what they did so well, he'd taken every precaution he could take to put Operation Tiebreaker on the road.

But like Ashmead's people who, once they'd agreed to sign on, had snapped to with drill-team precision and let Beck brief them on specifics, everyone had to understand exactly what was expected of him and be willing to do precisely what he was told.

Even Chris Patrick, with whom he was having dinner, was going to have to realize that.

Chapter 6

Spying for Beck on her fellow reporters that afternoon in the English-style bar across from the Overseas Press Club in the Old City was beginning to make Chris Patrick feel slimy.

The world was dying around her, and she was worried about ethical conduct, the repercussions of the disinformation she'd been spreading for no better reason than personal advantage, and whether the tiny .25 caliber Colt automatic she'd bought and now carried everywhere in her purse would really do the job, if she dared to try it.

She'd rather count on it than on the mercifully clear film badge she now wore next to her press pass or the clip-on Geiger counter attached to her belt, or any other placebo Beck had given her, including the once-over of her apartment by one of his people: Chris Patrick had watched her mother die of cancer; she had no intention of reliving the experience, or living it. But everybody said that was what was in store for all the "lucky" survivors—everybody in the press corps, everybody who favored places like this and got drunk earlier than they'd used to, grousing now about the chances of getting some real money—not paper or plastic—so they could get out of Israel and about the transAtlantic phone calls they couldn't seem to make to their home offices like a bunch of shell-shocked refugees which, by and large, they were.

In the Mandate gloom of the Disraeli Bar's Happy Hour, she was nursing a beer and staring at herself in the mirror, sandwiched between a BBC stand-up correspondent and a friend of his from the *Manchester Guardian*, trying to determine if she looked like a spy, if there was anything feral or furtive about her face.

But it was her same old face that peered back, tired but still gamin; not the face of somebody who would sell out friends and colleagues just to get laid. But that was what she was doing, she told herself harshly—it wasn't Beck's patriotic pep talk, his influential position, or his power base—none of that mattered any more. It was Beck himself—who had offered to take control of her life when she no longer wanted it, who was free from doubt and burning with purpose when everything seemed doubtful and purposeless—for whom she spied. When he'd left town, she'd panicked, though he'd told her he would. She'd called the consulate every day like a shameless teenager, using one excuse after another, but he was never there and she'd thought he was avoiding her.

Then the honey-haired Sabra girl had knocked on her door carrying a box full of filters, mechanical parts, rolls of silver tape and a message: "Yes, he's just back now. He sent me to see to your windows; also, your air conditioner. Call him to make certain, yes; it's perfectly all right; I'll wait here."

By then Chris had been resentful of Beck, of the way he'd used her and discarded her. The appearance of the beautiful, deep-eyed Sabra at her door, calling him "he" in that way women had, made Chris Patrick achingly jealous. But when Beck took her call and she heard the pause, then the protectiveness in his voice as he made her describe her visitor, then his subterranean amusement, she was lost all over again—headlong in love, and bereft of a single bit of information worth his attention.

By tonight, she had to have something good, to prove to him she'd never doubted, although she'd done nothing *but* doubt, for tonight he was taking her to dinner: "Let's make a celebration of it; wear something glitzy and I'll show you what a government expense account can do."

She should have been shopping for something suitable, a designer original like his wife might have; maybe she could still charge it to the bureau and reimburse them later, if there was anyone left in accounting back home to question her expenditures.

Instead, she'd panicked—she had nothing to report—and come down to the bar where she lurked like a fat spider, listening to her friends with new ears.

"This, then," said the Brit on her right, with whom she'd spent a night behind sandbags in Samaria taking Syrian fire and comfort in each other, "is assuredly the meaning of life." He was holding up an empty glass laced with beer foam in a pigskin-gloved hand.

It was a press-corps riff, a long-standing game they played: a spent AK round that had penetrated your luggage, the ubiquitous yellow grit regrinding your camera lenses, a spike order for a story you'd sweated blood to write—all of these, at one time or another, were declared to be the one true meaning of life, then discarded in favor of some subsequent oracle.

"What is?" she rose to the Brit's bait desultorily. "That?" She sniffed at the glass. "Only if it's full." And then she pumped him: "What about the casualty estimates—if you don't like mine, what's your guess?"

"Christine," he called her that because he'd screwed her, this lord's nephew, "it can't be that your sources have all dried up, can it? Is that what you're on about?" He leaned close enough to sniff her hair: "It's not cricket, you know, to grieve openly when your country is summarily demoted— take a leaf from our book; we're professionals at the stiff upper lip." Then, louder, his head drawing back, to include the rest of the newsies at the bar: "My sources say the US casualty count is about fifty-five million and rising steadily; they'll never admit to that, of course. But we'll know better after the fact-finding tour. I'd give my sodding peerage to be on that plane—"

"Yours, is it, now?" she quipped, filing away the data. "Was Knightsbridge nuked too, then?"

"Rule Britannia, no," he said it like profanity: "We NATO blokies walked away without a scratch— from the big stuff, at least; we've just the weather-borne radiation to worry about. A diplomatic victory, thanks to the—"

A soft mid-European accent intervened: "NATO refused to fire its missiles, used the hot line to let Moscow know their position—and the Warsaw Pact, too, deliberately delayed firing. . . . It's either the first step toward European independence of the superpowers or flagrant treaty violations by former allies and satellites, depending on whose rhetoric one chooses to believe."

Chris could see the speaker in the bar mirror: a dark, brooding Mediterranean type who could have been Greek or Semitic, with a stocky, muscular body of the sort they breed on the Aegean or the kibbutz and which always looks uncomfortable in city clothes, and a shock of black curls; on his jacket pocket, his ID said *Jerusalem Post*, NY.

The Brit scowled down at him with all the intimidating superiority of the Empire: "You're the new one, aren't you? What in bloody hell, if you don't mind me asking, is the use of putting on a new boy for the New York edition when New York is—"

"Elint; everybody calls me Elint," said the newcomer brightly, thrusting out a browned hand—remarkable in that it was not gloved when everyone but Chris, it seemed, wore gloves now, even indoors—that took the Brit's pale, limp one in a surprise attack, pumped it smartly, and then went on to seize Chris's and draw it to his lips.

She hated men who kissed your hand; the gesture blew away all the years of struggling toward women's rights in one dismissive moment.

"Elat?" she repeated what she thought she'd heard; his badge said "Levy."

"Elint," he corrected firmly as he lowered her

hand but didn't release it; his eyes burned on her like an Arab's, black and smouldering. "And you are the famous Christine Patrick, my idol, my role model among the Western—"

The Brit let out a derisive whoop and as he trumpeted an exact quote of Elint's words like an urgent bulletin to the rest of the bar, the *Post* reporter bristled: "If you'll allow me the pleasure, Miss Patrick, a drink? In a quiet corner? There?"

There was something in the manner of the *Post* reporter that made her go with him to the corner he'd chosen, let him pick her up—if that was what he was doing; the way he moved her through the crowd reminded her of the time she'd been led across the Green Line into a west Beirut stronghold by a Palestinian fighter.... maybe it was something about the eyes, which seemed to scan everything from cover.

Not until they sat together did she realize he had a briefcase with him; in the briefcase was a gaily wrapped package with blue ribbon, the sort you get in a souvenir shop. He put it not on the table, but on the button-tuck bench seat between them.

"A present," he explained. "From our mutual friend, Beck." He showed big white teeth.

Chris's heart was pounding, her pulse racing: "From—he's cancelling? How did you find me? Who are—"

"On the contrary," Harold "Elint" Levy said smoothly as the waiter came and he ordered another round for her and the same for himself, though she couldn't understand how he knew what she drank. "He asks that you allow me to drive you to the restaurant—in fact, to drive you wherever you need to go today." His glance said: *This is for your own protection;* it was fond and possessive. "Now open your gift, please."

Christ, she thought, *I should have pretended I didn't know what he was talking about.* But it was too late for that. Some spy.

His dark, strong fingers tapped the package between them and she stared at it as if it were a poisonous snake. A bomb? No, he was obviously going to sit right there while she opened it. But she was afraid now, afraid that this compact person with the soulful eyes was Beck's enemy and, by association, her own.

"I'm sorry," she said, half rising before his fingers caught her elbow and pain lanced up her arm as if she'd hit her funny bone, and she sank back with a feeling of helplessness in no way mitigated by the crowd of newsies around her. She tried again: "I'm sorry; this is really impossible. I don't know you, I don't know what your game is, or the State Department's, but if Mister Beck wants to cancel our interview, he can consider it done. I don't take bribes from government officials, Mister—"

"Elint."

"Elint. And I don't get into cars with strangers, especially in the Middle East."

In a flash the gift-wrapped package was on the table between them and her mouth dried up like the desert. Out of the corner of her eye, she could see the BBC Brit watching them, glass in hand, elbows on the bar, and making nasty cracks—she could tell from the swoop of his mouth.

Nothing for it, then, she decided, and tugged at the wrappings while Elint nodded approvingly.

There were two small boxes nested in the tissue

of the larger cardboard box, she found when she'd removed its lid. In the first was a black chrome watch, very expensive, everything-proof, like Beck's.

"Christ, it *is* from him," she muttered, flattery flushing her cheeks. She clasped it around her wrist, afraid it might not fit.

But it fit perfectly and Elint was saying, "It is indeed. If you'll press in on the winding stem, you'll see a small red light appear where the hands join."

She did and it did: "Gee," she looked up with a lopsided grin, "my very own Dick Tracy watch. What—?"

"This is deadly serious, Miss Patrick." Now she knew that those were fighter's eyes which watched her like a specimen while at the same time they watched the room at her back. "Now, small talk, please, while our drinks are served."

She made some and never remembered what she'd said, then chugged half her Budweiser and slapped the glass down. "Deadly serious, you were saying. What does the light mean?"

"That you've activated a tracer/transmitter: it will let us know where you are and allow us to keep track of your conversations."

"Oh," she said, too stunned even to object.

"Anyone with a sophisticated antibugging device will detect it, so do not use it casually—only when you feel threatened, or if you want a conversation monitored."

"Anyone with a sophisticated antibugging device?" she parroted numbly.

"We sincerely hope—" he toasted her with his beer, "that our enemies are unsophisticated."

Enemies? Our enemies? "How do I turn it off?"

"Press the winding stem again; a green light will replace the red one, then go out."

She did and again the watch performed as Elint predicted; this time, when she looked up, it was the watch, not her, at which he gazed fondly, like a favorite child, before taking a pack of Players from his breast pocket and saying, "Open the other package and give me a light."

She reached into her bag for her disposable lighter, but a flicker of displeasure crossed his face: follow orders, his expression implored; do not improvise.

So she brought out only her own cigarettes and then opened the second box, in which was a silver pocket lighter of the old-fashioned sort, with a flip-open lid. She noticed, as she brushed the wheel with her thumb and a flame rose obediently, that there was a small green dot, hardly a light at all, behind the wheel.

He cupped her hands and the lighter in his own, though there was no wind, a habitual gesture of someone who had lit many cigarettes in the open dark where a flame must be hidden. When he sat back, the cigarette dangling from his sensual lips, he said: "This will let you know if you yourself are being bugged by such an unsophisticated enemy—I would give you a better one, but it would register your own watch and defeat the purpose."

"The purpose?"

"Your protection, Miss Patrick. Only that."

"If you say so, Elint. That's a funny name. Is it a Jewish one?" It would be, she thought; this quiet man no taller than herself, with his rounded arms and deep lines like white scars around his recessed eyes, must be one of the fabled Mossad operatives, part of the Israeli apparatus. And Beck had sent him—or had he?

"It's a funny name," he agreed, "for a Jew. Jews should die in Israel, don't you agree? This is the meaning of life, for a Jew."

So Elint had been listening to her conversation long before he'd butted into it. Her mouth wouldn't moisten; her pulse wouldn't ease. *Beck, what are you doing to me?* "Are you an Israeli, Elint?" She'd meant to ask flatly if he were an Israeli agent; she became a coward at the last instant.

"Sometimes," he smiled. "Right now, I must be your newest beau; we shall stroll out together; you will show signs of feminine disposition toward me—a kiss on the cheek, a brush of hips, a holding of hands—whatever is natural. In the vestibule, you may call our mutual friend from a phone booth to verify my good will, but I hope you trust me better than to feel the need. Then we will go to my car and then your apartment, and then I will drive you to your dinner date. This is acceptable?"

All of that he said as he leaned forward in an intimate and courtly way, a bit too close for her American tastes, as Arabs and Israelis tended to do.

"I have to get a new dress, Elint—shop, find something to wear." But her ploy produced an unexpected result from this odd, somehow charming, little man.

"Good. Good. I will help you; I know many fine shops and I have funds for just such contingencies."

As he helped her out of the booth, she could have sworn that he was actually looking forward to taking her shopping for a date with another man.

By the time she had shopped, showered, and changed, she was quite used to Elint, who was used to making people comfortable and very used to waiting. He never once seemed impatient; she never felt she had to apologize.

She hadn't insisted on making the phone call; somehow it seemed like an insult, a breach of faith. Even in her apartment he seemed comfortable, staring out the window into East Jerusalem as if it interested him more than she did.

She wanted to resent his intrusion into her life, her privacy, to suspect him and disrespect him, but she couldn't: he made it impossible, putting her so much at ease she realized she was singing in the shower as if he weren't out there, watching the streets, watching everything with supremely wise and patient eyes.

When she appeared in her new silk dress, he nodded conspiratorially as if he'd expected her to look so elegant, when she'd never had a dress like that before, and forebore compliments that might have made her self-conscious.

"Exactly time to go," he told her, and the way he said it made her check her own watch, itself the perfect complement to her elegantly understated commando-camouflage shirtwaist with its military flair. But then he was holding her hooded, poly-coated raincoat for her and she remembered that she didn't like to go outside any more, that every time she did she was exposing herself, and her excitement bled away.

Only when they reached the King David did Elint give her another disconcerting moment: he parked his mid-size Chevrolet with its open-faced air conditioner across the street and said, "You must go the rest of your way on your own. I will be around, looking out for your safety, all the time."

"But—"

He was already reaching across her to open her door.

Flustered, she got out, fumbling the last of her disposable masks up over her mouth and nose, her handbag with the little Colt in it clutched to her stomach; what if she needed him? But then, she'd never needed him before today. How could she get in touch with him, she wanted to ask. His expression made it an intrusion as he waited for her to close the car door again, then locked it and sat there, staring straight ahead, his motor idling.

She nearly got hit by a car running across the street.

The King David was full of dazed, unhappy tourists bundled up as if it were the dead of winter. She realized she didn't know Beck's proper title, though it was part of her job to know such things—she'd attributed the propaganda she'd floated for him to "State Department sources"—and had to ask the maitre d' for "Mister Beck's table, please."

This evidently made her seem charmingly naive, for the maitre d' smiled unctuously and escorted her there himself.

One look at Beck and all her doubts fled; his physical proximity was like an electric shock; she felt a flush of pleasure when he stood up, complimented her appearance, and waited for the maitre d' to push her chair in under her before he sat down again.

"How are you?" From him, the banal courtesy meant something more: how was his spy, how was his agent, how was his *poule de luxe?*

For she felt very de luxe in her new dress, having dinner with this eminently civilized man who managed to be sexy even in a conservative dark blue suit and tie, until she clutched her bag in her lap and felt the unequivocal weight of the Colt there.

"A little queasy," she admitted. "I hope it's not . . . you know what."

"The excitement, more likely—good old stress." He reached out and took the fingers of her left hand in his tanned ones; he wore no wedding ring; she hadn't thought to notice before. But she did notice the smudges of weariness under his taut eyes and deep shadows at the corners of his mouth; his hair was just the tiniest bit shaggy; she could see a few silver hairs. "Let's figure out what we're having; then we can talk."

She didn't care, she told him, and he made her feel as if she should while he scanned the wine list and menu and then looked up: "Have a drink? It'll relax you."

"Is it so obvious? I don't know where to begin, what I can tell you here. . . . I mean, is it safe to talk?"

"In a moment it will be," he said encouragingly, and ordered her a white wine spritzer when the cocktail waiter came.

Then: "Tell me about your day, Chris. Did my rookie collect any intelligence?" A grin crinkled the corners of his eyes.

She blurted: "Intelligence!" too loudly; he sat back. He wasn't being fair; she wanted a more personal discussion. "Intelligence. Let me tell you something, Beck: all that crap you fed me—casualty estimates and brave propaganda about how well the US is holding up—it's bullshit. One of my friends knows some ham radio operators and they've heard from American and European hams ... things are," her voice choked up; she cleared her throat, "a hell of a lot worse than you led me to believe."

He chuckled softly, his head to one side: "That's the Chris Patrick I remember."

"It's me, all right. A BBC friend of mine says the estimate's more like fifty-five million and rising."

His hand was on the white tablecloth; he studied it, not looking up: "Intelligence leaks better than it disseminates—that's why I need you."

He needed her. Despite herself, she sat straighter. "You've heard," she said, "that the Shi'ites are saying it's the will of God, punishing the American Satans and their Israeli puppets—that God is going to punish the Israelis further? There's going to be another Arab–Israeli war, maybe more than one."

His mouth twitched: "Your colleagues read this as a probable result of the upstepping in terrorist activies?"

"Some do, some don't really give a damn any more. Somebody said to me today that a Jew should die in Israel. I'm not Jewish."

"Who said that?" His posture didn't change; he just became very still, even to the eyes.

"Your friend Elint. Oh, I forgot to thank you for—"

"*Who?*" It was his turn to snap.

A cold dread reached up from her spine: "Elint," she said uncertainly, one hand around the listening device that was the watch on her wrist. "You didn't send somebody called Elint, alias Harold Levy, to me with 'presents'?"

He'd relaxed now; he said, "Yes and no. Elint's one of ours. What were the presents?"

She showed him, relieved beyond measure that she hadn't made some terrible mistake, and he shook his head in a curious mixture of appreciation, pride, and amusement: "That's just fine. You do exactly what Elint tells you and you can't go wrong."

"But he lied to me, he said this," she tapped the watch, "was from you." She was disappointed.

"It is, after a fashion. Wear it in good health."

"You know, you're just too fucking mysterious for your own good. I'm not—"

Their drinks came and she grasped hers like someone dying of thirst.

When the waiter was gone, he said, "You're not what?"

"I'm not telling you anything else until you tell me something."

Again he leaned back: "Shoot." The steady, unflinching gaze told her she could ask him anything and get a straight answer.

"What is it I'm doing for you? What's the point of floating all this disinformation?"

"The point, not to give you a lecture, is that all governments and their ears—intelligence services—have a tendency to tweak their shots, to selectively deliver intelligence to support policy. That can't happen here—it's too dangerous. And it's equally dangerous to let our enemies in ComBloc think that we're in total disarray."

"So it *is* for God and Country."

"Most exactly, that's what it's for. On the trip, if you're still game, it's going to be a lot harder; you're going to have to listen very carefully and do precisely as you're told, while at the same time improvising with all your heart to attain certain objectives."

"Such as?" Her fingers were still on the watch; she wanted a cigarette but didn't want to use the gimmicked lighter; then she did, and its little indicator was blithely green.

"It won't make sense to you yet; we've got a lot more talking to do."

She didn't like it when he got tutorial. She said, "Then tell me something I can understand: tell me about your wife—any kids?" She wanted to know about her competition.

His stare flickered, then steadied: "I've been trying not to think about them; everybody has survival tricks, and mine is discipline." As he spoke, he was pulling a crocodile wallet from his jacket's inside pocket.

Then she realized what he was intimating: "You mean, they're over *there*? In the *States*? Oh, Christ, I'm sorry. I didn't mean to pry. . . ."

"It's all right." He took out a family snapshot—a blond woman in her early thirties on a sloop with a jauntily cocked captain's cap and children under either arm: a teenage boy with his father's angular, fine-featured face, and a chubby-cheeked girl with golden curls, perhaps ten. "If they were lucky, they were incinerated, vaporized in some strike zone, rather than being downwind and taking five hundred or a thousand Rems in a day."

She felt horrid and petty and didn't take the photo from him. His finger pointed them out: "Jennifer. Seth." His children. "Muffy." His wife.

"Ha!" The tense laugh exploded unbidden: "Muffy? Not Muffy, really!"

"Why not?" He took his photo back and put it and the wallet away.

"*Nobody's* actually named 'Muffy.' "

"Melissa, then. And you may be righter than you know." For the first time, she saw a deep sadness in him, deeper than her own, deeper than she'd ever seen in anyone but the factions fighting in the Middle East.

"I'm sorry," she offered lamely.

"So am I."

An anguishing silence ensued, broken only by the waiter who came to take their dinner order.

When the first course arrived, he said, "If you're willing, I'd like to take you back to my place to work later—that way, we can enjoy our meal."

Which was what he'd intended, she realized, before she'd put her foot in her mouth up to her knee. "That would be very nice," she said as tenderly as she could, trying to let him know that she'd realized her mistake and would never make another like it, and that she wanted to be with him, even comfort him if he'd let her.

When they left the King David, he pulled two of the rubber respirators with their replaceable filters that had become Jerusalem's new status symbol out of his raincoat pocket and handed her one as a limousine at the curb pulled obediently forward. By then, he'd lightened both their moods adroitly, helped along by Dom Perignon—"We're earning it, don't feel guilty"—and the festive meal itself.

"You're kidding me," she giggled, her voice muffled through the mask, leaning against him with his hand at the small of her back as the chauffeur, looking like a black-tie frogman, got out and smartly opened the door for them; she'd expected Elint in his Chevy, or Beck's own gunmetal Plymouth.

"Goes with the territory; when we're out together, it's got to be business as usual," he murmured into her hair before he took her hand to help her ease inside.

At his apartment, his jacket and tie came off and so did his gloss: "We've got lots to do. I'm sorry I was out of touch so long, but it's good for you. On the fact-finding mission, you and I can be friendly, though I'd really prefer antagonistic, but never intimate. You're no good to me if the IMF reps and the NATO honchos and the Japanese don't trust you implicitly, see you as the impartial observer, the member of the adversary press I want you to be."

"Oh," she replied with all-too-evident disappointment, "you're going to work me on the tour."

"Run you," he corrected absently as he collected pencils and notepads that said DEPARTMENT OF STATE in raised blue letters and then the tea kettle he'd put on screeched above the jazz from his stereo.

She followed him into the kitchen, watching as he filled a Melior with hot water. "Run you close at hand," he continued while, as if to demonstrate, he ran the taps and washed hands that didn't need washing, "the most difficult way. But don't worry, we'll manage."

Right. I don't know what he's talking about or why he thinks we'll live that long, but we'll manage. Anything you say, sir, as long as we end up in that bed of yours before dawn. Even in his suit pants, his tight buns were reminding her what had gotten her into this in the first place.

A bell rang somewhere and he shut off the water and turned to her: "Expecting someone? Tell anyone you'd be here?"

While she tried to convinced him that she'd done nothing of the kind, he leaned over the sink and peered out the window at the parking lot below, then knifed past her to hit the intercom button: "Yes?" His voice was terse and defensive.

She thought he was going to tell her to go hide in his closet, but a voice said, "Zaki," and his whole body slumped as he said into the mouthpiece, "Come on up," and pressed the button which would unlock the front door.

He seemed relieved, but she saw him run splayed fingers angrily through his hair as he went to wait at the front door, taking something from the single drawer of a table in the hallway, putting it on the tabletop and covering it with a newspaper.

A gun? She was almost sure it had been.

Without turning, he said, "Don't stand there. Go sit in the living room."

She did and soon the door opened, no shots rang out, and Elint came ambling in with his swinging gait and a broad grin on his unmasked face, carrying a small black bag: "Good evening, Miss Patrick. Just the person I wanted to see." For the first time she realized that Elint never bothered with any of the paraphernalia the Forty-Minute War had forced on the rest of them: no raincoat, no high boots, no radiation badge, nothing.

They'd spoken quietly in the hall and she hadn't been able to make out the words, but Beck was already rolling up his right sleeve when he told her, "We've both got to have shots; it's easier if we have them here. It won't take long."

Elint was taking alcohol and hypodermics of the single-use sort from the bag. Holding a bottle with a rubber top upside down, he drew viscous liquid into one hypodermic, squinting critically. "Very thick. It will leave a little bump for a week or so, but not to worry."

Beck was sitting on the sofa's back, his bare arm proferred for Elint to swab and stab. "First batch?" he said to Elint so softly she might have heard him wrong. "First time you've tried it?"

"All have had it but the three of us, no ill effects," Elint said in that same maddening undertone, so that the music from the stereo nearly overwhelmed his words as he pushed the plunger down slowly and with infinite care. Beck watched him as if it were someone else's arm, not his own.

"Hurts like a son of a bitch, Chris," Beck warned her when he rolled down his sleeve and Elint got out a second needle.

"Do I have to? I hate shots."

"You'll learn to love this one," Beck said mysteriously as Elint came toward her with that kindly, patient expression he must use on children and small animals and she rolled up her own silk sleeve.

It did hurt; the stuff they were injecting into her was as thick as honey and the muscle of her arm complained bitterly. She gnawed her lip and Elint told her she was very brave.

Then Beck said to Elint, "Okay, I guess I can give you yours."

The Semite shook his curly head: "Chassidim live or die according to God's will."

And Beck, who never let an argument go until he'd won it, said, "Suit yourself. Thanks. Thank the others for me."

"I will," said Elint. "And let me say that your Chris is all you told us and more. A fine girl. Well chosen. *Shalom*, Chris." He waved as, bag snapped shut, he headed for the door. "*Shalom*, Beck."

Beck followed him out and they whispered together again.

When he came back, she was slouched on his sofa, rubbing her arm, and he reached down from behind to kiss the top of her head. "I'm proud of you," he said, though she had no idea for what.

Two hours later, when the windows shook in their frames as if a jet had broken the sound barrier directly overhead and shock waves made the floor under them shiver, they were lying in his bed.

Beck vaulted over her and had his hand on the telephone before it rang.

"Right. I see. Right away."

The phone slammed down and he was pulling on his pants.

"What is it? What's happened? Christ, if it's another nuclear—"

"Conventional truck bomb. The consulate." Shoes in hand, he was running toward the door, protective gear forgotten, shirttails flying.

"*Wait!* I want to go with you! It's a story and you owe me—"

"Move, then," he called back. "Slam the door hard when you leave."

Trembling, she dressed—just the shirtwaist, no underwear, no stockings, shoes in hand so that she could run fast enough to catch him—and took the fire-exit stairs three at a time.

When she flung herself out the emergency exit,

he was sitting there, the Plymouth idling, its door open for her.

He drove like a NASCAR racer, fingers white on the wheel and silent, watching all his mirrors with fanatical concentration, bumping up over median strips and wheeling down one-way streets so that she crammed her knuckles in her mouth and fastened her seatbelt.

At the compound gates, he deserted her again, leaving the car before it had truly stopped, his door ajar.

Barefoot, she charged after him, only to pull up short: he was talking to the same Marine who'd been on duty the first day she'd met him—the day it had happened. Suddenly she wondered what the big deal was: it was a conventional bomb—nothing heavy when compared to what they'd already been through.

But inside she could see devastation: ambulances, men with masks and guns and helmets, stretchers, body bags, an Israeli army truck unloading men to help dig out survivors.

Her fingers itched for pencil and paper; she'd left her bag in his apartment; she'd depend on her memory, she thought as she edged up close and tugged on his sleeve.

As if it were the most natural thing in the world, he put one arm around her, never breaking the stride of his conversation.

"And Dickson? You're sure it's him? What was he doing in there at this time of night?"

"Whoever came flying through his office window's bagged and tagged as Dickson, Sir—only dental records'll tell for certain. But I ID'd his class ring on the corpse and I checked him through the gate earlier this evening. He had a lot of catching up to do, he said." The Marine had a hard helmet on, a government-issue respirator dangling unsnapped from one side of it; his face was grimy and streaked. "Sent Pickwick out for some of that Turkish coffee he likes, 'cause they ran out inside."

"Pickwick. Did he come back?"

"Ah—no, Sir, not to my knowledge." The Marine's gaze rested on her. "Hiya, Miss Patrick. Nice to see you—alive."

"Dickson's dead?" she piped up.

"Very, evidently, Chris. All right, Sergeant, thank you. Carry on."

Beck started to walk her back to his car.

"But . . . Sir? You're the highest grade surviving Int—"

Over his shoulder, Beck called back: "Tap the next fool in line, Sergeant. And find Pickwick; have him put under close arrest, my authority."

"Yes, Sir," said the Marine sergeant.

"What's hap—?" she started to ask.

Beck cut her off savagely: "Can you add, Chris? Two and two? If this isn't a diversion, I've never seen one. And I think I know from what. So you can stay here and work for your paper, or you can come along and watch the shit hit the fan."

She'd only seen that side of him once—when he'd held the hostage-taker at knife-point in the consulate, now a ruin of twisted metal and pulverized concrete behind them.

As they pulled away in the Plymouth, sirens began to scream.

Chapter 7

Ashmead was back in harness, sitting in a canvas-covered lorry pulled off the road out of the eastern campus of the Hebrew University, waiting for the twenty-millimeter tracers from Israeli air cover to signal that the terrorist raiding party was headed his way, barreling toward Jordan.

He shifted slightly and spoke into the voice-actuated transceiver threaded on the shoulder holster holding his SIG pistol and spare clips: "Test. This is Coach, check in."

Across the road, where a little rise was silvered in moonlight, there was no movement. But Slick's voice came out of the transceiver on Ashmead's shoulder preceded by the little snap and slight clipping of his first word as the transceiver's "send" mode kicked in: "Pitcher, check."

Then the rest of them, in terse succession: "Batter, check," said Jesse, lying prone at the bend in the road; "Catcher, check," said Thoreau, from the lorry's cab, dressed like an orange-grower but with his encrypt/decrypt communications gear, their link to one another and Netanayhu's Saiyeret teams, taped to the seat beside him, and an Uzi on his knee; "Outfield, check," said Yael, in her secondary command jeep, waiting with six of Zaki's Israeli agents, a cleanup squad to pick off anybody who jumped for open country: with their night-vision goggles and their position on the high ground, Yael Saadia's unit had the best seats in the house, with the possible exception of the Saiyeret chopper pilots, who had starlight-magnifiers and "tourist detection" radars that could spot a kefiya from a mile in the air.

Ashmead settled back, wiggling his arse to find a comfortable position despite his Saiyeret-issue uniform, complete with flash hood, all poly-sealed against radiation so that he was sweating like a pig, and his full kit—three extra magazines for his Galil, three flash-bang and three fragmentation grenades. As he ripped off the flash hood in disgust and stuffed it in his web belt—they were catching one and one half Rem per hour out here, no more than every American had caught unknowingly in the Fifties when the superpowers were testing—and rested his cheek against the infrared scope of the Galil rifle between his legs, Zaki chimed in too, though Ashmead hadn't expected him to make it.

"Left field, check," Zaki said laconically, and Slick let out a muffled whoop of pleasure to know that Zaki had finished his tasks in town in time to take up his position, opposite Jesse in a little gully beside the bend in the road around which the terrorists were going to come.

They really wanted this one—it would make up for losing Schvantz.

Ashmead's team had gotten wind of the terrorist operation the second day they'd been in Jerusalem, but because it was Dow's, they were told, an Agency operation—sort of, they were advised—Ashmead's team had spent thirty-six hours sourcing it and reconfirming that it wasn't official, wasn't on the books, was just Dow and his Palestinian network striking a tandem blow for West Bank autonomy and Dow's wallet. The whole time Ashmead's team had been confirming, they worked on their own, informing no one, torqued down tight in their own operational fervor while they checked and rechecked everything and everyone involved.

When it was confirmed that Dow was using his "indigs"—indigenous agents, in this case Palestinians from East Jerusalem—as well as six imported Shi'ites, to mount an operation to expropriate the anti-cancer drug being manufactured in the east-campus university lab, exactly as the plan had been leaked to Zaki's alerted network, Ashmead had looked at the numbers and realized he was going to have to have some help.

So he'd gone to Netanayhu, not Beck, who was too much the diplomat for what Ashmead had in mind.

At that time, there still had been pieces missing: the whys and whens, not the hows, of Dow's little romp.

But Netanayhu was an old desert fox, and if not exactly one of Ashmead's "agents of influence," then as close to that as he could be while retaining his intense Israeli pride.

They called it mutuality of interest, once Netanayhu had gotten over the shock of seeing Ashmead emerge from behind the curtains in his study when the colonel retired there for his customary sundown paperwork session.

Netanayhu had been glad to see him, though furious that no one—not an aide or a guard or his wife—had realized his uninvited visitor was there.

And there had been the little matter of Ashmead's team tailing Netanayhu to square away: "You think I need your cowboys to protect me? You think we are amateurs in need of babysitting by you, meshugganer? If I were not a patient man, and a friend of yours—if Beck had not confirmed my suspicion that it *was* you—what then? In jail, you would be. Cooling your arrogant heels, with your cocky young team beside you—or worse."

Netanayhu's glower had been fatherly and so Ashmead didn't push it by telling the colonel he knew all that—that he had one of Zaki's squeaky-clean bugs in place and so had a good idea of what Netanayhu had said to Morse, and to Beck, earlier today. There was no time for scoring vanity points.

"I just wanted you to know we were around, Colonel, so you could cover our asses for us—and that we thought things were pretty serious. They are. More serious than even we thought. My sources say there's going to be a truck-bombing at the American Consulate at 2340 hours, but that it's—"

"*Your* sources?" This was a sore subject. "You're not supposed to *have* such sources, not without approval from my office. . . ." But Netanayhu didn't have his heart in it tonight and Ashmead had to figure out why, and fast.

"Old sources, old friends. May I ask," he stretched

one leg up on the overstuffed couch, "why you aren't surprised—about the consulate, I mean?"

"Surprised? What could surprise me these days? Nuclear terrorists attacking your government's seat and touching off a superpower confrontation—one fears for the Knesset. Am I surprised when our Jewish friends in America who happen to have the ham radios tell us much that makes us think things in your country are far worse than we are told by your official reports? Am I surprised when I am warned away from internal disputes among Americans that are not explained, but come to my attention in unpleasant phone calls from Tel Aviv concerning an unspecified action I am *not* to take in response to an event of which no one has a clear picture—or, if they have, they will not say, just give scattered hints that *we* are not to be surprised if 'something untoward should befall the American delegation?' This 'untoward something,' Tel Aviv says, is not our business. Our business is seeing to the survival of the State of Israel, and right now that means the mobilization of all our forces." Netanayhu, having dropped his own bomb and feeling that now the score was evened for Ashmead's impolite penetration of his home's defenses, offered him a drink: "And your leg, Rafic? It is still bothering you? And your wrist, your shooter's arthritis?"

"Only when I have too much time to sit around and worry about what's bothering me, Colonel." Ashmead had accepted the two fingers of vodka gladly, moistened his lips, and regretfully put the glass down on the coffee table. With the vodka, Netanayhu, who seldom drank, was testing the waters further: was trouble so imminent that Ashmead would ask for coffee instead?

Ashmead did: "Black and as strong as Millie can make it—we don't have much time. I've got to know if you're going to stand around and twiddle your thumbs, like Tel Aviv wants, or if you're going to help me save Operation Tiebreaker—I can't imagine you're too busy with a couple of border incursions to pass up a counterterrorist operation; you're not going to be using Saiyeret on the front lines."

Netanayhu eased his bulk around his desk and went deliberately to the door, opened it a crack and bawled in his best battlefield voice for coffee for two, shut it and threw a deadbolt, then came slowly back: "Some things, Rafic, not even nuclear war between the superpowers can alter. Tel Aviv and I still have the same understanding: if I can think of something to do before they think to forbid me, then I do it." His old firehorse's eyes were sparkling.

"And in this particular case?" Ashmead asked softly.

"In this particular case, I was already helping Beck; Tel Aviv wants only not to attack your still powerful CIA." Netanayhu was treading carefully; he didn't know how much Ashmead knew or how he was going to take the revelation that Dow was using Palestinians against the State of Israel.

"If my intelligence is correct—" Ashmead smiled like a basking crocodile "—this agent of ours, Dow, is mentally unbalanced from the recent tragedy. It will be a favor to us if you'll help me retire him early—before he really hurts the relationship between our two services."

Netanayhu nodded happily: "Then we shall surround the consulate, and when—"

"I'd rather not do that, Colonel. Let's let 'em blow the consulate—it's an American acting against America, with Palestinians, proof that what we'll do then is justified. Anyway, I'd like to DX Dickson and as many of those involved in leaking Tiebreaker as I can."

Netanayhu pursed his lips: "What of our friend Beck?"

"We'll keep Beck out of it—in a state of ignorance, physically far removed from the action. I've got that part of it under control."

"So?" Netanayhu put on a puzzled look: "Then what are we to do about this Dow, whom Tel Aviv insists we do not touch?"

"Dow is going to be in the field dressed like one of his Palestinians. The real target is the university lab—the serum," Ashmead said carefully; Beck had taken great pains to keep the Israelis from finding out that what they were producing was an anti-cancer drug, not simply a medicine for radiation sickness. "Dow's realized that if he can preempt it, he can sell that stuff one dose at a time to various well-heeled folks and become the first rich man in the new society. And since it's the Hebrew University we're talking about, seems to me that Tel Aviv couldn't blame you if, in all ignorance and on barely five hour's notice, you put together an interdiction team to stop these terrorists ... with my help, at my instigation, or any other way you want to hand me the bag to hold."

A tap came on the door. Puffing, Netanayhu muttered, "Coffee; as if we had time for a coffee klatch," and went to unbolt it.

Millie herself had brought the tray; she craned her neck to see the visitor, then exclaimed with motherly disapproval: "Rafic! In my house, and no one tells me? You're staying for dinner, of course, though one meal won't put any flesh on—"

"Millie," Netanayhu gave her The Look: "He's not here, you didn't see him, and even I won't be home for dinner tonight." Firmly, before she could reply, he took the tray from her and shut the door with his hip.

"The responsibility—this bag, as you call it," Netanayhu said as he put down the tray and poured coffee from an ornate silver pot into the Rosenthal cups Millie had brought from Germany, "is not a problem. As you say, we are in all innocence interdicting terrorists, doing our jobs; and you, as in the past, are helping clandestinely. Are we not old friends? Officially, I know nothing of your unauthorized sorties into the Gulf after our mutual enemies." Netanayhu's sharp teeth clicked on his cup. "Now, tell me how much manpower, firepower, and air support you require."

By the time they'd finished the logistics and the phone calls, Ashmead had barely two hours to put a fine edge on his strategy.

But he had Israeli support—he wanted to look like part of Saiyeret, if possible never to report his participation. His team had to blend into the larger elite force, and they did, even down to the Israeli Military Industries brass casings they'd leave on the road and the Galil rifling on the bullets they'd leave in their targets, some of which were the new top-secret explosive rounds that would kill a man if they so much as grazed him.

Dow was going to get exactly what he was asking for: he was going to be cut down like a terrorist, stitched up the middle like a rabid dog. It really bothered Ashmead when Agency people used their positions to get rich, and Dow had shown tendencies before: he'd been playing the currency market like a trust fund; if the Forty-Minute War hadn't wiped him out, he'd probably have been able to retire in style. Now he was just going to retire early.

In the soft Jerusalem night, nothing moved as Ashmead's team got on with the business of waiting. Occasionally, from the truck's cab, Ashmead could hear the low crackle of static as Thoreau got status reports from the Israeli pilots on the location, number, and probably hair and eye color of their targets.

He rubbed his arm, where the inoculation was still a sore, warm bump: he didn't really believe it could do what Beck said it could, but Dow sure did. Ashmead had taken a chance with Netanayhu, not knowing how much the wily old colonel suspected about the long-range anti-cancer effects of Morse's serum, but trade-offs were a dime a dozen these days.

The com gear they had was more pertinent: most of their haute Agency gear was useless; the MOSFET-driven, satellite-bounced radiotelephones didn't work without a satellite to handle the signals. This didn't bother Ashmead so much as it did Zaki, who seemed to be sitting shiva for his dead equipment. So Ashmead had put Zaki on the streets; as Chris Patrick's handler-to-be and the team's case officer, there was plenty for him to do: Elint had activated his nets and brought agents to Yael for debriefing; when they'd sent him over to the university to pick up the serum, the glazed, shut-down look was gone from his eyes. It must have gone very smoothly for him to have rejoined the team in time for the action.

And, looking west toward the campus, Ashmead saw that Zaki was just in time: red tracers arced through the night and the sound of hostile fire, choppers, and an overflight jet two miles away pulverized the introspective silence of his waiting fighters.

Then Thoreau's lazy voice came out of Ashmead's transceiver: "Here they come, Coach; the jeep in front's got one American, Sky-Eye thinks, but even they can't see into a panel truck."

"Batter up, folks," he told them, and threw his assault rifle up to his shoulder, balancing his weight on one knee, so he could watch through the infra-red scope.

"Check, Coach; batter at the plate," came Jesse's reply before the others sounded off; Jesse, the sharpshooter, had a laser-targeting device mounted on his sniper rifle which put a dot on the target invisible to the naked eye and which Jesse had sworn he didn't need, when Saiyeret offered it, but had taken because the Saiyeret major had smiled like an elder brother and said, "Saves time; less time, more kills."

Only Slick failed to respond as the count-off continued; damned sulky kid: Slick had wanted Dow for himself, would have had a better chance at him if he'd been point instead of Jesse, but Ashmead was conserving Slick: if anything happened to Ashmead, Slick would have to step into the breach.

A full minute later than was proper, Slick said, "Check complete."

Ashmead had been beginning to sweat again, considering a quick run over there to see if Dow hadn't put some extra backup out and they'd come across Slick and killed him. He decided he'd beat some sense into Slick when this was over: it wasn't a free-for-all any more. It might not be the world they'd known and loved, but it was a world in which the old rules had to obtain.

Then they began to hear racing engines and he could feel his people hunker down.

Stray bullets from the Saiyeret herding the terrorists into their trap started flying; ricochets whined and muzzle flashes showed like distant fireworks, spattering the night with orange-yellow light so that even without the infrared scope, he could make out the terrorists in the jeep, running without lights, that came careening around the curve, a truck right behind and Israeli vehicles, lights blazing, in hot pursuit.

He couldn't pick out Jesse's first shot in the din of the fire fight, but he saw the lead jeep veer crazily and heard Jesse's murmured, "Gotcha!" come out of his transceiver.

A chopper swooped in from above, searchlights playing, twenty-millimeter cannon in its nose spraying the road carefully in hopes of slowing or turning the truck behind the jeep while, from the chopper's open side, a black-garbed figure took careful, placed shots with a semi-automatic rifle.

The jeep was back on the road, its driver hanging over the side as someone else struggled to push him out and take the wheel, and Jesse's head popped up from cover as he tried to shoot the replacement driver from behind.

A grunt, then a howl of animal rage issued from Ashmead's transceiver as the jeep roared past him, but he was too busy dodging incomings and spraying the jeep with full-auto fire to have his team count off: he'd find out who and what later.

"All yours, catcher," he said, hardly knowing that he did as Thoreau pulled onto the road, cutting in between the jeep and the truck behind in a maneuver that threw Ashmead, though he was expecting it, to his knees and smacked him in the eye with the scope housing.

Then he had plenty to shoot at, prone on the floor of the lorry with a panel truck full of terrorists behind him, returning fire as best they could while their driver tried to avoid crashing into the side of the lorry Thoreau had so inconsiderately wheeled into their path and which was now fishtailing, its rear wheels locked, directly ahead.

Knowing Thoreau, Ashmead ducked his head, cradling his rifle with his body's weight, and grabbed hold of the metal frame where the canvas was lashed to it just in time to avoid being thrown bodily onto the truck behind them as Thoreau slammed on the brakes and executed the collision he had in mind.

Ashmead vaulted up, spraying full-auto through the windshield behind him as he jumped onto the steaming, crinkled hood of the panel truck and emptied his clip into first the balaclava'd occupants of the front seat, then straight through the panel to take out whomever might be behind.

Rolling off the hood as he changed clips, he ran around to the rear of the terrorists' truck just as the Israeli pursuit vehicle behind panic-stopped, its nose sideways across the road, and six black-clad Saiyeret in flash hoods poured out.

Ashmead's grenade rolled into the panel truck a fraction of a second before a Saiyeret commando wrenched open its back door and threw a second one.

Ashmead hit the dirt, which was littered with spent brass, hands over his ears and his face turned away as the flash-bangs went off.

Good, disciplined boys, those Saiyeret fighters—they'd been told not to risk fragmentation grenades until they were sure there wasn't a case of serum inside, and they followed orders, even though one live terrorist was all it took to get you very dead.

The clap and flash made Ashmead's ears ring despite his protecting palms and showed him every vein in his eyelids, but he kept rolling toward the soft sand at the roadside, out of harm's way.

When he sat up there, Galil on his knee, he saw the Saiyeret leader, Uzi on his hip, standing back a little and watching his men boost themselves into the panel truck.

The chopper was landing, three men wearing bulky night-vision goggles that made them look like spacemen hopping out, and the noise of it helped mask the transceiver squawking on Ashmead's shoulder for another minute or two.

When the rotors slowed and stopped, he was already making his way to the Saiyeret leader's side, listening with one ear as Slick counted casualties in the jeep skewed in front of his position up the road.

The dark hood of the Saiyeret team leader dipped

in acknowledgement; his voice was muffled by the respirator that also contained his com unit: "Rafic. Nice job. Want to see your American?"

"Is he alive?"

"Not a chance: two through the chest, one through the skull. Here's his ID."

Dow's face stared up at Ashmead from an Agency badge. "Let's make a positive match."

They climbed into the ravaged panel truck and, while the Saiyeret major held a flashlight, Ashmead turned the crumpled figure from the wall against which his blood had splattered—very carefully, and with his SIG handgun on Dow the entire time.

Ashmead had seen men with holes in them a hand's breadth in diameter play dead and then get off one last shot when their killer got close enough: some guys just had so much guts they could stave off death long enough for a chance at revenge. But Dow was dead, the front of his skull blown off by a round that had entered from the rear.

It was only when Ashmead jumped back down from the panel truck that he realized Slick was calling the roll, but stuck at Zaki's name.

"Hey, Elint?" came Slick's voice from Ashmead's transceiver. "Zaki, you jive cocksucker, don't do this to me. You alive, then say so."

Ashmead beat Yael's jeep to Zaki's position by only seconds; Jesse reached the spot at the same time.

At first they couldn't find Zaki, and Yael, bareheaded and eyes blazing, cursed: "Fucking Elint. He never could take direction. Damned operations officers, always have to be in the thick of it."

But Jesse got the halogen lamp from the jeep and in its light they saw a smear of blood and traces in the sparse new grass as if something wounded had dragged itself to cover.

The cover was a little dry arroyo and in it Zaki was sprawled.

When Jesse's light fell on Zaki, his limbs sticking out at unlikely angles, the sharpshooter made a grab for Yael so quick she couldn't twist out of it, though she turned on him and started beating at his chest and kicking at his groin.

"You go on down, Sir," said Jesse, as if Yael wasn't struggling to neuter him, "and I'll bring Saadia along when she's calmer."

Yael was Zaki's cousin.

As Ashmead skidded down the ravine, he spoke into his transceiver: "Thoreau, get over here. Zaki's down and Yael isn't Jesse's problem."

He heard Slick's transceiver cut in: "Shit. And for what?"

He didn't bother to answer; the footing was tricky and he was going to need two good ankles for the arduous days ahead.

Zaki was about bled white, breathing rattlingly, too broken up from his fall to be worth the time of the medic aboard the Israeli bird that Ashmead called for: "What's the matter, you don't have any Type A? Get your useless butt down here; this isn't a vacation."

Slick was sliding down the ravine without concern for his bones by then, discarded flash hood flapping from his belt.

But Ashmead didn't say anything, or even look pointedly at the dosimeter wedged between his canteen and a spare clip on his utility belt: they could all spend a few hours in one of Saiyeret's underground decontamination chambers if they had to, though right then he didn't care much more than Slick about how many Rems they were taking.

He was sitting on the sandy ground beside Zaki's ruined body, wiping his operations officer's lips with a wet cloth from his kit, and the ground around them was dark with the blood it had sopped up. It was the sort of thing he always noticed at a time like this.

Ashmead looked up when Slick stood beside him and saw some of the Israeli commandos standing on the high ground, hands on their hips, staring down; between them, Yael was enfolded in Thoreau's arms as he started to ease her down the steep slope.

Slick squatted by Ashmead, fingering Zaki's caved-in chest, then putting his hand on the still throat: "We don't need the medic, Sir." Slick was telling him he was overreacting.

Ashmead ignored him; Zaki rattled; Ashmead leaned close, trying to feel his case officer's breath: "We're here, Zaki. Don't worry. Yael's coming. We got them—every one."

There was a flicker under Zaki's lids, then his mouth tried to form a word.

Ashmead put his ear to the lips, then said into an ear from which blood trickled: "You got the serum out and we got Dow—it's just that we'd like to know where you left it, Zaki. Can you hear me?"

Slick was colder: "If it's not in Beck's car, if you've been improvising again, better tell us."

Zaki started to choke, then got out: "One," and began to convulse weakly.

Ashmead, satisfied, sat back just as Yael broke free of Thoreau and pulled savagely at him: "Get away from him, give him air, give him—"

Then she saw Zaki's staring eyes and sat back on her haunches. "Right," she said softly. "Well, he always said a Jew should die in Israel. He wasn't even going to take his shot." Viciously, as if her own emotions were her enemy, she swiped at the tears running down her face.

Slick got up with a shake of his head and went to intercept the Israeli medic sliding down the slope, bag in hand.

Ashmead heard him say, *"One,* great," into his transceiver. "One fucking *what?* Plan One? One case? Even dying, he's giving me riddles."

Ashmead let his hand brush Yael's head as he went after Slick: nothing too comforting, just what he would have done if she'd been one of the guys.

Thoreau, flash goggles up on his forehead and mask down around his throat, gave him an eloquent look, then fell in beside him: "That's a bitch. Who's going to run that Patrick broad? Beck can't, not without a handler in between."

"You volunteering, Thoreau?"

"Well, maybe. . . . Yael can't help but blame her for some of this—" he gestured aimlessly around. "After all, if she'd kept Zaki busy, he wouldn't have been here. Left field. We didn't need him."

"Slick can handle her. You go handle Yael."

"Yes, Sir, if you say so, but that's a match made in hell."

He didn't answer. He knew that. Right now, he had other things on his mind.

At the top of the arroyo, he pulled the Saiyeret leader aside: "Morse is safe?"

The Israeli unlatched his com-unit/respirator so that they could talk privately, pulled off his hood and ran a hand through his short dark hair, then looked pointedly at Ashmead's shoulder-borne transceiver.

Ashmead switched it off.

Then the Israeli answered his question: "So far as we know. Netanayhu put him under house arrest, as you suggested." The team leader's eyes, in the chopper's spotlight, were full of unspoken sympathy: nobody knows what it means to lose a man like Zaki but another team leader who's had to replace one. "There's an ammo crate in the jeep you might want to look at, and another dead American."

"Really? Thanks. While you walk me over there, give me the damage report on the lab, Major."

The Israeli did, telling him that the facilities were essentially unharmed, since all the crucial equipment had been moved out beforehand and replaced with dummies, and the body count was seventeen terrorists, two counterterrorists.

Which meant that the Saiyeret leader had lost someone too, and prompted Ashmead to say, with the rebelliousness of a man who's trying to put a value on the lost life of a friend, "If that crate contains what I think it does, and you'll trust me and not ask any questions or tell anyone about it, and you can swear your men to silence, I think you and your team ought to all have a little shot. It won't take long."

The Saiyeret leader raised one eyebrow: "You're the commander, Rafic. If it's good for us, it would be good for Colonel Netanayhu, though, so I'll give him mine."

Ashmead knew he was walking a thin line, but he wanted the Israelis to figure out what the serum was for and, if possible, to continue producing enough of it, once Beck's mission was airborne, to inoculate every man, woman and child in Israel. One of the things he'd learned on his nation's Covert Action staff was that murder by inaction was just as bad as murder by direct action.

"I'll take care of Dov Netanayhu. We go back a long way."

"I'd heard that," said the fighter pacing him, with a quick grin. "You're something of a legend in a venue where that sort of distinction doesn't come easily."

"It comes expensive," Ashmead said gruffly.

And then they'd reached the jeep, where one splayed figure slumped in its seat turned out to be a little worm from the consulate named Pickwick, and Zaki's mysterious "One" explained itself:

Zaki had gotten one crate, and the terrorists had gotten the other.

Ashmead, with a whisper in his transceiver to Slick to bring the medic, began to pry it open with his combat knife while the Saiyeret major formed up his ranks to get their shots.

Chapter 8

There was no hail of bullets by the time Beck and Chris Patrick drove up to the interdiction site—the Saiyeret on the east campus had seen to it that Beck was sufficiently delayed, checking his credentials and Chris's, then double-checking, then making them wait until flak vests, replacement dosimeters and respirators for those Beck had left in his apartment, and a motorcycle escort to accompany them to the site could be found—and *that* only after Beck had thrown a diplomatic tantrum and called Netanayhu on a Saiyeret field phone.

Beck himself couldn't have executed a delaying action any better. Grudgingly, he gave the Israelis the credit they deserved: they'd been told to keep him out of harm's way and that security must be air-tight. They would and it was.

Even driving toward the site, beyond which lay Jericho and above it Jordan, Beck didn't know where the hell he was going. He just followed the blue flashing lights on the bikes before him and fumed.

Beside him, Chris Patrick looked irresistible in her Israeli flak vest over all that silk. Beck cautioned himself not to get too attached to his agent—people died on the sort of operation Tiebreaker was shaping up to be; and, in espionage, being a woman was no protection.

His escort held them—politely but firmly—in their car while one talked to an Israeli commander with a flash hood in his belt and a black sleeve rolled up. Beyond the little knot of commandos were wrecked cars, a chopper shining a blinding searchlight on body bags being loaded into a van and, farther down the road, a makeshift medical station by a ruined jeep.

Chris sat quietly beside him, taking notes on the back of a deposit slip she'd found in his glove compartment, her lips white in the Plymouth's courtesy lights.

When the Saiyeret leader came toward him, the commando slipped on his flash hood for anonymity and then leaned stiff-armed on the driver's side window well, rolling down his sleeve as he said, "Mister Beck, this is a classified operation and you have a news—a press person with you. You're welcome to look around, but she's got to stay here. We'll take good care of her."

Chris Patrick looked up at the man in the mask and actually growled, a low noise in her throat that made the Saiyeret duck his head to stare at her.

"It's standard procedure, Miss Patrick," the commando said before Beck could intervene. "We've got to protect our identities . . . terrorist reprisals. You understand."

"Do I look like a terrorist to you?" she demanded.

"Chris, in forty-eight hours you're going to have all the exclusives you can handle," Beck interjected before the Saiyeret could give her Counterterrorism 101, and touched her knee as the commando leader stood back so that Beck could get out of the car.

"Promises, promises," he heard her say when the car door slammed; as he was walking away with the Saiyeret, she was estimating loudly how much an interview with one of those commandos would have been worth. Then one of the commandos told her she'd better roll up her window or put on her mask; she rolled up her window.

The Israeli beside him, out of Chris's view, took off his flash hood and in the chopper's searchlight Beck could see his black anodized major's bars.

"Major, I'm going to need an explanation: if you people managed to be here in such well organized force, you could have been at the consulate. As far as I know, our intelligence-sharing agreement is still in effect."

The Saiyeret steered him around a shadowy patch that turned out to be a piece of twisted fender: "Explanations aren't my province; neither is intelligence. You wouldn't be here if Rafic hadn't cleared it—especially not with a girl newsie. You'll have to talk to him about what you need—Sir." The major's American English was flawless but his jaw muscles ticked, his resentment barely masked: it was all he could do to be civil; his disdain for the American diplomatic corps was palpable.

And Ashmead, bare-headed but in Saiyeret blacks and sitting on the ruined jeep swinging his legs

while to his left a masked Israeli medic gave commandos injections, barked at him: "What the *fuck*
are you doing here, kid? Is it your specialty, being
at the wrong place at the worst time?"

The medic gave a final stab and began putting a
half full vial, alcohol, and syringes in his bag.

"If that's what I think it is," Beck said, flicking his
eyes toward the medic and his bag as the Saiyeret
major edged away and began moving his men out
of earshot, "you're way out of bounds, Rafic."

Ashmead stopped swinging his legs and scratched
behind one ear: "Beck, this is no place to talk
about it, and you ought to know that." His head
turned: "Slick!"

Ashmead's handsome deputy, his face smudged
with powder residue, an Uzi swinging from his hip
and a rifle slung over his shoulder, came around
the jeep and gave Beck a cursory nod of acknowledgement.

"Slick, change clothes, then go introduce yourself to Miss Patrick as part of Beck's security force
and drive her home. Then take Beck's car to my
place and unload it. Beck's coming with me."

"Whose home—hers or his?" Slick asked with a
sardonic smile playing at the corners of his mouth.

"Anybody's but yours, Slick, okay? Go on, go."

Both men could hear the deputy swearing as he
trotted toward a lorry with a canvas top.

Beck, arms crossed, stared steadily at Ashmead,
waiting for some sort of explanation. The rough-
hewn CIA man stared back at him with sour
amusement. Finally Beck said, "Rafic, *what's* in
my car?"

Ashmead jumped down from the jeep's tailgate
and Beck could see an open ammo crate with vials

of serum in it. Ashmead patted it: "The other crate of serum. We wanted to slip them both out, but it had to look like we didn't know Dow's terrorists were coming—tried to put together some dummy serum but evidently it didn't pass muster, so Zaki had to leave one real case; he got the other one and put it in your car."

"Dow?" Beck now understood exactly what had happened. "Why the fuck didn't you warn me, Rafic? Dickson's dead, the consulate's—"

"Dickson was part of your problem. So was Pickwick, who, along with Dow, isn't going to cause any more trouble, beyond whether or not to ship their corpses back to the States."

"Okay . . . Dow, Pickwick, Dickson."

"And Zaki."

"Zaki? I'm sorry. But still, you let the consulate blow. Sometimes you really live up to your reputation, you know?"

"In this business you can't afford to get sloppy. As far as officialdom's concerned, it's a terrorist interdiction, a fait accompli that happened to accompli a couple of traitorous American scumsuckers along with a bunch of Shi'ites and Palestinians—I wasn't here, unless it gets to the point where I've got to be to get Dov off the hook: we don't want to ruin his day. Now, let's go write the after-action reports with the good colonel, and then you can tell me about our ETD and the aircraft you've got for us—I heard that one's a P-3B, one of those baby AWACs, and the other is a converted 727. That gives us zilch for active defense, in case somebody wants to make sure we never get there. And from the look of things, somebody probably does."

"Too many international honchos on board for

that." Beck, giving up all attempts to chastise Ashmead, whom he'd chosen because of his unconventional methods, fell in beside. "ETD's forty-eight hours, if it suits you. . . ."

"That's a lot of security arrangements in forty-eight hours."

"Plus the arrangements for Zaki's funeral," Beck agreed gently.

"Saiyeret will take care of that, give Zaki a military funeral as a Saiyeret hero, which is easier than making up some story about how he happened to get in the way of a Maadi AK round. Saiyeret aren't identified while they're alive, and it'll make his parents proud. We couldn't go to his funeral in any case: too much chance of a cohort of this bunch of martyrs being there hoping we'll do just that."

"Fine," Beck said in his most neutral diplomatic voice as he searched for a trace of hostility in Ashmead's eyes: he knew how deeply the Covert Action Chief cared about his operatives. "I've already started security checks on the dignitaries; your pilot can have his pick of the aircraft; my pilot will fly the other; co-pilots are you and me . . . we've got to keep this thing manageable. And, at the risk of 'ruining your day,' you ought to know that our best estimate is that the jet stream's no longer blocked—it's going to get hotter here, so we might as well put this show on the road."

Ashmead grunted as approvingly as if Beck had just shot a one-inch group at a hundred yards.

Slick trotted past them in nondescript khakis, face clean of powder smears and hair combed, rubber issue mask pushed rakishly up on his forehead.

Beck said, "Mind if I know why you're siccing Slick on Chris?"

"Slick's replacing Zaki."

"Damn, I forgot about Zaki. I'm sorry—"

"Plant a tree for him or something. Zaki won't be the last we'll lose on this fucking suicide mission of yours."

"*That's* why you gave those commandos the serum. You didn't tell them?"

"No. But I sure as fuck hope they figure it out. Somebody ought to get some good out of Morse's serum; it's five-to-one against that the Administration will, and that's my official strategic analysis."

"Morse!" Beck slapped his forehead. "He's—"

"Sleeping like a baby. Relax, Beck, don't sweat the small stuff. That's what you've got us for."

Book Two:
RED ZONES

Chapter 1

The P-3B AEW was an antisubmarine aircraft modified for early warning and control. It had a mission endurance of fourteen hours, a maximum range of forty-two hundred nautical miles, a maximum cruising speed of three hundred forty-six knots, and its takeoff distance of fifty-five hundred feet was approximately the same as the 727 full of multinational fact-finders it was escorting.

There all resemblance ended: the P-3B AEW's primary mission capabilities included, as well as early warning, passive detection, surveillance, C3I (command, control, communications), over-the-horizon targeting that could detect fighters and small surface vehicles in excess of one hundred fifty miles to the radar horizon, search and rescue, and miscellaneous other capabilities that allowed its use as an emergency command post.

For maximum efficiency, however, its crew had

to consist of a pilot, co-pilot, flight engineer, radar operator, and two air controllers, four of whom would always be working while two rotated aft to the galley or the pair of bunks provided.

This meant that, like everything else about Operation Tiebreaker's early stages, necessity took matters out of Beck's hands and put them squarely in Ashmead's.

Beck had wanted to divide Ashmead's people evenly between the two aircraft, the way the serum was divided, but Ashmead insisted on "full operational capability for the P-3B, Beck, or we might as well scrub this thing, here and now."

"Here and now" had been three hours before takeoff, when Beck was harried by the intermittent arrival of forty-three dignitaries and trying to go over Yael Saadia's outrageously detailed intelligence dossiers on each and every one of the IMF honchos, NATO guns, International Red Cross and UNESCO reps, and officers of the Japanese Ministry of Trade.

Saadia had puffy circles under her eyes and every now and then would bolt for the bathroom. During the third such incident, after which she'd come back with a freshly scrubbed face and smelling like a baby, Beck had voiced his fears to Ashmead: "Do you think it's the serum, Rafic? A bad reaction? Or too many Rems?" Vomiting was an early warning sign he'd been hoping not to see.

"It's worse than that," Rafic had muttered; "she's pregnant and she wants to have it. Best damned station chief I ever had, and Thoreau goes and knocks her up. Don't say anything about it."

The faucets, which couldn't quite mask the sound

of retching from the bathroom, were turned off; the toilet flushed.

Ashmead tapped the avalanche of paper on Beck's desk: "Come on, we've got to shred this stuff. Cave. It's my way or not at all: Thoreau's the P-3B pilot, I'm the co-pilot, Slick's the radar operator, Yael and Jesse are the flight controllers. That leaves room enough, even with what electronics we've pulled, for only six passengers—you, your girl Patrick, Morse, and three dips of your choice. Pick 'em out."

"Rafic, I need to be on the 727; so does Patrick; I'd like Slick there too . . . and Saadia. If we miss this opportunity to tell these people what we want them to think, we may not get another. And Chris's credibility isn't going to be helped if she's not on—"

"One more time, Marc, and then I'll just assume you're not listening: as far as I'm concerned, the 727 is a decoy. We can't protect it worth a damn; it's expendable. You're not. My people aren't; you tell me that Patrick girl's not. If we had Zaki, maybe I could have done without a full complement on the flight deck, but we don't. I need everybody. We've got to assume that both aircraft may not make it to Houston. If it were up to me, I wouldn't put that case of serum on the 727, but I'm—"

"Rafic." Beck gave Ashmead his best interrogator's stare. "If you know something you're not telling me—if this is another case, like the consulate, where you're holding back informa—"

Saadia came back with murmured apologies and flopped bonelessly down on Beck's couch: "Don't stop because of me, guys." She wiped swollen lips with the back of her hand.

"Yael," Beck said, resisting an impulse to touch her knee, lecture her about the madness of going into radiation red zones pregnant: "I'm trying to convince Rafic that I can handle one flight controller's station—probably both—and that I'd like you and Jesse on the 727 with Chris Patrick ... we need your propagandist talents more than we need another scope-watcher: you and Jesse, as 'reporters,' have an opportunity to assess and cut out the targets from this herd of—"

"Beck," Ashmead's rough-hewn face was expressionless, his gaze fixed on Yael Saadia, who was looking at him hopefully: "Go with Yael to the P-3B. If she checks you out, you've got your deployment of assets. But don't ever do this to me again. It was an intelligence failure that got us into this— yours. You want to go for two, that's fine, but not while I'm involved. If you think this is some fucking democracy I'm running here, you're deluded. Explain things to him, Yael."

Dismissed as if he were a member of Ashmead's team and not its controller, Beck had left quickly with Yael Saadia, who, in the hall of Beck's apartment building as they waited for the lift, touched his arm gently and said: "Rafic's never wrong about this sort of thing, you know."

"I know. And I know it's risky, but I want you where you can do the most good. Ashmead's letting his personal feelings intrude. I can't do that. I've got a mission to run."

Just then the lift chimed and its doors slid back to reveal Slick, his respirator dangling from one side of his motorcycle helmet: "A mission? No shit, Casper? Going to reactivate the 'Directorate for Science and Technology's' time travel project, are we? Roll the tape back and let us take those rag-heads out on the Riyadh runway like we wanted, like we could have done?" Slick's finger was on the elevator's "Emergency Stop" button and it was buzzing angrily.

"Slick, I don't know what you're talking about, and if I did, this is no place to discuss it." Beside Beck, Yael busied herself hunting for car keys in her purse. Task Force 159's time travel project had been an operational bust, just a flyer taken by a bunch of physics buffs with enough clout to convince a fondly permissive group of government agencies that their combined IQs were reason enough to fund their interagency project.

Slick's sarcasm twisted his pleasant grin as he continued: "You were in Task Force 159, seconded to CIA for that project, so tell me that's what this is really about, Casper. Otherwise," Slick let the button go and stepped over the lift's threshold, blocking their entry so that the doors closed, "you and I have to get one thing straight—"

"I can't tell you that—it's not true. 159 was bullshit; by God I wish it wasn't, Slick, and I wish you'd stop this—"

"Bullshit. Too bad. But that figures. You can bullshit the rest of 'em all you want, but it's clear to me that this whole half-assed operation of yours is just to ease your conscience, 'cause you can't live with the way you fucked up. Which is about one hundred per cent. And now, since we understand each other, you go ahead and piss into the wind all you want. I haven't got anything better to do, thanks to you, than watch from the upwind side." Punching the "Door Open" button, Slick stepped out of their path.

When the lift had closed and Beck was alone with Saadia, she tossed her long auburn mane back from her breasts and said: "Don't mind Slick; he's the best there is when there's something going down or if you're under his command. It's just that he's not used to orders from anyone but Rafic."

"You mean from someone he doesn't respect," Beck corrected, trying to shed his irritation but not quite succeeding.

"That's right," said Yael Saadia with equanimity. "Rafic keeps telling us how talented you are, but we haven't seen any sign of it. We've been together a long time. You can't expect us to just welcome you as a co-commander with open arms, not in this kind of life-and-death venue. Nobody's got *any* reason to trust you but we're stuck with you. Rafic's told us to be polite. . . ."

"*That's* polite?" He flicked his chin in the direction of the floors above as the lift descended.

"For Slick, yes. The rest, you'll have to earn." She smiled to make her words less stinging. "If you really can handle the P-3B's controller's station, that'll be a start. I'd much prefer to be rating those dips on the 727; I've done so much work on them it would be a shame to leave it to your Miss Patrick. . . ."

Saadia's smile was still there, but it was a Sabra's smile, full of desert wiles and killer instinct, that made Beck wish 159 *had* had more than "mildly encouraging" results, so that he could turn back the clock and make everything all right the way he'd once been able to, so that he wouldn't be in the unenviable position of placing his hopes and perhaps his survival in the hands of Rafic's operations team, who held him personally responsible for the Forty-Minute War and who harbored a despite for State Department people that he'd never be able to overcome.

But then, he didn't want to marry them; he wanted to deploy, enable, and activate them.

Which, in spite of Slick's open hostility and Ashmead's doubts and because of Beck's affinity for electronic countermeasures and familiarity with early warning aircraft, he was able to do: when the P-3B and the 727 finally took off from Jerusalem, he and Ashmead had reached a compromise which allowed Beck to put Jesse and Yael Saadia aboard the 727, although Chris Patrick, as well as Slick, Morse, and five dignitaries of Beck's choice, were on board the P-3B.

Nine hours into the flight and two hours after their refueling stop in Morocco, during which no one was allowed off their planes, he was grateful for the distraction Patrick and the diplomats provided: he kept thinking about Muffy and the kids. He hadn't realized what so long a confinement away from the workload he'd been using as a buffer was going to mean to his state of mind: a solitary meditation on radiation effects and the degree to which the American damage estimates had been laundered was the last thing he needed.

So he watched Patrick try to work the passengers and pretend she disliked him and Slick make frequent trips aft to whisper familiarly in her ear or bring her coffee or a drink like a solicitous flight attendant until the NATO Southern Commander, Dugard, and a Magyar named Nacht from the IMF trapped him into a post-mortem of the war.

He found it distressing that the Magyar, a ComBloc millionaire from Pest, knew more about Soviet damage estimates than he did, but not as distressing as phantoms of Muffy trying to shield Jennifer and Seth with her own body from the firestorm so that all that was left of them was a many-legged black silhouette etched into the concrete of the walkway leading to his club.

He listened with half an ear to Nacht's mid-European-accented English recitation of Soviet sites destroyed—Tyuratum, home of the Soviet shuttle program; the Sheremetyevo Airport; Moscow's antiballistic missile sites and the Pushkino phased-array battle management radars at Pechora and Abalakova, as well as the Saryshagan test facility. "In fact," said the Magyar with a degree of satisfaction Beck didn't understand, "the entire Maskirova program—the word means concealing, or masking —is no more."

It was Dugard, the NATO general, who said what Beck was thinking: "Why does this please you so, Nacht? Buda and Pest aren't going to profit from any of this—what use is being the Monte Carlo of ComBloc if the money's no good, those fancy pastry shops are baking with tainted flour, and all your capitalistic ventures depend on live consumers? Who will want a Rubik's cube now?"

Nacht pulled on his broad pug nose: "You think, because I am IMF, and because our economy is— was—successful, that I am either a usurer or a traitor. Not so. But with a projected kill-rate of forty per cent on incoming ballistic missiles, as the Politburo claimed, they should have come though this is in better shape, *nyet?* They did not. So maybe it was the much-vaunted EMP, confusing their electronics once the first air burst exploded, or maybe it was a purer failure of their equipment. But let me tell you," the Magyar sat forward, "the Bear has been neutered—nuked and neutered. No more will we stand in fear of eighty thousand soldiers of occupation in our country. No more will we send so much to the Soviet with so little in return. And, soon enough, while your American friends—" his watery gaze scalded Beck and returned to Dugard, "—were trying desperately to play the game of catch-up, the Soviet would have tried out their new and so-called 'anti-ballistic missile superiority.'"

"So you're saying, Secretary Nacht," Beck couldn't believe his ears and thus was considering all the reasons why someone would want to feed him this kind of disinformation, "that you're just as pleased we had this little war?"

Dugard scowled at Beck disapprovingly, but Nacht sat back with a deep sigh and crossed his legs, toying with a plastic glass that still had a half-inch of vodka in it: "No war, Assistant Secretary Beck, is 'little.'" The Magyar's tone was severe. "But ask among the Third Worlders and those of us from satellite nations and you will find no sympathy for either your country or the Soviet Union. Ask Iraq, and you will see that they wish to use this opportunity to sterilize every mullah in Iran with their own 'small' nuclear capability. Ask Poland, and you will see that they know the price of freedom is always high. A reign of terror has aptly ended by terror. You will soon find out that none of us who are in a position to be on this tour are overly anxious to help either the US or the USSR to regain their former glory. Too long the superpowers have held the rest of us in thrall. Surely you realize, Mister Beck, that it is a different world now, and a freer one."

Beck couldn't think of a thing to say that wasn't diplomatically inappropriate, so he just finished his coffee and hoped that Dugard would pick up the ball. If aid from the nations these men represented was not forthcoming—and if Nacht had his way, it would not be—not only the States and the USSR, but the entire world was in more trouble than it knew. Beck had expected some hesitancy, but not the elevation of generations of resentment into policy. It was madness, and he could do no more than mark Nacht as an enemy, one to watch, and smile patiently. Such was the nature of "frank and constructive" diplomatic dialogue: you let them insult you and you learned something.

Dugard was picking up on the Iraq–Iran angle, placing it in the context of a larger Middle East imbroglio that oil-consuming nations worldwide could ill afford, when Beck looked up and saw Slick, his hand on Chris Patrick's shoulder, surreptitiously trying to catch Beck's eye.

When Beck acknowledged him, Slick's gaze flicked to Nacht and he made a quick thumbs-down that the Saudi whom Chris was mesmerizing did not see: Nacht had just been targeted, and Beck didn't make a counter-motion which would have voided Slick's suggestion: unless Nacht's viewpoint changed drastically, he'd be better off dead than being allowed to spread his poison among the entire group.

"Excuse me," Beck said, coffee finished, and

headed forward; "duty calls," stopping only long enough to ask Morse—who'd been segregated from the other passengers by being given orders to play sick and stay in one of the two bunks—if he needed anything.

Morse's face, when the geneticist rolled over in response to Beck's question, was swollen and streaked with tears: "Nothing you can provide, evidently, Mister Beck," he said, and turned away again.

Since that was in general true, and Morse's remorse was due as much to having indirectly caused the truck-bombing of the consulate as to the treatment Ashmead's team was giving a "proven security risk," Beck didn't try to comfort Morse: now, after the fact, Morse had too many doubts about the side effects of the serum they'd all taken to earn him any sympathy. Ashmead had told Morse that if any of them died of these side effects, Morse would be next. Beck had been there, and hadn't argued: if this whole operation were a wild goose chase, he'd probably draw straws with the others for the privilege of blowing Morse away.

In the midst of so much death, in past, present, and future tenses, Beck was beginning to understand the team's operational fondness for dispensing it: chemically, one was forced to last resorts; emotionally, one became incapable of compassion; mercy was a rich man's game, and these days they were all paupers of the soul.

The galley and expanded "lounge" were in the plane's aft section, directly under the tail-mounted roto-dome; forward of the dome, the P-3B was still all business, and off limits to her passengers. Racks of electronics alternated with CRT terminals and

scopes in narrow niches where chairs were bolted
to sliding tracks.

Beck sat down at his traffic controller's station
and switched a toggle that took the system off
automatic "scan and inform," then put on a one-
ear headset and spoke into his throat-pad mike:
"Rafic, I'm back. Couldn't take much more of that."

He heard the static/clip of voice-actuation in his
right ear, then Ashmead said: "Learn anything,
cowboy?"

"That Nacht's a risk to the project. Slick's—"

Slick's voice cut in: "—got it well in hand. Either of you two geniuses see that blip at two-ten
o'clock on the horizon screen?"

Beck twisted in his seat and saw that Slick had
followed him forward and was sitting at his radar
station ten feet away, hunched over his control
panel, his handsome head awash in red and green
indicator spill. Beyond Beck's view was the flight
deck, where Thoreau and Ashmead were cloistered
behind closed doors.

"Yeah," Thoreau said, "now that you mention
it, I can pull it in on my heads-up, but it's not
exactly heading straight for us."

The P-3B had a "heads-up" display that allowed
the pilot to superimpose on his windshield any of
the electronics displays aft or, as a fighter pilot
might want to do, the instrumentation in front of
him. Unfortunately, none of that included active
defenses: the P-3B had no missiles, cannon, or any
other offensive weapons.

"Just for grins," Thoreau continued with his accustomed insouciance, "I'm going to piggyback the
727 and make us both disappear—or try real hard,
anyway."

The P-3B had sufficient radar jamming and counter-jamming to make it invisible in all spectrums, including heat, to any but the most sophisticated aircraft, but whether that protection could be extended to cover the 727 was questionable: Thoreau would have to interpose his aircraft between the 727 and the approaching unidentified aircraft in such a way that the P-3B's electronics masked not only its own radar-available signatures, but those of the differently shaped 727 also.

"Take notes, Beck," Slick cracked, "we're making aviation history and we need an unbiased observer."

Again, Slick's inference was that Beck wasn't part of the team.

Again, Beck let it pass: he was too busy trying to plot the vector of the approaching aircraft precisely enough to help Thoreau—who was now on a secure channel to the 727, telling it exactly what he wanted it to do—block the unidentified aircraft's view of the 727.

"This bogey of yours could be just another scheduled or nonscheduled flight, Slick," Beck said with neutral precision: "Everybody's having a rough time without radar handovers from ground controllers." The vector on which the other aircraft was approaching was not one that was commonly used for commercial traffic; no international airports had been able to rejoin the grid of international control radars which had once handled transoceanic traffic: the various militaries had pre-empted all available replacement electronics in a futile attempt to make up for lost satellites.

"Yeah," Slick gave back, "and your mother might have known your father." Then: "Here's the rest of their team—a trawler coming up over the horizon, three o'clock."

Beck had been adopted by an American couple in the Foreign Service, just one of countless war babies from Eastern Europe. He was about to let Slick know that, as far as Beck was concerned, Ashmead's deputy had just stepped over the line, when Ashmead cut in smoothly: "Come on, kids, this is no time for a family squabble. If I make this right, we're about to be in a heap o' trouble—that bogey's way too fast for a commercial anything and the trawler's there to pick up the pieces—the serum, if they're lucky—and pick off the survivors. Listen up, all stations: we'll hold this evasive course—" he gave new headings "—for five minutes. Over and out, El Al 10." When the 727 was off-line, Ashmead continued: "If after that time the bogey's still closing, we're going to veer off and get our tails out of here, maximum speed, maximum countermeasures."

Beck sat back and fiddled with his headset, casting a glance at Slick, who didn't look up from his radars. Then he said: "I can't let you do that, Rafic. Our responsibility is to bring that plane safely into Houston."

"Our responsibility, Beck, is to bring *this* plane safely into Houston."

"But the serum—"

"I told you," Ashmead reminded him patiently, "that I would have preferred to have both cases on board this aircraft. I *know* I can get this one home; I'm not sure about El Al 10."

El Al 10 was the flight designation for the 727.

"But Yael and Jesse . . ." Beck trailed off. Thoreau certainly knew that Ashmead was proposing to use the 727 as a decoy, sacrifice it and everyone on board in order to get the P-3B clear, and Thoreau wasn't arguing.

But it was too late to call back the words: "If it weren't for you, Casper," Slick said into his com mike, "Yael and Jesse would be here with us and your Magyar buddy and that Saudi sweetheart Patrick's mooning over would be with the rest of the sitting ducks."

Beck thought he heard Thoreau swearing softly, as if his hand were over his bead mike, but that was all.

Beck wasn't going to argue with Slick; he bent his head to his radars and worked desperately to come up with some piece of information that would invalidate Ashmead's theory that the approaching plane was an enemy attack aircraft.

He couldn't. Finally he sat back and said, "Look, let's try the International Hailing Frequency—what could it hurt?"

"If they don't see us any more," Thoreau responded, "it could hurt a lot. Anyway, Ivan doesn't let his pilots have International Hailing on the theory that it facilitates defection. I say we just stay on this heading and see if they fly by or indicate that they've scoped us. Three minutes, fifteen seconds more."

"*Soviets?*" Beck was trying to stay what seemed an ineluctable tide of paranoia coming over his headset in tight, short breaths. "Why assume that—"

"Beck," Ashmead said wearily, "stay off this channel unless you've got relevant technical data. The rest of us are trying to save our butts up here."

In the three minutes remaining, Beck thought of

Yael Saadia, pregnant and exhausted, and the impeccable dossiers she'd prepared on every member of the fact-finding commission; and of Thoreau, who loved her; and of Jesse, the sharpshooter from the Galilee, most easygoing of the team.

At two minutes he thought he heard murmured off-mike a short argument, something about search-and-rescue capability.

Then he heard Slick light a cigarette, the scratch of the match loud in his phones, and say, "Damn, it's gonna happen."

Then the P-3B veered sharply, banked, and climbed, and there was nothing he could do but watch the blips on his scope until the 727 fell abruptly off it.

At least he wasn't on the open com channel to hear the 727's pilot—Beck's pilot for the last three years—when he realized the P-3B was leaving him to fend for himself, or his attempts to contact the pilot of the attacking aircraft.

Watching it in silence wasn't any easier to take, but the silence didn't last long: from the flight deck came a heated argument between Thoreau and Ashmead as to whether it was worth it to go back and look for survivors.

"What'll we do if we find any, Thoreau? Wave? Just get our butts out of here and count your blessings."

It was another half hour before it was clear that the other aircraft was gone, on its way to Algeria or Libya, judging from its course, and Beck dared to leave his station long enough to go to the head and retch.

When he came back, Slick was standing by his console, headset collaring his throat: "Ready to go tell those five remaining dips how that 727 was shot down by a Soviet fighter escort, Casper? Or don't you have the stomach for it?"

"You can't prove it was a Soviet—"

"Look, Mister INR honcho, you've killed more friends of mine than the Forty-Minute War." Slick's eyes were very bright as he took off the headset. "I'm about out of patience with you altogether. If it weren't that I figure Thoreau's got the rightful first shot at you, I'd tell you just how and when you're going to die. If you could have kept your MIT mouth shut, Yael and Jesse would be right here, with us, safe—not down there." He pointed to the deck, below which was ocean. "Now, you and I have got to get something straight—smart doesn't cut it with me; I was at Oxford, read what I needed to at Baliol, and all I learned was that grades don't mean squat in the real world. And *you'd* better learn that when Rafic doesn't tell you something, he's telling you something."

"You mean you people knew this was going to happen?"

"Nobody *knows* this kind of thing's going to happen. We had some data, we interpolated, we took a calculated risk. What were we supposed to do, wait around to visually ID a Soviet Il-76 Main-stay AWAC fitted out to fuel-feed her Foxhound fighter escort, and get ourselves killed, maybe? Foxhounds have a look-down, shoot-down mode with radar-guided missiles. Now, you want to tell 'em, or shall I?"

"But why would the Soviets—"

Slick shook his head in disgust: "You just don't listen, do you? You think they want us to haul this serum home? When we wouldn't even share it with the Israelis? When they would have bought it from Dow for as many rubles as he could carry? Jesus, man, you're just plain functionally inept, you know that? Now, if you don't have enough balls to step out there and explain what just happened, I may not wait for Thoreau to decide whether he wants you for himself."

Beck was about to suggest to Slick that the two of them have it out then and there when the flight deck partition slid back and Thoreau came through it unsteadily.

Beck heard Slick mutter, "Shit," as he went to Thoreau and put his arms around him the way military men tended to do.

Rather than stand there gawking, Beck went aft to tell the five remaining diplomats that they were all alone up there.

Chapter 2

In the wee hours of the morning, when Nacht from the IMF, Dugard from NATO, Najeeb Thabet from the newly reconstituted UN, and Zenko Tsutsumi from Japan's Ministry of Trade and Industry, were all asleep and Prince Bandar bin Faisal's seemingly inexhaustible supply of amusing conversation had run down so that the Saudi prince sat staring moodily out the wing window, Slick came aft to see how Chris was doing.

"Hey there, sweetness, scoot over," Slick said, and she did. She knew by now that Slick's interest was professional; he described himself as her "handler," whatever that meant. But Slick's slow smile and his brilliant blue eyes in that handsome face had become a welcome sight; he made her feel safe and appreciated, like part of the team.

As Faisal looked up at them moodily from the window and then stared back out again, his expression obscured by his kefiya, Slick asked, "Did I ever tell you the one about the Iranian pilots? No? Well, these two Iranian pilots are coming in for a landing and the pilot says to the co-pilot, 'That runway seems terrible short. Give me one quarter flaps.' The co-pilot does, but thirty seconds later the pilot asks for half flaps, then says, 'Still, is very, very short. Give me three-quarter flaps.' The co-pilot does and it still looks like they'll overshoot, so the pilot yells: 'Full flaps, praise be to Allah!' at the top of his lungs and with the help of God, full flaps, and some serious braking, they make a safe landing, their nosewheel right on the edge of the runway. The pilot says to the co-pilot, 'Allah be praised, but this is the shortest runway ever I have seen.' Then the co-pilot looks to his left, then his right, and he says, 'Yes, this is so. But it is also very, very wide.' "

The Saudi, in spite of himself, chuckled. So did Chris: after the look on Beck's white face when he'd come out of the crew's compartment to tell them about the loss of the 727 and everyone aboard, she needed something to chuckle about.

She'd never seen Beck look that shaken; she'd seriously wondered if he was going to come apart. She'd wanted to go to him, comfort him, but Slick had been right there, reminding her of her job, of her pose as the nasty, wisecracking reporter, radiating moral support and intensity from every pore of his being.

And with Slick's help, she'd gotten through it, somehow; the ten hours airborne since the loss of the 727 had seemed endless, even though Slick had recruited her to help him feed the diplomats and used the opportunity for a little playful necking in the galley, which she wasn't entirely sure was an operational necessity. But with Beck sequestered in the off-limits crew area, she'd been grateful for Slick's strong arms and his casual courage: Slick, unlike Beck, was at ease and unworried, telling her so with his fighter's body.

Slick, she was beginning to realize, was about a dozen people, and he expected her to be able to play many roles as well.

He nuzzled her hair and whispered to her until the Saudi put on the spidery headset that provided a narrow selection of recorded music, the only amenity aboard the P-3B that in any way resembled commercial air travel.

Then Slick said: "In about five minutes, go to the head and leave your full cassettes there; there are new ones in the right-hand drawer. Find out anything urgent?"

"Prince Faisal's offered to marry me, which would make me . . . let's see . . . his fourth, I believe."

"I'll marry you," Slick grinned. "Soon as we land, which will be in about an hour, hour and a half."

She looked at her watch, still on Jerusalem time—Zaki had neglected to show her how to reset it and she didn't want to break it. "Thank God." She groaned and stretched, knowing he was watching her breasts appreciatively, and not minding.

"Thank Ashmead," Slick corrected.

"Not Beck?" She got out her cigarettes and lit two with her new lighter, whose indicator was blithely green, then handed one to Slick.

"No comment. Look, when we land, you're to stick close to me, no matter where the dips are taken. We're going to risk letting you be a little late for the Presidential briefing because of a lovers' tryst. Okay?" His lips were next to her ear, his breath tickled her neck.

"How's Beck doing?" she asked. "He didn't look too—" Then she realized the significance of what Slick had said. "You mean we're over the US?" She knifed forward in her seat and put her nose to the glass so that the Saudi glanced at her quizzically. "But there're no *lights!* There should be lights. *Some* lights. *Some*—"

"Easy, easy." Slick's strong hand was on her shoulder; he pulled her back and put his palms to her cheeks, forcing her to look at him: "No hysterics, okay? I'll tell you when to worry. You can trust me to do that. There's a lot of low cloud cover, that's all."

"You mean . . ." She sat back, trembling, feeling the sudden wetness of nervous perspiration under her arms. ". . . it's not all dark—not the whole East Coast?"

His gaze didn't waver. "I don't imagine it's anything like it used to look at night, but it's not all dark, no."

"Can you tell me how much worse it is than the garbage I've been feeding these dips?"

"Shh," he warned, yet his gaze was fond and his expression teasing. "Let's not take a chance that anybody's awake, okay? Let's get some coffee."

She went aft with him to the galley in the P-3B's tail, where he smelled the coffee which had been on its hot plate for hours, spilled it out, and started making a fresh pot.

"I'll do that," she said. "It's something I can handle."

"Ah, not liberated, to boot. You know, you just

might be my dream girl, if I can get you away from Beck."

She tore a plastic pack of coffee with her teeth: "Not a chance."

"Just a friendly warning—don't get too attached to him. He's made an awful lot of bad judgment calls. In this sort of context, he may not survive all of them."

"What are you saying?" She turned and stared at Slick, who was watching her with his arms crossed.

"I'm telling you that he's accruing a lot of guilt he's not built to handle. He'll either toughen up real fast or we'll lose him—I've seen men commit suicide lots of times, lots of ways that don't look like it, for less reason than he's got. So you be careful. Don't go off with him alone. Make sure I know where you are when you're with him, all the time, not just some of the time, no matter how innocent it seems. Copy?"

She poured coffee grounds from the plastic pack into the coffee maker: "Affirmative, Sir," she said teasingly, to cover her fear: it was Beck she'd been holding onto all this time, Beck's calm, Beck's competency. To hear Slick coldly suggest that Beck was crumbling meant to her that what was left of her world was crumbling. When Beck had announced that the 727 had gone down she'd been dry-eyed and proud of it; now she blinked back tears.

"Hey, lady," Slick said, and turned her to him, "I'm just trying to keep you informed. If you don't want to—"

"No, that's fine." She pulled back and shook him off. "You do that—keep me informed. About everything. As a matter of fact, I'd like to be informed as to why you people arranged to have us overfly the East Coast at night, and how bad it really—"

Slick sighed, "Newsies. Chris, we honestly don't *know* how bad it is ourselves. There's probably some guy from Langley sitting in the Houston White House with lots of hypothetical damage estimates prepared before the war, reading whatever he likes onto a tape, which then goes to the White House briefing office. Do you understand? Nobody knows squat yet about how bad it is. But you can be sure right now everybody down there who's expecting us is trying like hell to find as many undamaged or slightly damaged areas as possible to show these five guys we've got left, even though *they* only want to see the worst we've got to show 'em."

"But I *don't* understand. If we want their money and their help—"

"We want them to tell their countries that we're in pretty good shape, still the big, bad US of A. We'll show you some medium-rough stuff, but there won't be any red zones in the official tour—too dangerous, politically if not physically. If you want that, come with us while we go after Morse's family. But if you want in, you can't print it. It's that simple. Me, I'd as soon see you pass. Radiation may not be forever, but it sure can take years off your life. You never applied for this kind of job; don't let Beck make you think you owe it to your country. Okay?"

"I— No, it's not okay. I need to see as much as I can. As for what I report, I've agreed to security restrictions in exchange for an exclusive when . . . when . . ."

She turned away and began pouring water into the coffee maker.

Slick finished for her: "When it's appropriate? That's a long wait."

"Don't make fun of me."

"Fun of you? I'd like somebody I know to live through this, that's all. You say you don't care if it's you, I've got to respect that. It's just that I've lost a lot of friends in the last week."

"So has everybody else, Slick," came a voice from behind them.

"Beck!" Though she wasn't supposed to, she launched herself past Slick and into his arms. And he hugged her tightly.

"Come *on*, you two," Slick whispered urgently, "you're going to blow this whole thing," as he sidled past them to block any passing diplomat's view.

Reluctantly, Beck pushed her away. His eyes were bloodshot and his mouth a thin white line: "How are you?"

"Fine." She straightened her shoulders. "Just fine. Did you know that Ashmead's sister is married to a Saudi prince? That Faisal, out there, says that whatever help he wants from their ministers, all *he*—that doesn't mean the rest of us, or the Administration, or anyone else—has to do is ask?"

Slick spoke before Beck could answer: "There's a slew of Saudi princes, lady. And Ashmead would never do that."

Beck ignored Slick: "We'll be landing in forty-five minutes. There's a Presidential briefing scheduled for 0600; we've a rest period before that. If you're not too tired, Slick will bring you to—"

"It's all taken care of, Beck. Get out of here,

back up to the flight deck where you belong."
Slick's voice was soft but terse.

Wordlessly, on the verge of tears again, Chris
turned away and pulled the glass coffee pot from
its housing, thrusting a styrofoam cup under the
fresh stream that had been dripping into the pot.

"Check," Beck said evenly. "Just as soon as I get
my coffee."

Chris handed the cup to him, oblivious of the
scalding liquid that dripped onto her hand as she
pulled the cup back and replaced it with the pot.
"See you later, then," she said hopefully, and realized as she did that the possibility of a Presidential briefing with herself as the only reporter in
attendance was nothing compared to the possibility of even twenty minutes with him alone.

When he'd gone, she told Slick she had to fix her
face and spent half the time remaining before she
was to meet Beggs, the new President of the United
States, face to face, crying her heart out in the
cramped rest room of the P-3B.

Chapter 3

Ashmead's aircraft was in a blind spot, as far as ground control and radar contact, and he didn't want to think about why. Fort Bragg Control had told him not to worry about it—the P-3B would be picked up by Lackland Air Force Base and then handed over to Houston.

There was just this little, lonely space to get through, a solitary overflight of Alabama and Mississippi. After that, the P-3B would have an F-15 escort the rest of the way to Dugout, the Houston White House—as they'd had a Special Forces honor guard from Bragg until the squadron leader had peeled off with a cheerful, "Have a nice day, fellas: we burn fuel about as fast as our tankers can pump it, so this is as far as we go," and headed back to base, leaving Ashmead with the feeling that he was flying this mission over the

Sahara or Central Africa, listening to virgin static in his phones.

It was downright disconcerting to find dead air even on the prerecorded flight information channels when all the pre-war flight charts they had aboard told them that they were in busy air corridors dotted with Prohibited and Restricted sectors over which a dozen civilian and military controllers ought to be keeping caerful and possessive watch.

Thoreau kept punching in new frequencies from those suggested on his area sectional, trying to raise some tower chatter or even ATIS weather advisories; but otherwise, the ex-SEAL pilot was holding up better than Ashmead had any right to expect, considering that Yael had been carrying his child and it was Ashmead's decision—not Beck's—that had put her on the doomed 727 when he ought to have known better and that they had only forty-five minutes' worth of fuel to spare; not much room for error in the projected landing at the secret facility west of Houston.

"Go get some coffee, Thoreau. Stretch your legs. Hit the head. And bring me a cup, black, when you come back," Ashmead said easily.

"Great, thanks," Thoreau said without enthusiasm, slipping off his headset and slipping out of his crash harness to stand, slumped so he wouldn't bump his head, hand to the small of his back. Then he touched Ashmead's arm. "Rafic . . . I . . . It's nobody's fault."

"Hold that thought, Thoreau, and we'll get through this just fine."

"Yes, sir. Want Slick up here while I'm gone?"

"Beck, actually." Ashmead craned his neck to watch his pilot.

Thoreau grimaced: "Just don't let him touch anything while you're debriefing him. One degree off heading and we're looking at a dead-stick landing, which I could do without, considering they expect me to put this baby right in the decontamination washbay. On second thought . . ." Thoreau leaned forward, punched buttons, and stood up again, "leave it on autopilot while he's up here. You know where the revert-to-manual is, if you need it."

"Unfortunately, I'm not going to need it," Ashmead said gently. It was time to talk about what they were both feeling: "Real eerie, up here, like having the East River Drive all to yourself."

"Yes Sir, well . . . jet fuel's got to be at a real premium. Back in five," Thoreau promised with a desultory salute.

Alone, Ashmead leaned back, staring at the control-studded panels above the windshield, then closed his eyes and rubbed them with the palms of his hands. The worst part of this mission was that no one had any privacy in which to react to the various tragedies as they occurred—twenty-one hours of flight time, plus the Moroccan stopover the slow P-3B had needed because its mission-capability limit was only fourteen hours, was altogether too long sitting around on low-level alert status to do any of his team much good.

What was *left* of his team, he amended gloomily, and told himself that Thoreau's and Slick's morale was holding up better than his own: he kept trying to find a way to justify the sacrifice of Zaki, Yael, and Jesse to Beck's cockamamie mission, and he couldn't; the only way to do that was to win unequivocally, and all the data he was collecting told him that wasn't possible. There was too much wrong and not enough chance that they could restore the status quo ante. It would take a miracle to do that, and he wasn't a miracle worker.

In spite of twenty-two years of government service and a top-secret verbal report from an analyst named Watkins whom Ashmead knew to be close to infallible, the lack of seaboard lights and air traffic had shocked Ashmead to the core. He'd known it was bad, but he was an optimist in his way, as a field commander must be, and he was also human: damage estimates were just words and concepts; his mind kept minimizing their significance until he saw the dark swath in the Northeast Corridor with his own eyes.

When Beck came in and slipped into the pilot's seat, Ashmead couldn't help thinking that, if not for Beck, he and his team would be somewhere in the Persian Gulf, happily greasing terrorists where, if they took casualties, those casualties would have been acceptable, taken in a venue and for a reason all of them could easily understand.

Beck said: "I've been listening to Chris's tapes. She got some good stuff from Dugard on NATO's extant war-fighting capability; he and that Nacht from IMF got into an informative little wrangle about relative throw-weights in NATO and the Warsaw Pact and the possibility that NATO might yet launch if it feels their—or *our*—remaining interests are threatened."

"Shit, Beck, what are you telling me? That those fools haven't had enough boom-boom to suit them?"

"That there's still violent polarity, and where

there's polarity, there's room for diplomacy and, in this case, a chance of freezing the balance of power . . . national identities, integrities—borders, if you will."

"Well, that makes me feel a whole lot better."

"Good." Beck grinned ingenuously. "That's what I'm here for."

"Life goes on, eh?"

"Let's hope so, Rafic. Otherwise, this whole thing . . ."

Beck spread his hands and then curled them around the P-3B's yoke so that Ashmead snapped to: the return-to-manual was on the yoke and Ashmead wasn't entirely sure that Beck was taking this as well as he pretended: crashing a plane is the easiest thing in the world.

". . . Tiebreaker, I mean," Beck continued, "is useless. And I really don't want to think that. It's cost us so much already . . ."

"You know what Thoreau said to me just now?" Ashmead was watching Beck's hands. "He said it's nobody's fault. And he's right. It's real natural to get solipsistic at a time like this—I'm fighting it myself. You think it's all your fault. So does probably everybody else in positions similar to ours."

"But if I'd countered the negatives on your report, pushed it through . . ." Beck's knuckles were white and as he spoke he was staring out into the 0200 dark. "There wouldn't have *been* any nuking of Home Plate, no—"

"And if I'd ignored the pull-back order," Ashmead said wearily, "same thing. God knows I've done it before. But intelligence failures happen; they're a consequence of a bureaucracy removed from the action and overly sensitized to non-operational matters: political repercussions, budgets, adverse publicity. We thought somebody else would take over, that they wanted a clean kill over the ocean with no one to blame rather than a counterterrorist operation at the Riyadh airport where, if the bomb was detonated during the action, a lot of moderate Arbas would have been very unhappy. We reacted in a politico–military context which doesn't exist any more—all of us, you as well as me and my people. It's easy to forget that now that we're stuck with the consequences and the context is so radically altered."

"Slick sure has." Now Beck was looking at him, and Ashmead could see the results of his impromptu pep talk: Beck's stare was bright and steady; the dull defensiveness of shock was gone; Beck was beginning to let his emotions cycle—a healthy sign.

Seeing that, Ashmead began to relax: he needed every watt of Beck's mental power plant for what lay ahead: "Slick is . . . Slick. When we need him, you're going to appreciate him. Until then, don't take him too seriously. He always bitches when he has nothing much to do, gets depressed if he's not in the middle of a high-risk operation or a fire fight. But under pressure, I've never seen anybody with as much—"

Just then Ashmead heard somebody come forward and twisted in his seat, at first seeing only Thoreau, who hadn't brought his coffee.

"Thoreau, where's my damned coffee? Do I have to—"

Then he saw that Thoreau was not alone; in back of the tall pilot was Morse, the fat little geneticist.

Thoreau said, "I'm sorry, Rafic, I'm really sorry, but this guy's got a homemade bomb he says will—"

Beck didn't even turn around; with one hand he rubbed his eyes with thumb and forefinger and with the other casually punched up the intercom.

Morse was saying, "Just shut up, pilot, if that's what you are." The little man's voice was high and shaky with pent-up hostility and fear. "We're going to change course, land in Atlanta, and find my family—*now*. Or I'll blow us all to—"

"We can't do that," Beck said smoothly, slowly turning in his seat. "Tell him, Ashmead."

Ashmead had been noticing that Thoreau's side-arm wasn't in his cross-draw holster anymore and wondering if he could risk either a shot from his own pistol, which might or might not go through Thoreau and kill Morse, or a leap at Thoreau, which might pin Morse to the deck but which would probably also end in the pilot's death or the abrupt depressurization of the cockpit from a shot gone wild or the detonation of the bomb—most likely all three. Even if the bomb didn't go off, and if Ashmead emerged unharmed, he doubted his ability to wrestle what would then be a rapidly crashing aircraft back onto some acceptable heading.

So he said to Morse: "Beck's telling you the truth. We were stretching it, anyway, from Morocco to Houston. I've only got forty-five minutes' worth of reserve fuel at cruising speed, and that's not enough to get us back to Atlanta. If you'd have pulled this little stunt an hour ago, you might have had a chance. As it is, you're just giving us a choice of ways to die, and I'd rather be blown up than crash in a red zone." The point, he knew, was to keep Morse talking, so he added, "What kind of a bomb did you whip up, anyway? And why? We've been taking care of you pretty good."

"Taking *care* of me?" Morse's voice approached soprano. "Never you mind what kind of bomb I've got, just take my word for it, unless you're a chemist. And I don't believe you about the fuel, any more than I think that the way you've been treating me is acceptable or that you really have any intention of helping me get to my family once you've delivered your precious cargo to that murdering President, who's got no right to special treatment, not on my sweat, when somewhere my wife and—"

Slick grabbed Morse in a choke hold, his elbow crooked around Morse's throat with a force that snapped his neck back, his other hand twisting a vial from the little geneticist's left hand, then released the choke hold in time to grab Thoreau's gun as it fell from Morse's limp fingers.

The geneticist slumped to the floor.

"Sometimes," said Slick, stepping over Morse, who lay motionless, his neck at an unlikely angle, "I wonder how you guys ever got along without me." He handed Thoreau his pistol, butt first. "Good thing the safety was on." Then: "Whoever turned on that intercom was thinking on his feet."

"Beck," Ashmead said. "Let's see the bomb."

"Beck? No shit?" Slick grinned wolfishly as he maneuvered around the prostrate geneticist and Thoreau in the narrow confines of the flight deck and carefully handed Ashmead the vial of yellow liquid.

"He's dead," came Thoreau's uninflected judgment from where he crouched over the corpse.

"I had to save your ass, didn't I?" Slick said defensively. "Otherwise I would have had to stand there while he told me if I didn't let go and give him back his bomb he'd shoot you."

"No problem," Beck told them. "We got the formula from the Israelis; even if we hadn't, we could always analyze—"

"Piss," said Ashmead critically, holding the vial up and shining his penlight into it. Then carefully he began to open it.

"Don't do that," Thoreau objected. "What if it's air-activated?"

"I told you," Ashmead said, "it's piss. And there's a half-inch of air in this bottle. He didn't have anything, not a damned thing. Just scare tactics."

"He had my gun," Thoreau said sheepishly.

Slick grabbed for the vial: "Let me see that."

Ashmead gave it to him: "Go pour it in the toilet."

"Sure thing, Rafic," said Slick, eyes downcast.

"And, Slick? Nice job."

"Thanks to Beck, yeah, not bad." Slick clapped Beck on the shoulder as he scrambled aft, muttering to Thoreau to help him get Morse back into his bunk without alarming the dips.

"Too late for that. Beck, you'd better go tell them what happened." Ashmead glanced at the intercom control. "When did you turn that off?"

"As soon as Slick grabbed him. Don't worry, they'll be glad he's dead. As far as the bomb being nonexistent, let's not tell anybody."

"Fine. Thoreau, after you've helped Slick, get back up here. And bring my damned coffee this time."

Chapter 4

Touchdown at Dugout, west of Houston, was so surreal that Beck had his hands full shepherding the five remaining diplomats through the decontamination tube and out of the washbay without incident. He couldn't help wondering what he would have done if the 727 hadn't gone down and he'd had the entire original complement to deal with.

As it was, with no one on hand to greet them at 0300 hours except security people intent on performing intensive searches that brought to light Chris Patrick's .25 caliber Colt, Beck's charges' feathers were seriously ruffled.

The NATO general, Dugard, demanded to see one of the Joint Chiefs of Staff to personally lodge a formal complaint when his uniform was confiscated and he was issued a stiff white contamination suit with wristband dosimeter just like everyone else. Bandar bin Faisal wouldn't give up his kefiya, despite the fact that his hood didn't fit well over it and thus his breathing equipment couldn't pass its final checkout. Nacht from the IMF demanded a personal bodyguard and the UN rep, Najeeb Thabet, insisted that he'd come here to see the UN's "putatively destroyed" site with his own eyes and he had no interest in Presidential breakfasts or anything else but an overflight of New York, posthaste.

And Zenko Tsutsumi, with consummate politeness, told Beck to fuck off: "All that we see here is a further result," the pockmarked Japanese declared, "of your nation's *sakoku ishiko*," looking around him at the pure white arrival lounge where armed guards in respirators were stationed at intervals. "Until this changes, nothing will avail you."

Sakoku ishiko translated as *closed country consciousness* and the Japanese minister was telling Beck to expect no help from the Japanese.

The Morse incident had shaken Beck's five charges more than the shoot-down of the 727: none of them was certain of their security. In fact, Beck admitted glumly, they were scared half to death, and when diplomats are frightened they turn aggressive and hostile and that didn't bode well for what was to follow.

Even Chris Patrick, usually the bright spot, was so angry and flustered over the discovery of her gun and her subsequent body search by a horse-faced matron that Beck was afraid he'd lost her. So he got her gun back and pulled her aside as they were being herded into a tunnel which came out at what looked like a twenty-first-century subway station.

"Sorry about that, Chris. If you'd have told me about it, we could have avoided—"

She snatched it from his hand, her face flushed: "You can't expect to treat people this way, Secretary Beck, and get away with it. If you want any kind of neutral press, especially on that Morse story, you'd better do something about it, and fast."

The dignitaries were close at hand and here, underground where no one needed to wear headgear, they could all hear her.

He backed away, wondering if she realized how much power she had at that juncture, if she was still playing his game or her own, and whether she was cueing the others or taking her cues from them. Then Slick went smoothly into gear, stepping into the ugly pause and possible breach by going up to her, putting an arm around her waist, and whispering in her ear.

Operation or not, Beck didn't like it when Chris turned in to the embrace of Ashmead's deputy.

Great. I asked for this. He honestly couldn't tell at that moment if she was acting or not.

Forty minutes later, with the dignitaries safe in their quarters, an armed guard at each door, he found out.

"Twenty minutes, you two, okay?" said Slick easily when Beck opened his door. "Everybody else is already in the situation room but we'll cover for you."

Chris stood uncertainly beside Slick in the doorway, looking like an errant schoolgirl in her baggy white coveralls with her shoulder bag held by its strap in front of her so that it nearly dragged on the floor. She didn't say a word or look up from her rubber-soled boots.

Beck said, "Thanks, Slick. We'll be right down."

"You're bringing her? There'll be somebody from DDS&T there, lots of other types—it's going to get real classified."

DDS&T was the Agency's Directorate for Science and Technology.

"Perhaps not, then. We'll see," he said, and turned to Chris: "If you'll come in now?" It sounded too formal, but he didn't know if Slick was trying to warn him off her, or just playing a part for the sentries stationed in the hallway.

He found that his mouth was dry and although he almost never drank he was wondering what his room's bar was stocked with. As Slick closed the door he turned and headed toward it, saying over his shoulder: "Chris, I'm terribly sorry about—"

And then she was in his arms, demanding that he hold her tight, and dry sobs were wracking her.

He ran his hands up and down her spine, feeling relief flood over him: he really needed her; she was possibly the only person who could turn this diplomatic disaster into a victory.

"It's all right," he told her over and over until she stopped shaking her head when he said it, then risked kissing her gently on the brow and tipping her chin up so that he could see her face.

"Dear Christ, I was so frightened when it came over the intercom. . . . Morse, the bomb, everything. And you were so calm. How can you be so calm?"

"I wasn't. I'm not. I'm just good at pretending. You're not really angry about the strip-search? The gun? If you want a gun, we'll get you something with real stopping power—"

She was shaking her head again so that her hair flew about her face: "I don't want anything, I just want you. I want some time alone. I want to forget all this. I haven't fucked—screwed up, have I? Anything? Slick said it was okay, what I did back there, but . . . I'm so confused." This last was a whisper, and he was already unzipping her contamination suit.

Even if he hadn't felt the same way, though she didn't realize it, there was nothing she could have asked for that he wouldn't have given her just then.

Her firm breasts and her honest healthy sweat let him forget everything—the excessive security procedures in effect at Dugout (which, his belt-mounted Geiger counter told him, was cleaner than Jerusalem had been), the silent sentries in the hall, his diplomats and his family, whom he either would or would not be able to find during this trip.

And he really wanted to forget it all.

It was as if she were starving for him; she was frenzied and demanding so that he felt like some prisoner's last meal and pulled her up by the hair: "Hey, hey, slow down. We've got plenty of time. It's not the end of the world."

It was the wrong thing to say: she shuddered, crouched over him, and suddenly collapsed on him, weeping. "Oh, Christ," he heard her say. "I love you. Isn't that ridiculous? The human spirit, against all logic, finding things to hold onto." She was talking to his armpit, trying to burrow into it.

"It's not ridiculous," he managed, forcing her head up gently so that he could look into her bleary eyes. "But we've got a classified briefing in ten minutes and I'd like you to be there," he said softly, kissing her temples, the bridge of her nose, her cheeks, and finally her lips. "So we'd better finish this and get going, or it'll be all too obvious what we've been doing up here."

Neatly having avoided declaring himself or voicing his own confusion, he let his hands do the rest of his talking for him. At least he had enough confidence in her now to bring her to the briefing; love had motivated more successful agents than money or patriotism.

As for the rest of it: "Chris," he said as they toweled off from the world's fastest shower and he looked at his watch, "I'm going to propose a side trip: I have to know how my family is . . . if they're safe."

He saw her stiffen, one leg in her suit. Then she pulled it up around her thighs: "Of course."

"Now don't go all defensive and distant on me. What about you—parents, siblings?"

"No, thanks. I don't want to know. My mom's dead and my dad is—was—a practicing drunkard who remarried. It would be hypocritical of me to put people in danger to find someone I went out of my way to avoid. . . ."

"I understand."

"What about Morse's—"

"We don't owe him anything at this point. Not after what he tried to pull. Come on, we're late."

On the way out, she said, "Can I go with you, to find them? Good human interest story." Her tone was pure investigative reporter, there in the hall with two soldiers who looked like snowmen with M16s ahead of them and two more behind.

"We'll see."

Inside a red door marked RESTRICTED: NO ACCESS WITHOUT PERMIT above a slot into which Beck slipped his laminated access card, Ashmead's team was waiting, seated on one side of a table by two empty chairs.

On the other side sat President Beggs himself.

The President, the only one in the room not dressed in white, was shaggy-haired and harried-looking, polishing eyeglasses which had left angry red indentations on either side of his nose. On his left was Watkins from Tel Aviv, who had an analyst's noncommittal smile on his face as he stood up in the presence of a lady; on his right, a thirtyish Navy commander Beck didn't know and, on the commander's right, Sam Nye from the Agency's Directorate for Science and Technology, looking no older than he had when he and Beck had been running Task Force 159 out of Langley's basement together.

Nye left the table to greet them, a wide grin cracking his Teutonic face, arms outstretched to hug Beck: "Man, you and your cloak-and-dagger cliffhangers. If you ever scare me like that again, I'm going to trash you worse than I used to at practice."

Disentangling himself from Nye's long-armed hug, Beck said, "Nye, here, was a tight end at—"

"He still is," Beggs boomed in his best campaign-trail voice. "Ours. Will you introduce the lady so that we can sit down, Mister Beck?"

Beck couldn't quite tell if Beggs was annoyed that he'd brought her—Ashmead should have filled them in on her status by then. But Beggs would naturally disapprove of women in meetings of this nature. He ignored it, introduced her as his "best and at this moment only asset," and went around the table until he came to the Navy man.

"I'm sorry, Commander, but I don't believe we've ever met."

"My old boss," Thoreau said easily before the clear-eyed man with the military haircut could speak for himself, "Richard McGrath."

"Mac will do," said the Navy SEAL commander with a slight inclination of his head; "this is pretty informal. Miss Patrick, are you sure you want to stay for this meeting?"

Beck put a hand to the small of her back and prodded her toward the two empty chairs; Nye, on her other side, whispered, "Don't let them intimidate you, Madame," so low that no one at the table could hear.

She took her cue from Nye: "Why wouldn't I, Commander McGrath?"

Beggs was watching surreptitiously while he reamed his pipe.

Watkins said with a disarming smile, "I'll handle this, Mac. What the commander is trying to say is that if you sit in on this meeting, Miss Patrick, you'll be giving up your First Amendment rights: you'll have to sign a short secrecy oath which we've prepared." He tapped a file folder in front of him. "You'll hardly be the impartial reporter."

"She's not that now," Beck said, remembering Watkins and Dow in Tel Aviv and wondering what the hell was going on here. "And she's already signed everything but exit papers."

"You can speak for yourself, can't you, Miss Patrick?" Beggs said suddenly.

"Ah . . . yes, Sir, Mister President. And I realize that nothing I learn here can become public knowledge."

"Fine," Beggs sighed. "Give her the paper then, Watkins, and we'll get on with this."

Beck wished fervently that Chris was a real operative, that she could spot a factional dispute when she saw one, realize that it was significant that no one from the State Department was present while CIA had two supergrades—three, if you counted Ashmead, which Beck was hesitant to do—at the table.

When Watkins slid the form across the table to Chris, Beck saw the Agency crest on its letterhead and took a deep breath. Hardball they wanted, hardball they'd get: "There's no need for this; she's on State's role already."

Ashmead, for the first time, looked Beck's way with a cautionary glance. And Beck, reading the urgency there, began to worry about the Administration's reaction to the shoot-down: after all, they'd lost a whole 727 full of multinational fact-finders. If there was to be an attempt to apportion blame or minimize damage, even a discussion of possible lateral escalation, then muzzling Chris or removing her before the fact made good sense.

Watkins said smoothly, "Yes, well, that was before the airborne . . . incidents. We need more stringent control of—"

"Watkins, unless you want to talk about Tel Aviv, back off. Excuse me, Mister President, but this is unnecessary and divisive." He turned to Chris: "Miss Patrick, until now your contribution has been voluntary, with limits decided between us— flexible, if you like. Once you've signed that document, you'll be subject to Agency pre-publication review for the rest of your life. That's no way to win a Pulitzer Prize."

Slick crossed his legs and took out a pocket fingernail file, head down, a smile flickering at the corners of his mouth.

Chris scanned the document, looked up blandly, and smiled: "In that case, gentlemen, I'm afraid I'll have to leave."

Ashmead said quickly: "Good idea. Slick, take your lady friend to her room and come right back."

Everyone sat in silence until they'd gone, then Nye got up and ostentatiously took Chris's vacant seat next to Beck.

Watkins said, "Beck, you traitorous bastard. Now she can go tell it on the mountain—all about Morse and the way an Agency Covert Action team killed an American citizen—a goddam hero, if that serum's all it's cracked up to be."

"She's my asset, Watkins. I trust her."

"All right, gentlemen," Beggs said. "Whatever your personal feelings, it's done now. Is it acceptable to you, Ashmead, that she be allowed to continue in whatever capacity without signing that document?"

Ashmead grunted: "It was fine with me before; I haven't changed my mind. Can we get through this debrief, please? All my people are tired and cranky, Beck included."

It was a gentle way to find out he'd been demoted, but Beck stiffened. Then Nye's hand touched his thigh under the table and tapped insistently until Beck reached down and took the pack of cigarettes Nye was using to prod him with.

"Fine with me," Beggs was saying impatiently. "Let's have the rundown on these dips you've brought, then we'll open the table to comments."

As Ashmead began reciting Yael Saadia's dossiers from memory, Beck got out his lighter, put the cigarettes next to it on the table, and lit a cigarette, near the front of the pack, which had a crimped filter. His hands were shaking.

Casually, as Ashmead talked, Beck watched the coal burn up past the old Morse-code SOS scribed in brown fine-point marker near its tip.

When Ashmead had finished, Beck added nothing to his briefing, uncertain as to what Nye's warning could mean. There was a possibility that any negative assessment of the surviving fact-finding party's motives or attitudes given in the tense mood of this room could lead to the loss of the five dignitaries left from "natural causes." Until Beck was sure that wasn't what Nye was trying to tell him, he would keep his own counsel.

He had a good excuse: he'd been a working flight controller for the entire trip, and his agent had been refused accreditation. He used it and Watkins grew livid.

That didn't bother Beck; he'd cut his teeth on paper wars.

Beggs was impatient with the whole process: "Commander McGrath, will you give us the intinerary you've prepared and fill us in on your security preparations? I've got a breakfast meeting with those dips and I'd prefer not to be late."

As McGrath got up, telescoping a pointer to its full length and stepping toward a screen where he punched up prepared computer maps filling half of one wall, on which "clear" zones comprising about forty percent of the nation and "survivable zones" comprising another forty were clearly marked, Beggs said: "Mister Beck, this baby's your brainchild and you've said almost nothing during this entire meeting. Would you like to tell me why that is, or make some relevant comments?"

"Mister President, I've been the flight controller on the P-3B for the last twenty-odd hours. Before that, I had the work of ten people to do. I can't remember when I last had a good night's sleep. It seems to me that you're pretty well informed as it is."

Beggs leaned forward: "Watkins, here, can be a little prickly, but I want to thank you personally for bringing that serum home where it belongs." Beggs patted his left arm and winced slightly. "A job well done. With Ashmead's team members aboard that 727, no one can accuse us of a cover-up or suspect a sacrifice play. We've got the P-3B's tape and picture verification that the 727 was shot down by Soviet aircraft and, believe me, those Russkies are going to pay through the nose for it—it wasn't just Americans they murdered: this is a crime of international proportions. So, by and large, we're very grateful. Grateful enough that when Ashmead proposed we take the second helicopter we aren't going to need for diplomatic taxi service and use it to try to find your family, we agreed that, under the circumstances, we ought to make it a national priority."

President Beggs sat back, beaming as if he'd just kissed three orphans and opened an old-folks' home.

Beck's gut had tensed when Beggs started talking about retaliation. He'd known that Beggs was dangerous. He stared at the President, wanting to demand reassurances that Beggs wasn't about to touch off a second nuclear exchange—the new Commander in Chief was capable of it, in Beck's estimation, and so was America: the second-strike capability would have been the first thing to be put back on line, no matter how much damage the country's war-fighting hardware had taken.

But Beck's training wouldn't let him say any of that. He said, "Thank you, Sir; that's very kind of you. But I have to stay with my diplomats. Maybe when they're—"

"Don't argue with me, Beck," said the President. "I'm not Watkins. You and your teammates are going to go find your family while Miss Patrick and her multinational buddies get the guided tour of what sights are fit for them to see. Capiche?"

Beck did, and he didn't like the sound of it one bit.

Just then Slick came back and squeezed his arm as he slid into his seat: "She's a good guy, Beck. She knows just what to do."

He sat bleary-eyed and dry-mouthed through McGrath's detailed briefing, listening with one ear to mileage stats and radiation-hardness estimates for the Black Hawk helicopters, each of which could carry eleven people and had been modified to burn methane and brought up to helicopter-gunship specs.

When the meeting finally adjourned, he said casually to Nye, "I can't face any more bureaucratese on an empty stomach and with all these honchos to coddle those dips, they don't need me. Let's get some breakfast, Sam, and talk over old times."

"I'd like that, Marc," said Nye heartily. "Just hold on a minute while I clear it with the Chief."

Nye went not to Watkins but to Beggs himself and came away with a clap on the back: "All set. We're excused from the breakfast." Then, without moving his lips: "Just you and me, nobody else."

So when Ashmead, with a quizzical smile, asked them if they wanted company, Beck begged off: "Not unless you're up for a nice long talk about such scintillating subjects as spacetime manifolds, electron slip, and geochronometry. Us eggheads have got to relax every once in a while, and we like to do it with numbers. It's been too long since I've been around somebody else who speaks math."

Nye, when Beck turned back, had a sour look on his face that said Beck had chosen his words badly, but Beck didn't understand why until they were alone in a lived-in looking suite that Nye had been occupying, he said, "for the past three weeks."

"So long? You were here before the Forty-Minute War?"

Nye was stretched out on his leather couch, jacket off, tie off, shoes off. "Sure was. And this room is absolutely secure, though I can't vouch for any-place else in the building. Punch up a 6-5-7-3-9-K there by the door and watch what happens."

Beck walked over to the normal-looking computer-lock panel and did as he was told. An LCD screen appeared beside the lock-plate and started checking the security system, which consisted of six components. When it had run through every wavelength its electro-optics could scan, it hummed and winked green, then went blank.

"Okay," Beck sighed, "I'm impressed, Sam, but I wasn't kidding—I'm dead tired."

"I know. So tired you didn't even notice when they slipped figures by you that normally you'd have questioned. It's worse than they're telling you, Marc—all that intelligence is E-5."

E-5: Information the accuracy of which was

improbable, from an unreliable source—in this case, the United States Government.

"I know that. But you didn't bring me here to cry in our beer."

"Do you know that those maps were bogus—that we've got maybe nineteen per cent clear zones and forty-seven per cent survivable—*if* you're willing to accept the new definition of survivable, which knocks twenty years off the average lifespan of American citizens? Do you know that plenty of our citizens *aren't* willing to accept it—that a significant portion of the population has decided the hell with the funny suits and masks and are just running around in their street clothes—not to mention the loonies cavorting jaybird naked except for their "Impeach Beggs" placards? Or that the good old Communist Party USA is having a field day, so much so that Beggs is scared to death that there won't *be* an American government by the time his term's complete—that he'll be the guy who goes down in the history books as the man who killed democracy? Do you know that the red zones include not only Seattle, the Colorado Space Defense Command, NORAD, Groton and Newport News, but Langley—all our bases?"

"What are you worried about, Sam? Where to spend your next vacation? Try Kansas City or Denton."

"I'm worried that Beggs is going to do something stupid. Lord knows he's capable of it. I'm not the only one, either—the Agency's trying to keep him in line, but everybody's nervous about him—whatever else he is, he's still our President." Nye sighed glumly and shook his head. "Coffee. Come on, let's make some."

Beck almost wept for joy when he saw Nye's espresso maker; as it was, he bent down and rested his cheek against the brass: "I should have known I could count on you," he murmured with ersatz passion.

"Brioche, too. I can get anything I want—except what I need."

"What's that? Come on, Sam, don't play me. Just tell me what the SOS was about."

"You almost blew it back there—'talk math.' Shit, didn't you realize that that's exactly what I want to do—that we're about *it* . . . all that's left of 159?"

"What's that got to do with anything?" Beck took the can of espresso Sam handed him and began filling the strainer.

"Ask me that when you've analyzed the *real* damage reports and when we've estimated the probability of follow-up strikes or unrelated detonations in the Middle East and elsewhere. Since we're never going to get a chance to build a Ballistic Missile Defense now, and when we could those cheap sons of bitches in Congress wouldn't let us, 159's about the only hope we've got left."

"What are you saying, Sam? You're not seriously considering reactivating 159? We couldn't send a paper clip back through time when I left the project."

"That's right, we couldn't. When you left the project. Marc, forgive me if I change the subject— we'll have plenty of time to come back to it later, but there's something you've got to know . . . and I might as well tell you before somebody you don't know does: Muffy and the kids were with Jeanie at my house."

Beck dropped the strainer full of espresso on the floor. Ignoring it, he put both hands on the counter of Nye's little pullman kitchen and leaned there, vertigo threatening to topple him, his stomach lurching.

Nye put a steadying hand on Beck's shoulder. "It's fine if you want to fall apart here. I did."

But he didn't: "In Georgetown. You're sure?"

"Wish I wasn't. I've already checked fringe-area hospitals. They didn't make it to any. But we can go there, if you want."

"Is that what you want?"

"It is."

"Just to collect the ashes?"

"No." Sam Nye's square jaw quivered. "I want to go down under Langley with you and see if any of that equipment from 159 is salvageable."

"Are you crazy? We wouldn't last a day. It's red hot there; even McGrath's maps, the ones you say are sanitized, showed that whole area as a red zone."

"When you've seen what I've got to show you, or seen some of what I've seen, it won't matter."

"I don't believe this. Sam, everybody dies."

"For something or because of something, yes—I mean, that's acceptable. Look, I didn't mean to do it this way. If I can't convince you, then . . ." Nye shrugged and Beck, watching his face closely, began to notice signs of strain: deep webbed lines around Nye's eyes, pinned pupils, bloodless lips.

Concerned that his friend was going to commit suicide trying to resurrect a dead project for no better reason than a delusion that the project might in turn resurrect his incinerated family, Beck said, "Sure thing, Sam. You tell me and we'll go over the numbers. The least I can do is brainstorm it with you."

Then he got down on his hands and knees and began scooping up the spilled espresso grounds with his hands.

Sam Nye crouched down beside him, dustpan and whisk broom in hand: "You think I'm crazy, flipped. You won't. I've got time ... as much as anybody else, at any rate. Here."

Beck took the whisk broom and the dustpan and realized that Nye was shaking worse than he was.

But he had to ask: "What I saw in the situation room, that's not *it*, is it—what's left of the Cabinet?"

Sam Nye laughed a trifle hysterically. "I wish it were. We're the sane ones. Old Beggs doesn't trust anybody much, not since his Vice President hijacked Air Force Two to Brazil and the next guy in line tried to kill Beggs. We've got plenty of people spread out at the different sites, but there's too much trauma in the ranks. We need time and we haven't got it. We've got martial law and riots over paper masks that you used to be able to buy by the boxful—I told you, the whole damned country's falling apart."

"But what about the clean zones? Even if the percentage is smaller, there's bound to be some stable areas."

"Sure, but the people in them are all armed to the teeth and protecting their year's worth of food— remember the survivalist movement?"

"So what are we going to show the IMF and—"

"You heard McGrath—mostly overflights. Those damned diplomats of yours are bound and determined to see the worst, not the best, we've got. We'll try to reason with them, but the UN in Sydney has forwarded explicit instructions—they don't want clean zones, they want America on her knees . . . you know how the UN loves us." Nye smiled sourly. "At least Prick McGrath will be going with them himself—he'll make the best of it. He's a good man. You can trust him."

"And Watkins?" Beck asked, testing the waters.

"The National Intelligence Officer? He's—"

"What!" Beck was horrified. "NIO in charge of what?"

"Soviet Union and Domestic Affairs—everybody's had to double up."

Beck just stood up and resumed the process of making espresso. If Sam was telling him the truth, then the United States was in the hands of one shell-shocked bureaucrat too many; Beggs and Watkins added up to a disaster Beck wasn't capable of contemplating objectively.

But then Sam Nye, who'd given him a coded cigarette and thought that the answer to all their problems lay under tons of radioactive rubble in the old 159 lab at CIA headquarters in Langley, might be unwittingly giving Beck tweaked data: for all Beck knew, Nye could be certifiably non compos mentis. He'd been under a terrible strain.

But then, who hadn't?

Chapter 5

Dick McGrath, the Navy SEAL commander, could have been Supreme Allied Commander–Europe by now if he'd wanted the job, Ashmead knew; the fact that he'd sidestepped promotion to stay in his operational berth accounted for his youthful appearance, his behind-the-back nickname of Prick, and Ashmead's recognition of him as a kindred soul.

Mac was forty-odd and a straight arrow; even though Ashmead had leveraged Thoreau away from him five years before, McGrath qualified as the single person in the above-ground Houston White House—or below it for that matter—that Ashmead knew he could trust implicitly.

"What say we rescue Patrick and qualify her with a serious handgun? I can't have one of my people running around with a pea-shooter, especially if I'm not going to be there to back her up," Ashmead said to him once he'd mashed his Eggs

Benedict sufficiently that it would seem as if he'd eaten some.

Mac put a linen napkin to his lips. "Sounds good to me. We've got some new ammo you might like— depleted uranium instead of lead shot as an upgrade—that gets the density back up where it ought to be. Bring your boys and we'll see if any of them can hit the paper with it."

Real casual, real nice. Ashmead collected Slick, Thoreau and Patrick, telling Chris to put her watch on transmit as soon as they saw daylight in case anything transpired he'd later like Beck to hear, and they all trailed along behind Mac into an elevator which took them back underground to a RESTRICTED—REQUISITIONS BY PERMIT ONLY warehouse full of everything from armored personnel carriers to miniaturized microwave-surveillance shotgun mikes until they stopped before a counter under a stenciled sign that said ORDNANCE where Mac rang a bell to summon the duty officer.

When a big-eared fellow with no neck and his hair shaved almost to the skin said with a grin, "Yes, Sir, Mac, what'll it be?" the SEAL commander turned to Chris Patrick.

"Hold out your hand, Miss Patrick."

Ashmead held his breath but Chris extended her right, not her left with the watch clasped to it.

Mac asked her to squeeze his hand as hard as she could and then to try to hold his hand down as he raised it so that he could assess the strength in her wrist.

Then he turned back to the ordnance clerk: "Give me a Detonics Mark VI in nine millimeter, and a Galco Jak-Slide . . . cross-draw, I guess."

"Right," the clerk was filling out the form: "Jak-

Slide 2 holster." He looked up inquiringly, waiting for the rest.

"What's your waist size, Miss Patrick?"

"Chris; call me Chris. It's ... ah ... twenty-four," she said.

Behind her, Slick leaned an elbow on the counter, grinning fondly at her.

"Twenty-*four?*" Mac rubbed his neck and told the clerk: "Give me the smallest Gelco belt you've got and a hole-puncher, two spare magazines in a Seventrees magnetic holder, an Aim-Point that'll fit and a mounting kit, and three boxes of Glaser DU."

The clerk looked with a pained expression at Ashmead's team. "Sir, you know we don't have any DU—"

"Mister, this man," he gestured to Ashmead, "has a security clearance with four T's in front of the S. Let's not play 'I've Got a Secret.'" He turned to Ashmead: "You still carrying that SIG in .45, Rafic?"

"Yep," Ashmead said. "We're all standardized as to caliber."

"Good enough. Add five boxes of DU .45ACP, and that'll be it."

"If you say so, Sir," said the clerk doubtfully; he was still shaking his head as he disappeared between the tall rows of shelves to his rear.

Mac leaned on the counter facing the team: "DU's still classified, Miss Patrick, but under the circumstances your word will be a sufficient guarantee."

Chris looked at him with a dazed expression: "I have no idea what you're talking about, any of it. I've never shot a gun ... I just bought that one when I realized suicide might be a viable alternative to ... to ..." She bit her lip. "So I'm going to look pretty foolish in front of all of you."

"Don't worry about it. Everybody starts sometime," Mac assured her avuncularly. "You're getting a cross-draw with no thumb-release strap because you're a beginner and we don't want you to shoot yourself when you draw fast; and if you can't punch paper without it, we'll mount the Aim-Point—it's a scope that puts a red dot on the target so that you can't miss, as long as you can hold your weapon steady with the extra weight."

"Aim-Points are for old guys whose eyes are failing so they can't focus on three things at once," Slick told her. "You won't need it."

And, on the outdoor range, under Ashmead's tutelage, she proved she didn't, once they'd gotten around the problem of her small waist and the curve outward below to her hips.

While she stood at the firing line with Thoreau and Slick, all three wearing ear protectors over their white radiation hoods, and shot paper bull's-eyes at twenty-five yards, Ashmead and Mac sat in Mac's hardened staff car with one eye on the clock: "I don't want them out in this three-Rem wind more than another few minutes," Ashmead said, jingling spent brass in his palm from his own trial firing of the DU. "So let's get serious."

"What do you want to know, Rafic?" Mac turned sideways behind the wheel and met his gaze.

"Why Beggs and Watkins are so anxious to cut Patrick out of my herd—you're not going to grease those dips, are you?"

"I've no orders to that effect at present," the Navy commando leader said levelly, "but you never can tell."

"I want to take her home with me in one piece."

"Then keep her with you. It's nasty out there—not the radiation so much, but the public mood. Civilians . . ." His mouth twisted. "We've got the National Guard out trying to get the wrecks off the roads, and our citizens are looting everything in sight as well as sniping at those of us who're trying to help them. You'd think we were the enemy. They'll kill each other for a priority placement in a Medevac line or a hospital bed or even a pound of rice or a jug of bottled water. No discipline, no morality. There's just not enough standing army to maintain order, and the local cops are as bad as the people they're supposed to be policing. It may calm down now that they've got their telephones and TV reception back—it took us too long to get something like a network with regular programming and controllable news up and running. They felt cut off, I guess. Scared. And the Emergency Broadcast Network—when and where it functioned —didn't help much. All you need is a couple hysterics and it spreads like chemical warfare."

Ashmead could see Mac's frustration; every soldier fears anarchy more than death. "Keep her with us, you said. Any idea how I might be able to do that without disobeying a direct Presidential order?"

Mac cocked his head, "Did you hear an order like that? In all the commotion, you must have been mistaken." His teeth flashed: "From the heart, Rafic: do what you damn well please where, in your judgment, national interest isn't at stake. What we've got left of an Administration doesn't know its best interest from a latrine. If I were you I'd get in that P-3B and haul ass back where I came from with what's left of that team of yours and do what you know how to do: covert action includes drop-ping right out of the picture, doesn't it?"

"Could be. Want to join us?"

"I'd truly love to, but I've got too many boys to look after and I can't bring them all with me. What the hell happened, anyway? *You* don't *make* mistakes like the one that fried Home Plate."

"That's right, I don't. But other people do. I followed an order I should have ignored because I'd been taking a lot of heat over insubordination."

Mac was looking out the window now, binocu-lars up to his eyes, "Damn, but that Slick can shoot."

"You should have seen Jesse." Ashmead, too, looked out at Slick's white-suited figure limned against the new spring grass of the outdoor range, the horizon distant and empty beyond him. Empty was about how Ashmead felt: the loss of Elint, Jesse and Yael was something he'd come to terms with later. Maybe it was for the best, kinder; maybe Morse's serum wasn't all it was cracked up to be. It certainly wasn't going to be efficacious against the sort of radiation hazard they'd be exposed to in Georgetown. But, like Slick and Thoreau, Ash-mead had to believe that the sacrifices were worth the price.

"I heard," Mac was saying. "Did you train him?"

"Slick? He trains me, half the time—he's a natural. Want to rate Watkins's record for me?"

Mac put down the glasses slowly and shook his head: "I can't think of a single nice thing to say."

"Gotcha. That's what I thought. But what about Watkins and Beck? Why the vendetta? Without Beck, none of you guys would be sitting around rubbing your inoculations."

"Something happened in Tel Aviv, Beck said. Beyond that, I don't know anything except that Beggs trusts Watkins like I wouldn't trust my own mother. It's like CIA's running the country—no offense personally, of course."

"None taken. Suits or no suits, I'm ready to get those kids in out of the wind. Then I'd like to go over the Black Hawks, inside and out, with you."

"I've got my own people standing over them—there won't be any tampering. Everybody's so high-tensile, I couldn't sleep if I'd done it any other way. But you don't have to take my word for it—I'll be in one of those birds; I'd as soon get a hands-on, myself, before we take your dips sightseeing. And we don't have much time." Mac looked at his watch. "We're cleared for takeoff in three hours for the first leg." He started the Lincoln's engine and looked straight at Ashmead: "When we get to Bragg, there'll be plenty of time to stage enough of a little mixup that Patrick will end up in your Black Hawk instead of mine—just in case I'm getting complacent in my old age and you're right about a scratch order coming down."

"Thanks, Mac. I owe you one."

"If this inoculation's what it's cracked up to be, I'm going to do my damnedest to find you in a year or two, when things calm down, and collect."

"You're on," Ashmead promised with real affection. Then he opened the car door, whose armored windows wouldn't roll down, and motioned to Slick, who was reloading and looking their way, to bring the team in out of the radioactive spring wind blowing in off the panhandle.

Chapter 6

Beck had finally put Sam Nye's story into perspective and two and two together: it wasn't that Nye was addled, it was that he was acting under orders.

Sam hadn't admitted it, of course, which just proved that the Agency was still paranoid and Beck, more than ever with Watkins running the show, was still considered an outsider.

But the Agency, and Nye, who had worked on 159 for two years after Beck had left, apparently thought it was feasible to revive 159 in a last ditch attempt to turn back the clock, to literally correct the intelligence failure that had led to the Forty-Minute War *before* it occurred.

Beck still didn't believe it could be done, but Nye had evidently convinced the Agency that it was worth a try. That was why Chris Patrick was on the other chopper with the sightseers rather than in the Black Hawk carrying Beck, Nye, Ashmead, Slick and Thoreau to Fort Bragg that night, and that was why it was going to be very difficult to get any time alone with her at Bragg or find a way to sneak her aboard his chopper in the morning.

And Beck wasn't so sure he wanted her along. Not only was the mission at a security level that defied classification, but it was almost certainly one from which none of the participants would return.

Langley was simply too hot. No radiation suit, not even the black ones which they'd been issued to separate them from the dips and Patrick in their white ones and provide some operational cover if they ended up running through city streets at night, could protect them totally in a red zone like Langley, where ambient ionizing radiation was the least of their worries. If, by some miracle, he got out of Langley alive, it wasn't just a matter of a shortened lifespan: Beck wouldn't be producing any more children; Morse's serum wasn't effective against genetic damage or sterilization.

He was feeling resentful and paranoid; he knew he was shocky with grief over Muffy and the kids, but the Agency could have leveled with him, not tried to manipulate him like a civilian and use his best friend to do it.

Still, if Nye was right and President Beggs was seriously considering a second strike, what difference did it make?

Two years ago, when the ancient cat he'd gotten Muffy on returning from their honeymoon had been put to sleep, Beck's wife had broken down so completely she was sure for a number of hours that the vet had just told them their cat had to be put to sleep so that he could sell it to an animal experimentation program: that sort of paranoia was a function of physiological grief and, though intellectually he understood what was happening to him, Beck couldn't help but wonder if Nye was telling him the truth about Muffy and Seth and little Jen. For all he knew they were really alive somewhere, in an Agency holding facility or a burn hospital like the one they'd taken the dips through earlier today en route to Bragg in a nicely orchestrated bit of psychwar that silenced all accusations that the fact-finding tour wasn't going to be shown anything embarrassing to America.

The burn hospital had done more than that: it had silenced all conversation and brought Dugard, the NATO honcho, to tears.

For Beck, it had been a personal nightmare: he kept looking for familiar faces among those laved in cream and gel and once, standing above the bed of a woman who had only one side of her face left and merely a handful of remaining hair, he'd thought he saw one.

But the woman wasn't his wife; not only the chart at the foot of her bed but the look in her single eye told him that.

Still, he'd had all he could do not to bolt when he excused himself to find the men's room, and then he'd seen Chris Patrick, a white-swathed lonely figure in the hall, packing a Detonics in a strap holster and leaning her head against the tiled corridor wall while tears streamed unheeded down her face.

He couldn't help himself; he took her in his arms and held her head against his chest: if he'd broken her cover, he didn't care about it at that moment; any man would have held a total stranger in those circumstances.

She said to him, "What I don't understand is why the sky looks so friendly. The clouds are white, the air smells sweet, and it's all a lie."

"Shh," he said. "Shh."

"If it weren't for you, I'd use this thing," she pushed her hip, where the pistol nestled, against him. "Please, let's get out of here, go home, go back to Israel, together, alive."

"We will," he'd promised. "In three days' time. Just hold on. We need you so badly. America's counting on you."

"Fuck America."

He didn't say that America was pretty well fucked already; he said: "*I'm* counting on you."

She could relate to that. She pulled back from him of her own accord as they heard footsteps and pushed her way into the ladies' room, a gamin if puffy-lipped smile on her face: "Right," she said in an imitation of Slick. "Check."

It wasn't until they'd piled back into the two Black Hawks waiting outside the burn hospital and lifted vertically into a magnificent sunset that Beck began to feel guilty about lying to her, about caring about her when his own family remained unaccounted for, about the degree to which her presence made him willing to accept at face value Nye's—CIA's—assurances that his wife and kids were dead in Georgetown.

The rest of the trip to Bragg had been a nightmare the like of which he had never experienced—not during the entire aftermath of the war.

He couldn't talk; if he opened his mouth he was

going to start screaming; he just stared out the window at the sparse lights below and listened in his radiation hood's phones to Ashmead's people bantering; even though he should have been trying to pinpoint a moment in time at which Ashmead's team could change history, he didn't bother. Nye's plan seemed like a hopeless, absurd game, the only result of which would be more death: his, Ashmead's, Slick's, Thoreau's. And Nye's, but that was okay because Nye didn't care any more.

He kept seeing a death's head grin on Slick's beautiful face and Ashmead with only half a head of hair and wondering if he was finally going mad.

But he wasn't that lucky. He calmed down and the cowboy talk around him became no more than an annoyance as his body cycled him into a different phase of shock, in which he could float, detached, superior and at ease: he knew what was going to happen; none of these macho types around him had any idea what lay in store for them.

At Bragg, among the Delta and Ranger personnel on post, life seemed almost normal except for the radiation precautions—respirators and gloves and raincoats and boots, no worse than Jerusalem had been: Bragg, due to serendipity and favorable winds, was a low-risk survivable zone.

Bragg's commanding officer had them to dinner and showed Beck's dignitaries that life at an American military base could be civilized. NATO General Dugard had retrieved his uniform and strutted around happily, at ease in his bailiwick, and his gratefully gleeful mood infected everyone but the Japanese: Zenko Tsutsumi remembered Nagasaki and Hiroshima and his eyes were full of ghosts as he came up to Beck and pulled him aside.

"Secretary Beck," the Japanese trade minister said, "I apologize most sincerely for my boorish comments and my insensitivity of yesterday. We will do all we can to help your people, even though . . ." Tsutsumi squeezed his eyes shut; his pock-marked cheeks quivered. Then he opened them and said: "I have a confession to make. I had expected to enjoy this, to see your country suffer as it made my country suffer. But revenge is sour when one stands eye to eye with such horror. Accept my apologies and the condolences of my people, please."

"Accepted and understood, Minister. We're all a little shaken," Beck said gently, his mouth on diplomatic autopilot while his mind dwelled on his own problems, of which the little Japanese didn't then seem a part. "Try to distance yourself from it. It sounds heartless, but it's all we can do. From now on, you'll just be overflying sites, not staring casualties in the face. In fact, for most of the rest of your time here, radiation suits will be optional except when directly over red zones: the Black Hawk's hardened and there's no reason for you or any of the others to feel apprehensive. It should be easier from here on in, but we had to prove to you we aren't pulling any punches. If you'd simply take our word for it that we've lost both coasts but that the country is by-and-large intact, it would be easier still—on everybody. Have a pleasant evening, Sir."

Walking away, Beck caught Ashmead's eye and the two of them retired to a corner, drinks in hand, of the officers' mess. "I have to talk to you, Rafic."

"Talk."

There was low music playing, the chatter of men and even a few officers' wives.

"If we had it to do over again—the interdiction of the Islamic Jihad and their bomb—what would be the last possible moment at which you could have turned things around?".

Ashmead's brooding eyes measured Beck soberly. Then he said: "Hypothetically? Twenty-two hours before that plane took off from Riyadh, Slick and I were sitting in our hotel room with the team deployed and Elint called in and I had to tell him we'd gotten a pull-back order. Three hours after that we were in our Jetstream on the way to Nicosia. That close enough for you?"

"Rafic, I need numbers—a spread of time, 0600 to 0900, or whatever. That sort of thing."

"Fuck all, Beck, are you asking what I think you're asking?"

"Probably. Can you give it to me?"

"Can you tell me if giving it to you is going to do any good, or just end us up digging through hot rubble in Langley?"

"Certainly the latter; as to the former . . . who the fuck knows? Didn't Watkins brief you?"

"Not on this, which is a good sign. Okay, let me get my two boys and we'll see if we can't get down to hours, minutes, and seconds for you."

Ashmead turned away to do just that.

"Rafic," Beck called softly.

Ashmead came back, hands on hips: "Yeah?"

"Tell me it's not worth the risk and I'll blow it off. I still can—I'm the only one who can."

"Why should I tell you that? You're the walking brain trust. Let's give it a go."

Ashmead gave him a thumb's-up and began collecting his operations team from the video games in one corner of the officers' mess.

Four hours later, after the team had left his room and Beck was trying to fall asleep in the stuffy guest room whose air purifier sounded like a Formula-1 car, there was a knock at his door.

In just his briefs, he opened it: he'd been told to sleep fully clothed, but he was still full of grief and resentful, questioning everything, especially whether he wanted to undertake a foray into Langley for CIA, Nye or no Nye, second strike or no second strike.

When he opened it, Ashmead was standing there with Chris Patrick, who was as white as her radiation suit.

"I thought you two ought to have a talk before we split up tomorrow. Unless Chris is coming with us?" Ashmead's voice was gruff but his eyes were smiling.

"You bastard. All right. Come in, Chris. This is terrible security, Rafic."

"Tsk, tsk," said Ashmead as he reached in to pull the door shut after Chris had stepped inside.

"What *is* it?" she whispered, obviously terrified. "This morning Rafic was going to move heaven and earth to keep me off that diplomatic Black Hawk, now everything's changed. What's happening? What do I have to know that *he* couldn't tell me and Slick wouldn't tell me?"

"A number of things. Sit down, please, Chris." Beck could have strangled Ashmead with his bare hands. He remembered Slick's warning that when Ashmead wasn't telling him something, he was telling him something. Beck had no idea how much Ashmead knew of what Nye had told Beck, or what he expected Beck to tell Chris Patrick. But Beck wasn't going to tell her any more than she needed to know. He didn't have the heart for it.

"Oh, Christ, don't give me that State Department voice. You're scaring me half to death."

"On the bed, okay?" He sat beside her and slapped a cassette into the tape deck on the nightstand without bothering to see which one it was. "Do you still have your lighter?"

She fumbled in her purse for it with a plucky grin and lit a cigarette before she showed him its green light. "Safe as can be, see?"

"First, I have to explain about the shot that Elint gave both of us in Jerusalem," he said quietly.

When he'd done that and she finally realized that she'd been given a dose of serum which, augmented by reasonable precautionary measures on her part, would reduce her chances of developing cancer to even less than they had been before the Forty-Minute War, she was overcome with joy, effusive in her gratitude, ready to crawl into his lap: "So we do have a chance—for a normal life, I mean," she exulted. "You and me. That is, if you're . . . if your family . . . oh, Christ, you know what I mean . . ."

"A chance, yes." Then he started to tell her the fable that duty demanded, composed partly of truth and partly of wishful thinking, which he wanted her to disseminate to the dips and to her newspaper—if Nye was right and a second strike was imminent, it was useless disinformation, but it might buy them some time; if Nye was wrong, protecting America by projecting a perception of relative strength was the most important thing he could do right now, surely what Ashmead wanted him to do. "I'm going to begin by explaining that no one actually knows yet what our current state of readiness is or how extensively our war-fighting capability's been damaged, let alone how long it will take to put America back on track. . . ."

He talked to her for two and a half hours and when he was done he still couldn't bring himself to tell her about the trip to Langley, so he didn't, just intimated that tomorrow's trip was too dangerous for her and that he'd catch up with her and the dignitaries later.

And then he took her to bed. If he was going to sacrifice everything tomorrow on a long shot, he wanted to leave something behind, even if it was only a pleasant memory.

Chapter 7

When Slick came to Beck's room to get Chris it was an hour before sunrise and she was so groggy with sleep that she didn't have the presence of mind even to tell Beck how much she loved him. She just struggled into her radiation suit and cursed security measures of every sort.

Never mind, she'd have plenty of time to tell him later, now that she was sure that he loved her too. He'd loved her all along, or else he'd never have given her a dose of the precious serum that was earmarked for those crucial to the functioning of the US Government.

In the dimly lit barracks hallway with Slick she was almost euphoric, hardly listening. He had to tell her twice to activate the tracer—"homer," he called it—that was part of her black chrome watch, so that they could find her if anything went wrong and she got separated from her party, and to remember that if she wanted to contact him, all she had to do was speak into it.

"I've got a vibrator on my belt," he grinned, showing her a metal clip, "that will let me know if you've activated the transmitter or if you've switched the homer on or off. So don't fiddle with it unless you're in trouble."

"Right. Never cry wolf," she nodded.

"Now, when we get out there, we'll take off our masks and I'm going to give you a big goodbye kiss in front of Mac and the others, and you're going to return it, okay? You've still got your job to do with those diplomats and we have to protect Beck's cover."

They were coming out onto the barracks steps and as they did, Slick finished settling his own mask on his head and checked hers, paying special attention to the filters below her jaw.

"Good enough, you're getting the hang of it; great, considering that this is just a drill and you know it's not much worse than Jerusalem out here. That's what we want you to do—build up habitual reactions, even if the dips aren't smart enough to follow your lead," he said, his voice sounding odd because she was receiving it through her hood's communication system as well as through the air.

"That's nice to hear." She let him take her hand, feeling detached, as if everything beyond the plastic in front of her eyes was happening on a video screen, as if none of it were dangerous, as if none of it could hurt her.

Beck loved her; she'd play her part. She shied away from thinking about his family—her woman's intuition told her that they were dead and that she shouldn't be happy about it, but she was. They were going to get through this and go back to the Middle East and live as normal a life as possible.

All the way to the chopper pad where the fact-finding tour was assembling, she kept seeing Beck's face: his deep eyes with their inherent calm and soothing intelligence, his quick smile, the way he could make you pledge allegiance with a stare. Not only did he care about her as a woman, he respected her as a person—he'd brought her along because she could be useful, because she was capable, because he respected her.

She hadn't been so optimistic since before she'd heard the first rumors of the war.

In front of the diplomats and their Delta body-guards, she and Slick took off their masks and kissed fervently; she thought she even felt his penis stir against her and wondered just how far Ashmead's deputy would go for operational veri-similitude. She liked Slick, she really did; he just wasn't Beck.

Commander McGrath broke up their theatrical embrace: "That's enough, you two. You don't have to make the rest of us feel lonely. Save it for tomorrow night, when we get back here."

Slick gave her a long, regretful look as he fitted his mask over his face and she let Mac lead her to the Black Hawk.

Once inside, strapped into a makeshift passenger seat between Zenko Tsutsumi and Dugard, her elation over the events of last evening quickly faded. Across from her sat five flinty-eyed bodyguards, Delta commandos of the same stripe as the Saiyeret she'd encountered on the dirt road north of Jericho when Beck had let her go with him to the interdiction site. All of that made better sense now, but the presence of these black-suited fighters, armed to the teeth and bulky with electronics and she-didn't-know-what strapped to their chests and waists, made her nervous, especially because they had their masks hanging around their necks like horse collars as if to say: *Who gives a shit what happens in twenty years; we don't expect to be around long enough to worry about it.*

Chris was incapable of not worrying about it: she wanted to have a baby, some day—soon, if she could. Beck's baby, if he was willing. Hesitantly, when Commander McGrath came up to her and gently told her to take her mask off, saying, "It's safe as a grave in here, Chris, you've got my word on it," his eyes kind but teasing, she complied.

Only Mac was a friendly face; Bandar bin Faisal ignored her, nursing his injured pride: how, his eyes seemed to say, could she have chosen the attentions of such a person as Slick over his own? Such men, in his country, were bought by the kilogram, expended as Allah willed.

Once the Black Hawk lifted off with a shiver and an escalating whine of rotors and Mac, his mask dangling around his neck and his harness unbuckled, had convinced the dignitaries to do the same and relax while the pilots gave them a running commentary on points of interest over the intercom, he invited her "aft" with him.

Aft they went, crouching in the diminished headroom toward the chopper's tail, where he assured her it was safe to smoke a cigarette and offered his calloused palm as their common ashtray.

Crouched on her haunches, the handgun Mac had chosen for her jabbed her hip; the holster which secured it to her belt was merely a strap of molded leather, unidentifiable as what it was when no weapon rested in it.

They talked about her "qualifying shoot" for a while, going over the procedures Ashmead had taught her while Mac had stood by.

"Just remember," Mac said now, "that it's got no grip safety and one up the spout, so if you squeeze that trigger while it's cocked and your thumb safety's not engaged, it's going to go bang."

"Bang?" she repeated, looking down at her side askance.

"That's right, soldier. Bang. So let's not have any accidents."

He was still looking at the weapon on her hip and finally she realized why and engaged the thumb safety as she'd been taught.

"Thank you," said the SEAL commander with equanimity. "I feel a lot better now. This may be none of my business, but if you and Slick aren't a permanent item, I might be tempted to pull out all the stops myself." He watched her as he spoke, his pale eyes cool and glinting with amusement and something more intimate.

"Sorry," she said firmly. "I'm flattered, but I'm an old-fashioned girl." She hadn't been, not until Beck.

"Me, too. War makes people forward. . . ."

"I bet you've got a girl in every port. Isn't that the Navy way?"

"Yep. But on board this bird, I don't. Just so you'll know there's no hard feelings, I'm going to appoint myself your personal bodyguard for the duration—you have any problems, you come directly to me with them. Rafic thinks very highly of you and that's an automatic rating in my book."

Just then one of the commandos came toward them, crouching as he got closer: "Sir, somebody on board's using electronics that are fouling up the pilot's instruments." The commando was eyeing her steadily.

Her hand went to her watch, cradling it. She didn't know whether to surreptitiously turn it off or explain.

Mac said, "Shit, I thought we searched that bunch," rising into a crouch. Then she tugged at his sleeve and he looked at her over his shoulder and shook his head infinitesimally. "I'll handle this, Lieutenant. You stay here with the lady."

Uncertain as to what she was supposed to do, she tapped the winding stem which would silence her watch's homing device and wriggled sideways so that the Delta commando would have room to sit without touching her.

He had longish hair and a short beard and through it he said, "Old Prick's going to have our butts for breakfast tomorrow about this, lady. If you're one of Rafic's little girls, make my life easy—turn whatever you've got off before we crash into some damn tree or a mountain peak. This is no terrain for a three-day hike with a hot wind blowing."

"I don't know what you mean, Lieutenant," she said and saw from his narrowing eyes that he didn't believe her but that for some reason his esteem for her was increased.

Almost immediately, after talking quietly to each dignitary in turn, Mac came back and said: "All taken care of, Lieutenant. And it's time all of us rejoined the others. Miss Patrick is from *The New*

York Times and she's got work to do that had
better not include interviews with any of us."

"Sir." The Delta commando scrambled away from
her and forward, and she followed. Mac was right:
she had work to do.

But without using her tape recorder, Mac warned
her: "The old way—take notes. That's an order."

She didn't ask why, and since no one mentioned
the electronics Elint had given her again, she assumed she'd done the right thing. The most infuri-
ating part of dealing with these people was that
they hardly ever told you anything. It was as if
declarative sentences were against their religion.

The dignitaries weren't much better: Zenko
Tsutsumi's eyes were bloodshot; the little Japanese was still upset over what he'd seen the day
before and every time the intercom crackled with
instructions to look to their left or right, he started
in his seat. Nacht, the IMF ComBloc rep, was belli-
cose and defensive, spewing the party line at her
whenever she asked a question. Najeeb Thabet was
obviously in fear for his life, twisting his fingers in
his lap, the knuckles fish-white against his dark
Mediterranean skin. And the Saudi prince and
Dugard from NATO were involved in a long, unpleasant wrangle about how much of the burden
of rebuilding the US would be taken on NATO's
shoulders and how much borne by the Arab League.

She should have recorded all of that, and since
she couldn't, her fingers and wrist soon numbed as
she took longhand notes.

Every so often, when she looked up, she caught
one of the Delta commandos staring at her and
was glad Mac had gone to the trouble of demonstrating his personal interest in her. She tried to

tell herself that she was the only female aboard and thus the most interesting thing to look at and that they meant no harm, but she was uncomfortable under their scrutiny. They sat so still, with their shooters' eyes resting on her like a target. She was glad she wasn't.

To cheer herself up, she thought about the serum again—she'd never get cancer; she'd survive all this and set up housekeeping with Marc Beck. It would happen; she'd make it happen.

Hours wore on, the drone of the rotors and the disconcerting banking of the helicopter as it swooped low to show the occasional functioning hamlet making her stomach queasy, until well after noon, when the Delta team started to bring out sandwiches and Thabet complained that he was airsick as it was and couldn't eat unless they put down on solid ground.

Mac handed him a Dramamine without a word.

Thabet took it, turning the tablet in his fingers until one of the Deltas handed him a canteen.

As he put it to his lips, one of the pilots in the cockpit called out, "Mac, you'd better take a look at this—I've got a visual on a non-registering bogey at fifty feet, underflying radar, headed our way just like trouble!"

Mac unfolded himself with uncanny speed and, crouched low, headed for the flight deck, where the pilots were now whispering together in an urgent undertone.

One of the Deltas stumbled to the window in the sliding door as the chopper veered suddenly and said, "Aw, shit."

Somebody on the flight deck called out: *"Incoming!"*

Then an explosion rocked the Black Hawk and flame spouted before Chris Patrick's eyes.

She had time for a momentary indrawn breath which brought fire into her lungs and to throw herself backwards as her vision registered a final image: flung bodies as silhouettes before an orange fireball.

Then she was falling, along with the tail-section of the Black Hawk, toward the trees, unconscious.

When she woke, she wished she hadn't. It was nearly impossible to breathe and something wet kept spouting up in her throat, choking her.

She couldn't see anything, couldn't tell if it was day or night. Her left arm was pinned under something and no matter how she tried she couldn't free it to activate the homing device on her left wrist; her right leg felt as if it were being twisted from her body.

Sitting up was out of the question; she was trapped. She'd never experienced so much pain. She'd never thought you could hurt that much and still be alive.

Mostly, she wanted to clear her throat, take a deep breath, but she couldn't do either. Whatever was welling up in her throat was salty and it just kept coming. After an interval, when she realized the gurglings she was hearing were coming from her, she decided that she was choking in her own blood.

She wondered how long it was going to take her to die. Then she tried to call Beck's name. Nothing came out but awful retching sounds, like a dying animal.

Then she thought about Jerusalem and everything she'd almost had.

And that caused her to remember that she had a side arm and that all she had to do was pull it out and thumb off the safety and it wouldn't hurt any more.

Her limbs were beginning to twitch of their own accord by the time she got it out of the holster; her body seemed like someone else's, but that person was in terrible pain.

She really wanted to say goodbye to Beck, to see him leaning over her, just in time, to have him stare at her in that way he had and tell her that everything was going to be all right. Even now, if he did that, she'd believe him and take the gun barrel out of her mouth.

But he didn't come.

Though Chris didn't know it, she was all alone on a Kentucky hillside except for dead bodies and pieces of helicopter and a sick horse that hid among the trees, flanks quivering, where it had run when the helicopter had exploded above its head.

The sound of the gunshot sent the horse bolting once more, toward a broken fence through which it had escaped days ago and the safety of its barn.

Chapter 8

In the Black Hawk as it circled over Georgetown, now a suburb of a red zone so close that the devastation beneath the descending chopper looked like the amorphous blob of a tightly shot group on a paper bull's-eye, Beck's nerves reached saturation and professionalism took over: he became completely calm, resigned to what lay ahead. He was part of the problem and its solution, a victim and a perpetrator, and yet none of these: his crisis management training demanded that he compartmentalize his emotions, divorce himself from the horror that lay ahead in order to function in its midst.

Once you've seen one holocaust, you've seen them all. Georgetown reminded him of Sabra and Shatilla—except that in Lebanon the dead were outnumbered by the living, who walked around in masks with dull eyes and impassive voices, as if sensory overload had made them deaf and blind to the human cost before them.

Even the charred woodframe homes and burial mounds of shattered concrete office and apartment buildings resembled Beirut, and that was a blessing—Beck knew how to deal with human tragedy on the scale of Georgetown. It was the overflight of Ground Zero Washington and its surroundings which left him breathless and numb, so that he found himself grateful when Thoreau put the chopper down on what was once a Georgetown street.

No one in the chopper had said a word since they'd decided to overfly the capital except Thoreau, who occasionally murmured positions into his helmet mike for the benefit of Fort Meade's ground controllers.

Now Sam Nye, beside Beck, fingered his Zone-I Class radiation mask, resembling a pilot's helmet with its clear plexiglass visor and throat-level filtration units above the seal that met his black contamination suit's collar: "Jesus, I'd give anything to wipe the sweat off my face. You're sure you want to go out there, Marc? We can still go straight to Langley."

Ashmead and Slick had their helmeted heads together, talking privately by means of the wave propagation that contact afforded, their com units off, on the flight deck, Ashmead squatting by Slick's co-pilot's seat.

"I need to see for myself, Sam. It won't take long." He'd said the same thing to so many distraught foreign nationals during his Mediterranean tours that the sense of déjà vu he experienced was comforting.

He'd gotten through at least a dozen scenes like

this—earthquakes in Turkey, revolutions in Iran, camps on the Pakistan–Afghanistan border—that he knew he could get through this one. It wasn't part of his mission, after all, just a prelude to clear his mind and put things in perspective.

"You're certain? It's going to be rough; Muffy wouldn't want you to risk your health; we've got to live for them, not die for . . ." Nye broke off.

Beck wondered how to explain. He didn't feel the need to exhume his family's corpses and hold them in his arms; he'd never been the type who got relief or absolution from funerals. When he had to go to them, he tried to avoid open caskets. Dead was forever and it didn't look anything like life on the bodies it claimed. Consonant with his world-view, he preferred his last memories of people he loved to be memories of them filled with life, not empty in death.

And yet there was a chance, vanishingly small, that someone—his kids, Nye's kids, his wife, Nye's wife—had survived: if they'd been in the cellar of Nye's solid brick home, it was barely possible. That was all he wanted to know—that he wasn't snuffing out a dim spark of life in order to save himself some grief. Once he'd seen that survival wasn't possible in Georgetown, he could leave for Langley.

He said only: "You're welcome to stay here with the chopper, Sam. I won't take offense and some-body probably should keep Thoreau company."

Through the double-thick, darkened glass of the Black Hawk's windscreen Beck could see jumbled wreckage as Thoreau put them down in the center of a street littered with cars and twisted hulks of metal much less recognizable.

There was a snap-pop as Ashmead and Slick reentered the com circuit: "Okay, Beck," Ashmead told him, "let's go ruin your day."

The Black Hawk's rotors slowed but did not stop; its powerful engines idled: Thoreau wasn't taking any chances that a mechanical failure would trap them here.

Slick unbuckled his harness and came aft to get shovels while Ashmead slid back the door: "Let's go, ghouls."

Thoreau's voice crackled in his ears as Beck hopped down onto the greasy, cracked pavement: "Good luck, Casper; hope you find what you're looking for." The tone, more expressive than Thoreau's flip words, said: *Us family men have got to stick together.*

"Thanks, Thoreau, we won't be long."

However long they'd be, they wouldn't be without recourse: along with shovels and pickaxes, Slick distributed Ingram M-10s with folding butt stocks and full thirty-round clips, demonstrating their use deftly: "Just in case, okay?"

Sam Nye looked at the weapon in his hand with distaste and gave it back to Slick: "I'd probably shoot my foot off."

"Bugger all, Rafic," Beck heard Slick mutter, "if he could fly we could leave him here and bring Thoreau."

"But he can't," Ashmead said as Beck rotated the cocking handle of the bolt through ninety degrees to safe the weapon and hung it over his shoulder by its web strap as Ashmead had long ago taught him.

Perhaps it was the shouldered weapon, but Beck

began to perspire so that salty drops ran into his eyes and the sides of his viewplate began to fog.

Slick, weapon at his hip, waved them forward, a map in one gloved hand; Nye paced Beck and Ashmead fell in behind them with a deep sigh that said Nye wasn't playing by Ashmead's rules.

But it was Sam who recognized the house—or what was left of it, among the ruins gleaming in the spring sunlight.

Above, the sky was "high," as pilots say, blue and cloudless, giving every shattered brick and downed telephone pole and shard of glass a hard, unnatural edge.

The pile of rubble that had been Nye's home of brick and finely fretted white woodwork was blackened and tumbled as if a giant's hand had swept it aside in a fit of pique. Not one wall stood higher than Beck's calf and two chimney stumps rose like amputated limbs from either side.

Support beams had fallen and floors were compacted upon one another.

Slick said needlessly: "This be it, gentlemen. I swore an oath never to step on anything looking remotely like that, and you should too: if what's left of that ground floor gives way, we'll never dig you out in time for you to thank us." But even as he spoke, Slick was unwinding coils of black nylon rope from around his waist.

They were standing on what had been the walkway. Beck could see a hole that had once been a basement window—just a darker shadow among the tumbled beams.

Ashmead came up to him and put a hand on his shoulder: "Talk to me, Beck. Quiet isn't good at a time like this." An uplifted palm stayed Slick's offer of a safety line. "You don't have to prove anything. You're here; there's not a sign of life. If you were one of mine, I'd order you back to the Black Hawk about now."

Sam Nye said suddenly: "Did you see that?"

"See fucking what?" Slick demanded curtly.

"The basement window—I could swear something moved."

"Rubble settles," Ashmead said to Nye. "Well, Beck?"

"I'll just . . . look in the window," Beck heard himself reply. He was telling himself he could see something in there—a gleam, a glow of eyewhites—something worth keeping the rest of them at risk. His heart was pounding like the Black Hawk's composite rotor blades as they cut the air.

Slick tossed him the rope and Beck, feeling foolish, hooked it to the safety harness at his waist.

Nye said: "I'm coming with you."

Beck shrugged.

Slick said: "Hold onto his line, then, fella—two heroes is more than I was prepared for."

Ashmead slapped the buttstock of his Ingram so that it unfolded and nestled the weapon, muzzle heavenward, in the crook of his arm. Then he gestured with it: "Gentlemen, be our guests."

Beck was already moving, not up the crazed walkway, but across the littered yard with Nye beside him.

When he stepped carefully over something and Nye gulped in a sharp breath as if he'd been struck, Beck realized that it was the handlebars of a tricycle.

He remembered asking Nye, back in Dugout, if this trip was just to collect the ashes.

Moments later, he was down on his knees and wishing that ashes were all there was to collect.

In the imploded window's frame was a hand. It was impossible to tell if an arm was still attached to it because it disappeared into blackness and the hand itself was blackened. In places charred bones showed through crispy skin, not white bones, but gray-brown like those of a well-cooked chicken.

On the hand's third finger was a single ring, a square-cut two-carat ruby that Beck had given Muffy because he'd not wanted a double-ring ceremony and the very idea of wedding bands distressed him. It was from Harry Winston's and there certainly wasn't another like it on this street in Georgetown.

He was on his knees, peering at it, unwilling to touch the dried and wizened finger for fear it would come off in his hand and he'd vomit all over himself inside the radiation helmet.

He just knelt there, his palms pressed against his knees, conscious that Nye, beside him, was breathing heavily.

After a time, Ashmead snapped: "What the fuck's going on over there?"

"I . . . found her."

"Damned convenient," Slick said. "You're sure?" And then, to Ashmead: "Here, hold the rope. If I don't get them out of there, they'll sit there till sundown."

He felt rather than heard Slick's footsteps and when he could see the toe of Slick's combat boot he reached out to take his wife's ring, eyes slitted almost closed.

"Aw, shit," Slick whispered as the entire hand came free in Beck's grasp and he sat back, holding it, face averted, so that he didn't see the dog, fangs bared, lips curled, come barreling out of the hole.

He first realized what was happening when Slick pushed him out of the way and he sprawled across some jagged brick.

The dog had its teeth in Slick's wrist and Slick was trying to lift it off the ground and shoot it with his free hand without shooting himself.

Beck's training reasserted itself: he had the Ingram by its pistol-grip, safety disengaged, the bolt already slamming home before he knew it.

The .45 caliber report was so loud that he could hear it through his helmet. What he couldn't hear was the howl of the shot and dying dog and the growls of its three compatriots—shepherd mixtures—who were leaping through the window after the leader of the pack.

Beck yelled to Nye to run but Ashmead countered: "Hit the dirt, fool," and then there was time only to shoot the dog leaping for his throat and roll out from under it, fully aware that Ashmead's bullets must be whizzing above his head and ricocheting off the rubble.

"Clear," came Ashmead's voice in his ears again. "Everybody out of there, *now*."

Beck was watching Slick, who was looking at his torn, bleeding wrist and the tatters of radiation suit around it.

"Well, fuck," said Ashmead's deputy, "that's that, I guess." His breathing was labored.

Tuning out Nye's sudden burst of hysterical non sequiturs, Beck said, "No—it doesn't have to be." He got up and went to Slick, who was staring doubtfully at his freely bleeding wrist. "The blood's washing it. We'll get you right back to the chopper and scrub it down, tape the suit.... Worst case it'll cut a year off your life, and if you're going with us into Langley, you ought not to be too worried about that."

Nye toed one dog: "It's rabies, not radiation he's worried about," Nye said. "You can't always tell from looking at a dog whether or not it's rabid."

Slick retorted: "I'm not *worried*, Nye; I'm dead on my feet, like Beck says, one way or the other. But come on, let's go. I want to see you guys safe to Langley—that's what I'm here for."

Ashmead had a hand on one hip and his Mac-10 on the other. Even from a distance, Beck could tell he was shaking his head in disgust while he covered their retreat from the building.

When Slick reached him, Ashmead lowered the gun, grabbed Slick's wrist, and then put an arm around Slick's shoulders. "After you two." Ashmead motioned with the weapon in his other hand and his voice was metallic: "Let's go; on the double."

Thoreau was already preparing to lift off as they scrambled aboard and Ashmead slammed the slider shut.

Only Nye strapped in. Wordlessly, Beck exchanged his M-10 for the medikit and they went through the motions of scrubbing Slick's exposed and bitten skin and then taping up the rents in his suit.

Slick, despite his protestations and even logic, looked worried, as white as a sheet.

While Ashmead fussed over Slick with the obsessiveness of a mother, Slick said: "Okay, Beck, maybe now you'll tell me just what it is in Langley that's worth all this." Sweat glittered among the stubble on the deputy's jaw.

"He can't . . ." Nye said.

"He's got a right to know, Sam," Beck interrupted, and was shocked to hear his own calm, decisive tone.

"I just meant that he wouldn't understand it," Nye said thickly.

"Try me," Slick challenged.

"We're going to try to get a message upstairs to Langley—the operational Langley of sixteen days ago: that's about all we can expect to handle, somewhere in the vicinity of a sixteen-day temporal skew. Nye says they managed a two-week send from computer to computer in the building during test—"

"They're not cleared for this. . . ."

"Nye, shut up." Then, to Slick: "The basement computers have gallium arsenide circuitry; that gives us a better chance that they'll have survived the pulse . . . that and the fact that they were probably shut down. But there are problems: it's going to be hot in there. Even if the emergency generators are all working, we won't be able to spare power for air conditioning, so we've got to do it right the first time, before the heat starts affecting the computers and we begin getting garbage or outright equipment failure. Which means lots of sitting around while we get everything up and running and do systems checks in a red zone which is going to read off the scale on that belt Geiger counter of yours. So it doesn't matter about the dog bite, unless you were going to sit outside in the chopper."

"I wasn't," Slick said easily. "But what about paradoxes—time travel, I mean . . . What's going to happen to us if it works?"

"Good question. This isn't a test signal we're sending—it'll change things if it works. Rafic, got a scratchpad?"

Ashmead did and when he handed it to him, Beck saw that Ashmead's eyes were bright and their lower lids flame-red. Slick was his favorite and bandaging Slick's wounds had brought ghosts of too many others out where Ashmead had to deal with them. Fighters will tell you that in their occupation they become inured to death, that your first kill is the one that haunts you and all the rest line up faceless behind, but that's the way it is only with enemies. With friends, and especially with a team like Ashmead's, losses cut as deep as in any family.

"You might want to see this too, Rafic—it'll make more sense to you . . . everything, I mean."

Nye was glaring at Beck fixedly, as if a security breach could endanger *anything* at this stage.

Beck was about to say something very hostile to his best friend when Thoreau interrupted, from the flight deck: "I'd really like Rafic up here. Not that I can't handle this bird single-pilot, but she's not really built for it."

Rafic's heavy features registered something like relief and he left them.

Beck took the scratchpad and began drawing a leafless tree with a thick trunk and many branches, on an axis like cross-hairs. As he drew, he said: "What will happen to us, on site, is most likely terminal overexposure—in *this* particular future. What we're going to do is try to create or hook into *another* future, one in which your team took out the Islamic Jihad who nuked Home Plate before they got out of Saudi Arabia. If it works, some theories suggest that we might not even have time for a long leisurely death." Beck pointed to the tree trunk and drew a line on the positive axis toward the future that meandered up the trunk and swung left onto a short branch that ended abruptly: "It could be that in a forced, unnatural situation like this, everything we know and are will just . . . stop. Zero, zilch, zip—end of the world. And, of course, if that son of a bitch Beggs goes ahead with his secondary strike, it might be just as well."

"Beck!" Nye's pejorative had a tinge of hopelessness.

"I'm telling you, Sam, it doesn't matter. CIA suggested that something like this might be possible in order to distract President Beggs from his primary intent: a second strike against the Soviets. Beggs authorized this little adventure, gentlemen, in order to instigate a *pre-emptive* strike against the Soviets."

"Shit," Ashmead's voice came out of Beck's helmet.

"But Nye—CIA—and I have an understanding," Beck continued. "We don't think there's a chance in hell we can make something like a pre-emptive strike work, or that it would make any substantive difference if we could—probably the same, or a very similar, time-line to this one would be the result. And that, we agree, is unacceptable." Beck took his pencil off the abruptly ending branch and tapped another, one a bit longer, which nevertheless dead-ended. "Like this one." Then he moved the pencil again: "However, we think that if we can *stop* the terrorists, we we might hook back into a time-line that has a chance of continuing." With the pencil, he traced a line from the bottom of the tree trunk that went up the main branch and disappeared off the paper: "An open-ended temporal flow, if you like."

"No shit," Slick grinned. "Well, we'll be alive again, then, right?"

"You bet, Slick. We may be, somewhere, anyway, doing that instead of this—multiple novels, remember? I can give you the math, run it down to you in positives and negatives. . . ." He began to jot x's and y's and complicate the diagram, but Slick put out his hand.

"That's fine, Casper. I'm convinced—and Ashmead's probably right about you being so smart you're worth all this trouble. But run that by me again: we're alive somewhere else?"

"Well, just mathematically, as far as I can prove. In the real sense, if we do this—make a temporal correction—we'll be alive in the there-and-then trying to prevent this particular here-and-now from ever occurring."

"So you're not sending *any*body—" Thoreau's voice entered the conversation, "—any person, that is, back in time. That's good news. I don't think you can do that—I mean, you'd be in two bodies at once, and that can't happen."

"That's right, Thoreau, it can't. But, even though we'll never find out if this works—because, if it does, we'll either just blink out of existence or die soon, wondering about it—you and Saadia and Jesse and Elint and Slick are going to get a second chance to save the world a lot of grief."

"You mean to take out our Islamic Jihad targets.

But we won't know about any of this?"

"If you do your jobs, it will never have happened. We've never sent anything but test messages. It may not work. Langley may ignore my priority 'go' order—I certainly am not going to risk trying to send them an explanation. Or it may work but not change anything—the future may be fixed, the end result the same whatever we do. Interdicting the Jihad may trigger a superpower nuclear exchange by means of a nuclear terrorism variant scenario; all it would take is for the Jihad's bomb to go off in Riyadh and—"

Nye cut in, "What he's trying to say, gentlemen, is that all we can do is counterfeit an order that could well have come from Beck, an override that will cancel your pull-back order either before it's sent or after. It won't matter. There's a chance that Beck will be contacted and deny it, that the past can't be changed. But we think we can time it so that there won't be any opportunity for that sort of thing until after the fact. There's also the chance that you'll fail, for one reason or another. . . ."

From Ashmead, on the flight deck, came a chuckle: "Beck, I hope your counterpart in the past isn't going to dump responsibility for this in my lap."

"He may well, Rafic—if it works. There's going to be a priority-flagged go order that should turn your people loose. What happens from then on is anybody's guess."

"Talk about long shots," Slick breathed. "Well, it's nice to know that you guys believe in what you're doing. As far as I can tell, it's going to make not one shit bit of difference to us in the here-and-now."

"But if you do your jobs in the there-and-then, it might make a hell of a difference to the civilized world," Nye said softly.

"*If* your message gets sent, and *if* somebody forwards it to us—they didn't, if you'll remember, which might mean they won't—and *if* we can interdict successfully," Slick said.

"I don't think," Beck replied, "that just because it didn't happen means it can't happen. If there'd been some attempt at floating a priority go order with my name on it, I'd have heard about it. So it hasn't happened—yet."

"You guys are making me dizzy," Thoreau complained.

"All I'm saying, Thoreau, is that mathematics—and logic—bear little relation to reality. They're just tools, and very limited tools at that. What happens—success or failure—will depend on reality, not mathematics."

"And if it does work, we'll never know it?" Slick's cowboy grin was firmly in place, but his face was still white and he clutched his injured wrist with his good hand. "Damn, think of the promotions we're going to miss—let alone raises, intelligence stars, tickertape parades. . . ."

The fact that everyone was accepting his child-simple explanation made Beck feel better. He still didn't really believe it was going to work. But now, with so much sacrificed, he couldn't bear to call it off—Ashmead and Slick had a right to die *for* something, and Slick, at least, was surely going to—that taped suit wasn't up to what Langley had to offer. Then he thought about Muffy's charred hand and the ring that was somewhere in the ruins at Georgetown and admitted that he did, too.

He said, "Thanks for the vote of confidence," and meant it. The Langley basement station was going to be hard to get into and hard to work in; it was probable that they'd never come out. At least he'd been able to divert Chris; he'd never have had the guts to go through with it if she were there beside him. She made him too anxious to live.

He looked outside, at the destruction below, and saw not destruction, but clean water.

Even as he was letting the chop of the sea below soothe him, Thoreau said, "We're out here so we can take off this headgear for a few minutes and relax a bit—it won't hurt us much. I'd suggest we all take this opportunity to pick our noses or whatever. And Beck, would you come forward?" Thoreau's voice sounded funny—sharp and clipped, not his usual slow drawl.

Ashmead slid out of the co-pilot's seat: "Sit down but don't touch anything. We've got something to tell you."

"I do," Thoreau said, his eyes never leaving his displays. "Slick lost Chris Patrick's homer before we put down in Georgetown. I've been working with a rescue team to try and find out why, and why we lost contact with the other Black Hawk."

Ashmead took over: "Beck, we've got people at the crash site in Kentucky now. There were no survivors."

Beck pulled off one glove after the other and palmed his eyes. "Sabotage? That bastard Watkins?"

"Maybe," Ashmead answered; "maybe not. These

methane-fueled engines are new, chancy. Could have been natural causes." Then he grinned bleakly. "But we don't think so. We think it was Watkins and, since I've killed people on suspicion of a lot less, I took the liberty of radioing a friend of mine—in my business it's handy to have as many friends as you've got enemies. So, just for your information, Watkins is as good as dead in the water. Prick McGrath," Ashmead added ruefully, "and I went over every inch of both birds, and we couldn't find any sign of tampering. We did that because we knew damn well that if Beggs wants to scream bloody murder about the Russian shoot-down, it'd be more convenient if there weren't any survivors to mention Morse and argue that we let the 727 go down in a sacrifice play. I'm sorry about Chris Patrick—we all liked her—and sorrier than you'll ever know about Prick, but at this point, if you believe what you're telling us, it ought not to matter."

Beck took his hands away from his face and looked into the blue, cloudless sky. "You know, there isn't anybody on earth I'd rather be doing this with than you and yours, Rafic."

He got up, went aft and, to take his mind off Chris Patrick, said to Nye: "Let's get going on those numbers. We don't have much time."

Nye, who'd heard the discussion on the flight deck, nodded. Then he said soberly: "Where there's a will, there's a way."

"Let's hope," Beck corrected, feeling as if his entire body were encased in cotton batting and his mouth belonged to a lizard.

When they put down in a park where a low stone building still stood among leafless trees, though the stenciled sign that had said PARK COMMISSION MAINTENANCE: NO ADMITTANCE was gone, everybody knew exactly what to do.

Slick forced open the building's steel door with Ashmead's help while Thoreau shut down the chopper and booby-trapped it with a radio-detonating device as well as a tamper-trigger.

When they'd slid the heavy door aside, Beck stepped in and shone his halogen lamp around: the emergency route in and out of Langley seemed untouched by the blast. But that was what its architects had intended.

Even the emergency generator functioned when Slick found its circuit breaker and tripped it, flooding the tunnel, its tracks and electric car, with red light.

Nye fed his Langley access card into a slot in the wall and the car whirred. Beyond it, a three-inch-thick steel door drew back to reveal the beginnings of the more than two miles of tunnel hewn from solid rock.

There wasn't a rockfall on the track for as far as they could see; the disaster-bracing above had held while hell broke loose on the surface.

And yet, somewhere, there was a breach: Beck's digital Geiger counter ran out of digits and he tapped Ashmead to bring it to the Covert Action Chief's attention. For some reason, he was hesitant to speak, as if he were in a tomb.

Ashmead didn't say anything either, just shrugged.

They all piled into the electric cart, Nye and Beck in the middle with the team around them, shielding them with their bodies from whatever they might encounter, Thoreau facing behind, Ashmead driving, Slick standing with legs spread and weapon at the ready, though everyone else in the car was seated.

Somehow, though Beck was sure no one could have broken in here and survived for long, the tactical caution of the team around him made Beck feel better.

Twenty minutes later, because the car crawled at a snail's pace and once in a while they did find a rock on the tracks which had to be moved, they drew to a halt before the door to Langley's subbasement, where Nye had to perform a more complicated entrance procedure: hand and voice print as well as card ID.

Beck saw him shiver as he took off his glove to press the plate and wince once he'd done it: hot is hot, and Langley was hot as hell. Like stigmata, red weals appeared on Nye's palm.

Beck saw them as he gloved it once more and touched his friend, who slumped against him, then recovered: "All in my mind, no doubt," Nye joked lamely as the door slid back and, leaving the cart, they stepped inside.

Above their heads was the executive garage and tons of collapsed building: Thoreau had given them a description of a photo-reconnaissance shot he'd seen to explain why he didn't want to bother with a flyby.

Beck couldn't have cared less about what existed or no longer existed above ground.

Down here, where 159 had flourished and then died of budget problems and lack of tangible, usable results, the condition of things mattered terribly.

Every time Beck saw crumbled concrete fallen from the ceiling it was as if someone jabbed him with a hot poker. When a passageway they needed to enter was blocked by a buckled steel door that would not be moved, Beck began to swear in Greek, the foulest of his store of epithets, until Nye told him, "Relax, we'll just go in the other way."

The two additional years Nye had spent down here had seen many changes. Without his first-hand knowledge, they'd never have made it to the proper corridor.

But eventually they did and, though everyone's breathing was raspy, Nye laughed like a delighted child: "Looks good as new."

It wasn't, behind the black door that demanded lock-plate and voice identification, but it was close enough.

They fired up the emergency power source and they all held their breath.

When the red lights came on and the dust covers came off the equipment, Slick said: "Looks like we're rolling," and stretched out in an ergonomic chair, his feet up on a communicator's Telex that wouldn't be telling anyone anything because there was no one upstairs to tell and soon there wouldn't be enough power left in the entire building to draw any of the steel doors back, let alone send out a message.

Looking around in the red light, with perspiration rolling down his skin so that it crawled, Beck said: "Okay, gentlemen. Time for the good news/bad news. The good news is that whatever we can do, we've got the power to do. The bad news is that once we do it, we're trapped in here."

"That ain't news to me, Casper," Slick said.

"Well, Nye and I think that there's no reason

you can't leave now if you want to: you too, Ashmead. Take your team and get out."

"We can't get past the voice ID. And you'll need all the power you can coax out of these things," said Ashmead, his face glistening with sweat in his helmet. "Don't get all humanitarian on us, kid. We're here to see that you do your job."

With a flick, Ashmead's submachine gun was trained on him. A glance out of the corner of his eye showed Beck that Thoreau had Nye similarly covered.

Slick yawned and stretched: "Not that we thought you'd punk out, but you never know how somebody's going to act under pressure."

"We're here to help," Thoreau put in, "and for the duration. So why don't you two brains get started?"

Suddenly, Beck remembered Slick telling him that if not for Thoreau, Slick would have killed him on the plane after Beck's intransigence had led to the deaths of Jesse and Yael.

And yet he didn't feel betrayed, or even nervous: there were all kinds of courage, and there were moments ahead in which he might well lose his nerve.

It was nice to know that Rafic and his boys were there to make sure that the job got done.

"Well, Sam, come on then, don't let them intimidate you." Beck bared his teeth and leveled his best stare at Nye, who was standing very still and breathing shallowly. "Time to get to work."

It took an hour and a half to make sure everything was ready and all systems go. Intermittently Beck thought about Chris Patrick, his wife and kids, and the casualties from Ashmead's team. But it didn't hurt his concentration—it may have helped it.

Finally Beck said, "Well, Sam, I think that's got it."

"Me, too," said Nye, "and just in time. I don't know about you, but I've about had it. Go ahead, Marc—push the button."

Beck, too, was feeling queasy from the heat, queasy enough that when the lights flickered, he wasn't sure if they really had or if it was eyestrain. Surges wouldn't bother this system, which had a backup emergency supply, but when it went down, it would be down for good.

"Ashmead?" Beck asked. "Thoreau? Slick?"

Only Ashmead answered: "Give it your best shot, Beck."

Slick had his head on his arm, slumped over a nonoperational console and Thoreau, on the floor with his back against the wall and the M-10 balanced on his updrawn knees, didn't open his eyes.

Beck tapped the "run" button on the mainframe computer before him and saw his reflection staring back at him. He gave it a thumbs-up.

Then the lights went out.

Book Three:
COVERT ACTION

Chapter 1

The Saudi fondness for preformed concrete had
made Riyadh a study in architectural culture clash
exceeded nowhere in the Middle East.

Through the window of his high-rise Riyadh
Marriott Hotel room, Ashmead watched the Cadil-
lacs, gleaming in the evening streetlights, cruise
by and waited for the phone to ring.

The connecting door to Slick's room was open
and Ashmead's deputy, in a show of optimism,
had finished laying out their operations gear and
was changing into his black fireproof jumpsuit
which was padded with neoprene at the elbows,
shoulders and knees and tailored to fit without
binding over his lightweight kevlar body armor.

The sun had set without bringing the telephone
call that Ashmead was expecting. He was beginning to worry it might never come—or come bearing the wrong message.

Anything could go wrong, and something usually did: Yael's informants might be in error and the Islamic Jihad's martyrs might never show up in the hotel lobby to check in one floor below; Zaki's agents might have swallowed Iranian/Palestinian/Libyan disinformation whole and thus misdirected Ashmead's team to the wrong city, the wrong airport, or even the wrong terrorists: the Libyans, at least, were getting better at tradecraft—the holy warriors his people were running to ground might be decoys carrying a suitcase loaded with lead bars and not the bomb.

One thing Ashmead *was* sure of: there was a bomb and there was a terrorist operation in progress that could change the face of the world, kick off a Gulf spasm war of hideous proportions, or even trigger a nuclear exchange. The fact that these risks were unacceptable to Langley and Ashmead's Stateside superiors in the National Intelligence Tasking office gave the Islamic Jihad a peculiar advantage upon which the Libyans certainly were counting. A successful nuking of Home Plate would tempt the US to retaliate against the nations involved—Libya and Iran, at least, since Palestine was wherever the exiles hung their AKs—and no American strategic analyst at home in McLean or field collector from Defense or State on-site could bring himself to believe that the budding Pan-Islamic front would risk nuclear annihilation by an aroused superpower.

But the desk boys didn't understand what martyrdom meant to the Muslims, except perhaps for Marc Beck, who was on the other side of a very high interagency fence but might just be Ashmead's best hope. Beck had the balls to go against the consensus and the clout to override Stateside qualms about taking action which wouldn't long remain covert, and taking it in a Gulf State.

Whether or not they got a go order, whether or not their information was correct, they were already inserted and Ashmead was pulling every string his puppeteers could hand him to make sure that if such an order was forthcoming, no Islamic Jihad members commandeered that jumbo bound for Washington International.

Slick, somewhere behind Ashmead, cleared his throat.

The Covert Action Chief turned and regarded his deputy: Slick had donned a *thobe*—the white, full-length Saudi shirt—which hid his black jumpsuit the way dark glasses hid his pale eyes and a red-and-white Saudi ghutra-and-aghal headdress covered his Western-cut hair. With his bearded chin and his deep tan, Slick would do, even if he had to carry on a conversation: even Ashmead's sister had been fooled by Slick's Omani-accented Arabic.

Slick said, "Salaam, Hajji," soberly; then in English: "I'm going to go check the car again."

Hajji meant *pilgrim* and it was Ashmead's code name for the operation. Slick wanted to check the Mercedes in the garage because it *was* in the garage, where anyone might slap a load of plastique up against the shocks or jimmy the locking gas cap to put any of a number of detonating devices in its gas tank. Slick had just returned from checking the bugs and passive surveillance equipment ready to monitor whatever might occur in the Islamic Jihad's suite directly below: since they hadn't been able to determine whether the bomb was radio detonated, they'd had to make sure that none of their own devices could trigger it.

What no one wanted, and what Ashmead had had to promise his brother-in-law—Turki ibn Abdul Aziz, head of the Saudi Secret Police—there would not be, was a nuclear explosion in the middle of Riyadh.

"Wait until we get a go or a no-go, Slick; I don't want to be sitting here wondering where the fuck you are."

"A no-go? You still think they'll pass? After everything we went through to get those heat and radiation signature detectors up and running? And calling in the Saudi National Guard? And the can-opener?" The "can-opener" could peel back the metal of an aircraft like a sardine can.

"Don't know, Slick." Ashmead switched to Arabic, telling Slick that the *ghazzu*—raid—would take place or not, *Insh'allah*—as God wills; that the *Ikhwan*—brothers of the army, in this case the Saudi National Guard's anti-terrorist squad—were ready, and so was the team.

Just then the phone rang, and Ashmead gestured in its direction.

Slick went to answer it, leaving Ashmead with his thoughts once again. It had been less than ten years since a Saudi princess and her unacceptable lover were marched, tranquilized, into a square and publicly beheaded. Ashmead had been there, with his sister and Turki. The veneer of civilization here was still perilously thin; anything could happen. Turki was trying his best to help Ashmead with this operation—not only were they brothers-in-law, but Ashmead had been pivotal to the negotiations that facilitated the training and equipping of the Saudi National Guard by a private American company in California with ties to the Agency. So Turki owed him one, but could easily be overruled by others higher in the House of Saud—there were too many members of the royal family in Riyadh to evacuate while maintaining security, and most of those wanted assurances Ashmead couldn't give that the bomb wouldn't explode within their territorial borders.

Slick palmed the phone: "It's Qadi. He wants to talk to you."

"Qadi" was Arabic for "judge," and Turki's code name.

Ashmead got up and took the receiver from Slick: Turki's voice was regretful as the police chief told Ashmead that the Saudi government had not yet given the operation its sanction. "Still, *Ikhwans* await with Elint, as we discussed—there is a higher law than that of the *Majlis al Shura*"—the Consultative Council—"and it is *Shariah*"—Islamic Law. "None wants to see the entire Kingdom become like *al rabba al khali*"—the barren lands. "*Salaam alaykum, Hajji.*"

"*Wa alaykum as salaam, Qadi*," Ashmead replied wryly—"And upon you be peace."

Slapping the phone irritably into its cradle, Ashmead hoped to hell it would be peace that came upon the Saudis, and not the cleansing peace of a nuclear fireball, either.

He shook his head when he encountered Slick's questioning gaze: "They're fighting it; they don't want it to happen here, and I can't say that I blame them."

"Then where?"

"Over clean water, maybe—a shoot-down. That's

what I'm hoping, anyway. But definitely not in this hotel—it's the airport or nothing."

Slick flopped down on the Marriott-modern couch: "Bugger all. That means Elint's got to go aboard."

"Unless we can cut that girl terrorist loose from her crew if she goes down to the restaurant for dinner; unless we can determine that there's no radio-detonation option; unless we can do better than a bomb blanket and a big apologetic smile if something goes wrong, I halfway agree with them: if the gas doesn't hit fast enough, and we can't be sure it will, one of them could still conceivably make it to that suitcase before we get in the doors and windows and grease 'em. So it's up to you and Jesse to see if you can't seduce her away from them so that we can interrogate her: if they lose her, they've lost their commander and the whole operation might well go on indefinite hold. *If* we get a go order."

"We'd better get it soon, or anything but trying to gas 'em and pry 'em out of that plane will be out of the question. That bitch is a Palestinian; I'm not holding my breath that she's going to fall madly in love with me at first sight."

Ignoring Slick, Ashmead began to dress. When he'd secreted all his equipment he pulled on a *mislah*—a long brown coat trimmed with gold thread—and headed for the door.

"Shit, Rafic, where do you think you're going? What if—"

The phone's ring interrupted Slick and he dived for it as if it were a live grenade that had just landed in front of him.

Slick said: *"Salaam."* Then: "Black Widow."

Then: "Say again?" Then: "We copy that, Uncle." Then he hung up.

Ashmead looked at him questioningly, his hand suddenly slippery on the doorknob: "So?" Slick's use of the recognition code "Black Widow" meant that it was the call they'd been waiting for—a go or no-go relayed from Ashmead's staff headquarters.

Slick looked up at him gloomily: "It's a no-go. Let's pack up and get out of here."

Ashmead's stomach sank: "Then they've found another way that sits better with the Saudis— probably a shoot-down in international waters. Sure."

Slick said nothing and Ashmead came back and began to strip, setting a stoic example but a silent one. If he opened his mouth again, all the resentment he felt for the Stateside desk jockeys who'd worked up a flow chart and subjected their data to analysis and then backed off would come pouring out. And Slick didn't need to hear it.

They worked without a word, like automatons: Slick had very little time to pack up Elint's electronics and the gas canisters whose lines Slick had fed with tubing through carefully drilled holes in the floor which exited above the ornate light fixtures in the ceilings of the rooms below.

They'd just finished wrestling the canisters into the huge steamer trunk they'd used to bring them upstairs when, once more, the phone rang.

"That's Elint," Slick predicted. "You tell him, Rafic. I haven't got the stomach for it."

Ashmead nodded and went slowly to the phone, picking it up on its fourth ring: "Scrub," he said simply in English, not waiting for the party on the other end of the line to identify himself.

"What?" said a guarded female voice: "This is Black Web to Widow. Say again?"

Ashmead snapped: "What the fuck now?"

"We've got a priority mail package for you, Widow; just came in and it contradicts the last letter you got. I say again: your uncle has had a change of heart. You're go."

"Affirmative and understood, sweetheart. See you tomorrow."

"That would be nice," said the female voice, wistful now. "Tell your nephew good luck and I'll be waiting for him."

"Will do."

Slick was watching him, narrow-eyed, hands on hips, by the time Ashmead cradled the phone gently. "Not Zaki?"

"Control. We got a priority override—Beck, I'll bet a month's expense-account vouchers. Well, don't just stand there. Let's put all this stuff back together again. Oh, yeah, that little girl of yours said to wish you good luck."

Surveying the jumble of equipment in the trunk and the cords he'd thrown in at random, Slick said: "Yeah? That's nice. We're going to need it."

Chapter 2

To most Foreign Service officers, even in the Mediterranean, word came earlier than it did to Marc Beck, who was babysitting a convention of genetic engineers with astronomical security clearances at a private estate on the Red Sea when an aide slipped him a note.

The State Department being what it was, the note was cryptic—SM/NSB B-1; RSVP—but the Israeli hand holding it out to him was as white as the paper and shaking like a leaf: one look at the blanched face of the Saiyeret commando was all Beck needed to confirm the urgency of the coded message.

The prefix SM was familiar, even routine: Shariah Mosque—Riyadh; following it, instead of an operation's cryptonym, was the acronym for Nuclear Surface Blast; after that came the standard letter-number intelligence appraisal, B-1, which

269

told Beck that the information was from a usually reliable source and confirmed by other sources; the RSVP appended was somebody's cynical joke.

Given the above, he left the genetic engineers to their Israeli hosts and RSVP'd toward Jerusalem at a hundred eighty klicks per hour, eschewing a driver and pushing his Corps Diplomatique Plymouth well beyond the laws of man and physics in exactly the way every new diplomat was warned against when first posted overseas.

He would never remember the cars he ran off the road into the soft sand, and later into one another; he only remembered the sky, which he watched through his double-gradient aviator's glasses for some sign of thermal shock wave, a flash of light, a mushroom cloud, a doomsday darkening in the southeast over the Gulf or northeast over Iran—and the radio, which was stubbornly refusing to confirm or deny what the little piece of State Department letterhead in his pocket said.

Beck wasn't naive, but he couldn't believe that the bombing of Saudi Arabia's capital wasn't newsworthy. Damn it to hell, Ashmead had ignored the pullback order and, though his report had been right, his tactics hadn't: a Gulf war which could render radioactive every barrel of oil on which the West depended was likely to be the result.

So the Islamic Jihad had actually done it! Nobody believed they could—or would ... nobody but a handful of Ashmead's field-weary counterterrorists, who couldn't write a grammatical report and didn't seem to understand that a nuclear blast in Riyadh was simply unacceptable and, under the conditions the counterterrorists had detailed in their situation report, probably unavoidable as soon as any interdiction plan was undertaken. His mind reeling with possible implications, Beck tromped the gas pedal. He hoped to hell that by the time he reached Jerusalem Ashmead and his team of cowboy operatives had been pulled in by the ears and were waiting for him. He was going to personally kick Ashmead's butt around the block.

Beck, in fifteen years of overseas postings, had never been party to an error of this magnitude. He'd signed off on a negative analysis of Ashmead's intelligence, along with everyone else whose opinion he respected, with Beck's own confidential notation appended that, despite Ashmead's record and predilections, Ashmead would obey a simple pullback order if it was given—a tragic misjudgment of the covert actor's character which had probably just destroyed years of productive relations between the US and the House of Saud. Beck had visions of himself standing rigidly while Aramco and Bechtel VPs helped his superiors decide just where Beck was going to be posted next—Greenland, if he was lucky; the Manchurian border, if he wasn't.

Because Beck had loyally stood up for Ashmead when others had questioned the wisdom of assuming that the area's Covert Action Staff Chief would simply follow orders, it wasn't going to look nearly as bad in Beck's superiors' files as it was in his. He wheeled the competent Plymouth past an Israeli convoy on the move, their desert camouflage reminding him, if he needed the reminder, that he was posted in a war zone.

The worst that could happen, he decided, was

that he'd be sent Stateside—headquarters wouldn't sack the lot of them, even if the entire House of Saud was a puff of radioactive dust wafting over the Empty Quarter by now.

And that wouldn't be all bad, as far as Beck was concerned—he was ready for a rest. He'd been here seventeen months as State's liaison without portfolio, trying to reduce friction among the various intelligence services crawling over Israel like ants on a picnic table.

And he'd been doing pretty well—Ashmead had trusted Beck, and Ashmead didn't trust anybody; Mossad and Shin Bet honchos invited Beck to weapons tests and gave him Saiyeret commandos, no questions asked, when he needed security boys, as he had for this conference—pretty well, until today.

Suddenly, wondering which way the wind was blowing, Beck focused through the Plymouth's tinted glass on the sun-baked road ahead, blinked, then cranked the steering wheel around and the Plymouth went up on two wheels to avoid a woman and a donkey crossing the road directly in his path. Beyond them, eucalyptus whispered, their leaves shimmying in a white-hot breeze blowing steadily to the southeast.

Pretty well, Beck knew, wasn't good enough when you were in the field. He had no doubt that, by qualifying CIA's high-priority-flagged warning of an imminent terrorist attack on Home Plate and Ashmead's ability to deal with it, the blame for this was going to end squarely in INR's—more specifically Beck's—lap.

Ashmead and his team had end-run themselves this time. Beck hoped to hell they hadn't end-run the whole intelligence community—or the whole blessed US of A: a "Nuclear Incident" like this could start a damned war. Worse, it could destroy the all-important "liaison service" relationships American intelligence enjoyed with a host of other nations, if word got out that a field agent had ignored a pullback.

The thought made him nervous and he began punching buttons on the Plymouth's multiband. When the radio chattered on blithely in Hebrew, Arabic and English of quotidian affairs between musical interludes, he could only assume that stringent Israeli security measures were in effect.

And that made good sense: only the parental and unceasing care of the US kept Israel from destruction by her enemies. But then again, it was ridiculous to assume that even the Israelis would censor news of this magnitude or that even Israeli paranoia could look at what had happened in Riyadh and assume it meant the destruction of the State of Israel. So it had to be something more: sensitive negotiations to keep the true situation top secret must be in progress.

And this, finally, cracked Beck's calm: in the air-conditioned sedan, he began to sweat. If Ashmead had really fucked up, and the bomb went off in downtown Riyadh, not only might the US have to pack up and go home, so far as the Gulf States were concerned, at least, and probably throughout the Middle East, but retaliation became a real possibility: if the Saudis demanded American help or used American weapons to go after Libya, Iran, and the Palestinians headquartered now in Jordan with nuclear or even conventional weapons, Beck was in on the beginning of World War III—the

Soviets couldn't stand by and let their client states take it on their collective chin.

By the time he careened into East Jerusalem, Beck was getting visual confirmation of a mobilized Israel and a deep security hush in place: too many of the wrong kind of official vehicles on the streets; too few of others.

Driving up to the new temporary American Consulate, he was praying in nonsectarian fashion for the English-language radio commentator to drop even a hint of the nuking of Riyadh—if it went public, that was a sign that repercussions had been or could be contained.

But it wasn't forthcoming. He told himself that there was no way it could be as bad as he was assuming it might be—a state of actual war in the Gulf ought to leak, even in Israel.

RSVP. Right. Check.

A pair of stone-faced Marines stopped him at the compound gates, their M16s on full auto. It was the weapons which told him for sure, before one Marine said, "I guess you know we'd really appreciate a confirm or deny on this, Sir, if and when you can—some sort of prognosis, damage estimates. . . ."

"As soon as I know, Sergeant. What are all those people doing in there?" Beyond the guardpost, a queue of civilians had formed. Beck could imagine what the Americans in their rumpled polyesters wanted—emergency travel arrangements home; he was just trying to cover his own confusion.

A glance in the rearview mirror showed him a taxi pulling up and a woman with a boyish haircut and the custom-tailored bush jacket of a press type getting out, a carryall in hand. Her face was pale and her jaw squared.

"Just citizens, sir; and newsies. You know you can't keep something like this . . . rumors, that is . . . quiet long," said the Marine sergeant thickly.

When Beck looked up at the guard, he saw that the man's chin had doubled and his lips were white. "Hey there," Beck caught the Marine's gaze and held it, "this isn't Teheran. And anyway . . . when the going gets tough . . . Right?"

The Marine squared his shoulders: "That's right, Sir," he replied. "As long as we've got a compound to protect . . . well, you know—it's got us."

Haven't lost your touch, anyway, Beck told himself.

By then the woman with the carryall was hiking up the drive, hallooing and breaking into a trot. She had on sensible tennis shoes and the bag was now over her shoulder.

Beck was about to put the Plymouth in gear when she put a hand holding a cassette recorder on its fender, then on the half-open glass of his window: "American Consular Corps?" Her voice was husky, but it might have been from emotion. She ducked her head to peer into his car and he decided she was very pretty—she shielded her eyes and said, "Thank God . . . I saw the CD on your car . . . look, let me go in with you. I can't stand in that line. I've got to get a statement. Please?"

The Marine was telling her with firm politeness not to bother Beck and the way was clear before him, the Plymouth idling. All he had to do was drive on.

But the woman was grasping the window, ignoring the Marine, leaning in so that the press credentials on her breast pocket were easy for him to read: *The New York Times*. "Come on," she said insistently, "give a fellow countryman some help: we've had a report of a nuclear bomb going off at the Riyadh airport. Can you confirm or deny? What's the chance of it touching off a war, Mister—?"

Newsie or not, she was exceptionally pretty. And she'd given him a piece of information. "Ms. . . . Patrick, you know I can't help you. You'll have to stand on line with the others. As for a statement, I'm afraid I can't comment at this point in time." He gave her a cool smile and from the driver's side pushed the button that caused the electric passenger window to roll slowly upward.

Taking her hand away, she said hopefully through the closing window, "Maybe later, then, Mister—?" as the Marine took her firmly by the shoulder and Beck accelerated away from the guardpost toward his parking slot.

As he walked around toward the front of the building he got a glimpse, through the open window of Dickson's office, of Ashmead, his deputy, and the leonine head of the Ambassador himself.

It was going to be one hell of a hairy meeting, with the Ambassador in attendance. The only consolations Beck could think of were that Ashmead and his deputy were alive to take the blame and that the meeting wasn't taking place in Tel Aviv—a sign that no one had any intention of making more of this mess than was absolutely necessary.

The RSVP had been an invitation to this "party" at which a cover story would be developed—that meant that they were going to need one, and that meant that State and Defense and CIA had decided the matter was containable.

No longer worried that he'd been instrumental in starting World War III, Beck began to get angry.

Ashmead and his deputy better have a damned good explanation for jumping that order.

Inside—once he'd threaded his way through the confusion of nervous tourists who had no intention of spending any longer than necessary in the volatile Middle East now that there'd been a nuclear incident, and reporters slavering for details—he learned that Ashmead didn't have any explanation whatsoever.

"I've got a goddamned tape on its way here from my station of the priority go order as it came in from Langley," Ashmead was saying through gritted teeth, his big hands trying to strangle the windowsill, as Beck came in and closed the door behind him.

Ashmead's deputy, whom Beck knew only by dossier, nodded from where he leaned insolently in a corner, arms folded across his chest.

"And I lost a man better than any of you," Ashmead continued, "at the airport—my electronics specialist, Zaki. And the last thing I want to hear is that that kid's relatives aren't going to get suitable compensation because of some fucking internecine squabble or glitch in the chain of command or—worse—that you gutless wonders have decided to put new meaning into the term 'total deniability.' We got our orders and we followed them. That's what we're paid to do, folks," Ashmead flashed a look of fond commiseration at Beck.

The Ambassador turned away from Ashmead with a shake of his huge head and said, patting his white mane, to Beck: "Marc, it seems we have a bit of a problem, as you may have gathered. Langley says you sent them a priority override, a go order on your authority. Did you? Without consulting anyone, not me or Chief Dickson or anyone whomsoever?"

"*What?*" Beck was astonished. "Jesus." He looked around for a vacant chair, realized that there were none because the three extras in the room were taken by others he didn't know—a honey-haired girl, a lanky pilot in a baseball cap, and a tall Semite with shooter's eyes, all of whom were watching him as he went to Dickson's desk and stood before it.

Beck's chief wouldn't meet his eyes, but it was the fond look Ashmead had shot him which made him understand exactly what was happening.

He considered for a moment trying to avoid the consequences, keeping up a protest that there had been an error though it was clear enough that someone, somewhere, had decided that the buck was going to stop with him.

Then he stopped trying to get Dickson, who was heroically suppressing a smirk, to meet his eyes and turned to the Ambassador.

"Mister Ambassador, I think we ought to consider what the consequences would have been if that nuke had gone off in Washington, don't you? And get started with a damage assessment so that we can do whatever is possible to minimize repercussions? Containment has to be our top priority. I'm sure Ashmead's contacts in Riyadh are security-minded. No one else has to know that American intelligence officers were involved. If we can leak this as an Islamic Jihad-sponsored terrorist action against the Arab moderates, we ought to be able to turn it to our advantage."

Dickson snorted.

Beck ignored him: Beck could always go into the

private sector, if this didn't work. Muffy had been after him to do that for years.

"So you don't deny taking matters into your own hands, Marc?" the Ambassador said slowly, his face reddening.

"How can I, Ambassador?"

Behind him, Beck heard the fellow with the baseball cap on backwards whisper to the woman beside him: "Told you. Rafic's never wrong."

From the window, Ashmead gave Beck a thumb's up.

Chapter 3

Chris Patrick was still waiting outside the Jerusalem US Consulate when Mercedes 600 limousines with privacy glass began to pull up out front.

Beside her was a sandy-haired BBC correspondent with whom she'd shared a passionate night under fire in Samaria and who, because he'd been a standup correspondent in the Middle East for five years and, some said, a stringer for British Intelligence, knew who was whom among the players of the various diplomatic corps.

When the Ambassador and his entourage began to file out of the mission to duck into the waiting limos, she was carried forward with the Brit and his cameraman and had just enough time to point out the impeccably-attired diplomat she'd accosted at the gatepost and ask her sometimes-lover, "Who's that?"

"That? That's sodding Marc Beck, State's wonder boy. Don't bother with him, he won't give you the time of day—he's INR as well as an Assistant Secretary in charge of no-one-knows-what."

Then the Brit was shoving his mike in the Ambassador's face and the cameraman muscled her aside with a muttered, "Sorry, then, but you'll excuse me," and the shove moved her up one step to where Beck was drifting sideways through the security men, briefcase in hand, toward a second limousine whose door was already open.

"Secretary Beck!" she called as she charged toward him, stumbling on a step.

A strong hand caught her by the elbow, before her knees hit the stone, and helped her to her feet.

Then Marc Beck was staring at her quizzically, and electricity shot through her as if her cassette deck had shorted.

"You must be more careful, Ms. Patrick," he said in an amused, but not taunting, voice.

His hand was still on her arm; it was his left hand and there was no wedding band on it.

Then he let her go and she looked back at his face. "A statement?" she asked hopefully. "From an unidentified State Department source?"

He chuckled briefly: "Sorry, Ms. Patrick. Your sources are too good as it is. Now, you'll have to excuse me. . . ."

And he ducked into his limousine along with a heavy-set, rough-featured man who wore a rumpled suit, and the car drew away with the purr of German automotive excellence.

She stood watching it, thinking that at least he hadn't given her a brusque "No comment," and that, in a town as small as Jerusalem, she was sure to run into him again.

PATRICK TILLEY
CLOUD WARRIOR

"Reminiscent of Stephen King's *The Stand*." —*Fantasy Review*

"Technology, magic, sex and excitement. . .when the annual rite of selection for the Hugos and Nebulas comes around, CLOUD WARRIOR is a good bet to be among the top choices." —*San Diego Union*

"A real page-turner!" —*Publishers Weekly*

Two centuries after the holocaust, the survivors are ready to leave their underground fortress and repossess the Blue Sky World. Its inhabitants have other ideas....

352 pp. • $3.50

The future of America depends on

MUTUAL ASSURED SURVIVAL

A space-age solution to nuclear annihilation

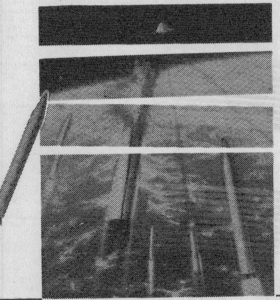

by Jerry Pournelle and Dean Ing

Based on the Citizens Advisory Council's Report to the President

"Dear Dr. Pournelle:
"You and your associates deserve high praise...efforts like this can assist us in achieving a safer and more stable future....
Thank you, and God bless you."
            —PRESIDENT RONALD REAGAN

This high-tech, non-fiction blockbuster could usher in a new era of peace and prosperity. Assured Survival is not an offensive strategy. It is a scientifically advanced defense system already in development that is capable of detecting—and disintegrating—nuclear warheads in flight...long before they reach their land-based destinations.

"To be or not to be" is the question:
MUTUAL ASSURED SURVIVAL is the answer.

A BAEN BOOK

November • 55923-0   256 pp. • $6.95

Distributed by Simon & Schuster Mass Merchandise Sales Company
1230 Avenue of the Americas • New York, N.Y. 10020

HAVE YOU FOUND YOURSELF ENJOYING A LOT OF BAEN BOOKS LATELY?

We at Baen Books like science fiction with real science in it and fantasy that reaches to the heart of the human soul—and we think a lot of you do, too. Why not let us know? We'll award $25 and a dozen Baen paperbacks of your choice to the reader who best tells us what he or she likes about Baen Books. We reserve the right to quote any or all of you...and we'll feature the best quote in an advertisement in <u>American Bookseller</u> and other magazines! Contest closes March 15, 1986. All letters should be addressed to Baen Books, 260 Fifth Avenue, New York, N.Y. 10001.

"Engrossing characters in a marvelous adventure." —C. Brown, LOCUS

"The amazing and erotic adventures of the most beautiful courtesan in tomorrow's universe."—Frederik Pohl

On a planet desperate for population, women hold the keys to power. These are the adventures of Estri, Well-Keepress of Astria, The High Couch of Silistra.

RETURNING CREATION

JANET MORRIS